17

)17

I8

INHERIT THE DEAD

A NOVEL

BY

MARK BILLINGHAM • LAWRENCE BLOCK • C. J. BOX

KEN BRUEN • ALAFAIR BURKE • STEPHEN L. CARTER

MARCIA CLARK • MARY HIGGINS CLARK • MAX ALLAN COLLINS

JOHN CONNOLLY • JAMES GRADY • HEATHER GRAHAM

BRYAN GRULEY • CHARLAINE HARRIS • VAL McDERMID

S. J. ROZAN • JONATHAN SANTLOFER • DANA STABENOW

LISA UNGER • SARAH WEINMAN

EDITED BY JONATHAN SANTLOFER

WITH AN INTRODUCTION BY LEE CHILD

AND AN AFTERWORD BY LINDA FAIRSTEIN

A TOUCHSTONE BOOK
PUBLISHED BY SIMON & SCHUSTER
NEW YORK   LONDON   TORONTO   SYDNEY   NEW DELHI

Touchstone
A Division of Simon & Schuster, Inc.
1230 Avenue of the Americas
New York, NY 10020

This book is a work of fiction. Any references to historical events, real people,
or real places are used fictitiously. Other names, characters, places, and events
are products of the author's imagination, and any resemblance to actual events
or places or persons, living or dead, is entirely coincidental.

First Touchstone hardcover edition October 2013

TOUCHSTONE and colophon are registered trademarks of Simon & Schuster, Inc.

For information about special discounts for bulk purchases, please contact
Simon & Schuster Special Sales at 1-866-506-1949 or business@simonandschuster.com.

The Simon & Schuster Speakers Bureau can bring authors to your live event.
For more information or to book an event contact the Simon & Schuster
Speakers Bureau at 1-866-248-3049 or visit our website at www.simonspeakers.com.

Designed by Akasha Archer

Manufactured in the United States of America

10 9 8 7 6 5 4 3 2 1

ISBN 978-1-4516-8475-9
ISBN 978-1-4516-8478-0 (ebook)

Contents

CONTENTS

Introduction

One of the most often repeated legends in the publishing world is that crime fiction writers are the nicest of all. The theory is that they work out all their angst and all their aggression on the page by killing made-up people in all kinds of gruesome ways, thereby leaving their real lives full of nothing but kindness, generosity, and gauzy goodwill. Consequently, they help, support, and encourage one another. The success of one is celebrated by all, and they're always ready to drop everything to help out with a good cause.

That's the legend.

Is it true?

Well, yes, it is. All of us were new to the scene once, and all of us can testify to the help and support and encouragement we received from those who came before. All of us remember being sincerely and genuinely congratulated on whatever small successes came our way both by those who left such milestones behind long ago and by those yet to reach them. All of us have had flat spots or difficulties, and all of us have been helped out of them by the others.

But what about dropping everything for a good cause?

That's true, too. You're holding the proof in your hands—a serial novel that combines the efforts of twenty great crime writers in a twisted noir tale so seamless it shows just how cooperative crime fiction writers can be when they put their talents together. *Inherit the Dead* is as nasty and dark as it is fun, every chapter a surprise yet inevitable.

But how did it come about?

Well, Linda Fairstein needs no introduction as an acclaimed crime writer, but she's also a real-life prosecutor on some very tragic criminal cases. Linda, being Linda, wanted to do more than just secure convictions. She wanted to draw attention to Safe Horizon, the largest victims' support charity in the United States, that provides assistance of every kind to victims of crime, long after the legal dust has settled.

And Jonathan Santlofer needs no introduction as an acclaimed crime writer either or as an acclaimed painter—which he is, too, by the way—and which helps make my point: he generally doesn't have much spare time on his hands. But Jonathan happily agreed to put the book together and to help the charity. The idea was to assemble an extraordinary cast of bestselling contributors who would combine their creative talents and help support Safe Horizon's vital work.

So he put out a call to his wish list of contributors—even though he knew that none of them was exactly sitting around doing nothing. At a rough guess, between them they'll publish about thirty or so novels this year, and I know there's major involvement in five or six TV series and a couple—or more—major movies; and they all have families, and they all have personal projects of their own.

So what did they all say?

They all said yes. Immediately. They dropped everything and rallied around a good cause. I'm proud to call them my friends, my peers, and my colleagues. And I'm delighted to have a good book to read. I hope you will be, too. And thank you for helping out by buying it.

Crime writers really are a great bunch of people.

Crime readers, too.

LEE CHILD
New York
2013

INHERIT
THE DEAD

1

JONATHAN SANTLOFER

The call had been unexpected. The reference—a friend of a friend of a friend—too complicated to follow. But the job—if it turned into a job—was simple enough, a missing person. Or so the caller had said. But Perry Christo, former NYPD homicide detective turned private investigator, knew nothing was ever simple.

It was six years now since he'd left the NYPD. That was the way he always said it: *I left the police department six years ago.* As opposed to the truth: that he had been fired. More specifically: asked to leave *before* he was fired.

Pericles Alexandros Christo, Perry to his friends (though he didn't have many—his choice). His mother was the only one who had dared call him Pericles (and live). Forty-four years old, disgraced cop, divorced, one of those men who saw his child every other weekend and sometimes less. His fault. He tugged his collar up against the wind as he cut across Third Avenue. It was the kind of winter day that reminded residents Manhattan was an island surrounded by water, icy water, an unprotected twenty-four square miles of land that had nothing to shield it from the chill other than glass and steel skyscrapers that only helped create wind tunnels and lonely corridors.

But the address Perry was headed for, 720 Park Avenue, only a dozen or so blocks from his Yorkville one-bedroom, could have been a hundred miles away in every conceivable way and buffered by something special: money.

The call had come the night before.

It's my daughter. She's missing and—

Did you call the police?

No. It's . . . a family matter. And I want to keep it that way.

How long?

How long . . . what?

How long has she been missing?

Oh. A week. No. Closer to two.

Perry thought: *Two weeks.* If his daughter were missing for two *days* he'd have called out the National Guard.

That's a long time.

A pause. *Well, my daughter, Angel, has a tendency to . . . wander. Now and then.*

Wander?

Yes. Take a trip, go off with a friend. She's not a child. She's twenty. And she doesn't live with me.

Who does she live with?

Her father.

And I presume he hasn't heard from her.

You presume correctly.

Have you checked with her friends?

Of course. The words barked.

Perry could tell this would be no ordinary mother-and-child reunion.

You will help me, Detective.

It was not a question. And Perry had not answered it. Instead, he waited for her next command, which followed.

Come see me. Now.

Now?

Is that a problem?

Now—as in ten at night—when he was already in his underwear, feet up, watching a *Law & Order* rerun. Clearly a woman used to getting what she wanted when she wanted it. But if she could wait nearly two weeks, she could wait another eight hours.

I'll see you in the morning.

But you will get started right away.

Again, not a question.

We'll see, he'd said, though he knew he would take the case. A job was a job. And with the current economy he needed every one, though he was doing okay. Four years now since he'd started his own PI firm. More than half of his tiny apartment was his ad hoc office: two computers, a scanner, video equipment, a digital camera with an extra-long telephoto lens, listening devices. Things he never imagined he'd be using, but necessary for the work he did for his biggest clients: insurance companies. Spent his days spying on people out dancing and climbing trees when they claimed they couldn't walk.

It's my daughter, she's missing . . .

The woman's words replayed in Perry's mind as he quickened his step against the cold.

He didn't particularly like missing persons—"locates," as they were called in the business. Most of them were people who didn't want to be found, embezzlers or ex-husbands behind on child support, the latter his least favorite and something he turned down when he could. Perry hadn't missed a child support payment in five years, even at his lowest point when it meant skipping meals—but a missing girl, even one twenty years old, was something else, something to worry about.

Unless she'd run away. Perry turned the corner, more icy wind in his face. Most runaways were teenagers, he knew that, young ones who didn't know yet how tough it could be out in the cold, cold world. Perry had found more than his share of them. Girls and boys out of the plains states, corn-fed innocents, pretty young things who'd run away because they hated their parents for good and bad reasons. A mistake either way, which they learned working Manhattan's mean streets. Most turning up scared and sick, ruined, a few who might be saved (though he was never sure); every one of them another scar on his soul, to see what the world could do to a kid.

Perry tugged the woolen scarf—a gift from Nicky—tighter around his neck.

It's not my birthday, kiddo.

Does it have to be your birthday to get a gift, Daddy? You give me things all the time.

Nicky had draped the scarf around his neck—soft wool, blue and tan stripes. *See, it matches your eyes, Daddy.*

Impossible. There's no red in this scarf, and my eyes are always bloodshot.

Oh, pul-leese, Daddy. Your eyes are blue, like mine!

The best kid in the world—and he had lost her. Well, not entirely. But every other weekend was like a prison sentence, though one he would wait out because in another three years she'd be eighteen and thinking about college. Barnard on the Upper West Side. Something Perry had suggested. He was already checking out two-bedroom apartments in the area.

The thought made him smile, but looking around at the passersby he noted he was the only one. Lexington Avenue was clogged with people trudging to work on streets slick with ice or stepping over gutters filled with blackened snow, all of them frowning.

A strong gust of wind made him shiver. He'd walked only a few blocks, but he was freezing. His winter coat, a three-year-old trench with a cheap zip-in lining, wasn't doing the trick. His gloveless hands—he'd lost the third pair he had bought on the street a week ago—were jammed into his pockets and going numb. If Nicky noticed, she'd be getting him a new pair for sure. God, how he loved that kid. His best work, for sure.

Last night's call played again as he crossed Lexington Avenue.

I'll expect you at nine, Detective.

One more time Perry had neglected to correct his status with the client he was about to see. Six years since he'd been a detective. A lifetime, though Perry still saw it like it was yesterday, that damn Bayer case immediately in his mind.

A taxi's blaring horn brought him back to the moment in the middle of the street, but not for long.

I know you would never do anything bad, Daddy.

The look on his daughter's face when she'd said that—bravery mixed with sadness mixed with confusion, trying to smile, to make *him* feel better.

You're right, sweetheart. I wouldn't. And I didn't.

The taxi beeped again, the driver leaning out his window, "Get out of the street, asshole!"

Perry flipped him the finger as he dodged and jogged across the street then headed on to Park Avenue.

Could it be that the cold was a little less bitter here, the air sweeter? No dirty snow in the gutters. No ice on the perfectly clean sidewalks.

The rich, thought Perry.

He took in the wide avenue lined with beautiful old apartment buildings and beautiful new ones. He made it only halfway across, stopped by traffic, on the center divider where there were tulips in spring and begonias in summer, trees all year round. The median was currently housing large Botero sculptures of bulky men and women, three or four to a block, bronze figures lightly dusted with last week's snow that gave them the look of huge Christmas ornaments. Perry noted one lone icicle hanging off the breast of a sculpted woman and wondered why the city needed sculptures of fat people in the middle of its ritziest avenue? Was it to make all the rich ladies, those social X-rays starving themselves to death, feel better, thinner? As if that were possible.

Perry flicked his finger at the icicle, watched it shatter. A woman beside him in a dark mink raised an eyebrow, or tried, her Botoxed mask as frozen as the ice. In a few months, he knew there would be other sculptures, then flowers, niceties few parts of the city could afford but apparently a requirement for this neighborhood.

Perry reconsidered what he had managed to glean from several hours on the Internet about Julia Drusilla. She was a socialite who was no longer very social, her name and face having disappeared from the society pages over the past few years. There'd been mention of her parents' deaths a decade ago, and the fact that her father had made—and married—a fortune. Plus a few references to Julia Drusilla's charitable giving. Beyond that, she remained a mystery. One he was about to confront.

Seven twenty Park was a limestone and sienna prewar building, solid and substantial-looking, with an arched entrance and canopied walkway. Huge urns with seasonal evergreens stood beside the double-door entrance. A doorman, red-nosed and with graying temples, white gloves, and a uniform so starched it could have stood on its own, opened the door while Perry attempted to smooth his own windblown hair into place. Suddenly everything about him felt wrong: his coat, his gloveless hands, his chewed cuticles, his old uniform dress shoes, which had surely lost their luster. Why hadn't he polished them?

A few steps inside were small heaters warming the foyer so residents did not have to freeze while waiting for cars and drivers or taxis, and right now Perry appreciated them. He rubbed his hands together while a second doorman, this one a young Latino, looked him up and down with something more than the usual doorman appraisal, though Perry wasn't sure what, or why.

"May I help you, sir?"

"I'm here to see Julia Drusilla."

Something ticked on the young man's face, barely noticeable but Perry caught it.

"Your name?"

"Perry Christo. She's expecting me."

"One moment, sir." The young doorman plucked the house phone off the wall. "Mrs. Drusilla—" Another tic, this one longer, eye blinking, corner of the mouth tipping up to meet it. "There is a Mr.— Excuse me, I'm sorry—"

"Christo."

"A Mr. Christo here to see you." The doorman nodded at Perry and offered a smile that actually seemed friendly. Then he angled his jaw toward a large lobby. "Just through there, sir." He replaced the phone with an audible sigh.

Perry wondered if it was the job or Julia Drusilla that had caused the sigh along with the facial tics.

"The elevator is at the rear. That's the top floor. Penthouse A."

Perry crossed the large lobby, its centerpiece a huge display of calla lilies arranged in an even huger vase. The room was overheated, Perry going from cold to hot in a matter of seconds, the flora adding an exotic, jungle quality. Behind it, he caught his reflection in floor-to-ceiling mirrors flecked with gold. He attempted to smooth the wrinkles out of his trench then gave up, took it off, and folded it over his arm. It didn't help. His shirt was wrinkled, too. He looked like a door-to-door salesman who'd come to the wrong door.

The elevator had more heat, more gold, and more mirrors, but

Perry didn't need another look to confirm that his wool sports jacket looked tatty, his out-of-date tie too wide.

The elevator deposited him into an equally overheated hallway leading to only two apartments—one to the east and one to the west. The door to the west apartment, directly opposite, was still adorned with a Christmas wreath and had a brand-new sisal doormat. The door to the east apartment, at the far end of the hallway, was bare, and there was no welcome mat.

Perry pressed the bell. There was a low chime from somewhere inside the apartment, and then the door opened and Julia Drusilla stood there, backlit, a dark skeleton.

"Come in," she said, her voice a rasping whisper.

Perry closed the door behind him. In contrast to the stuffy lobby and hallway, the penthouse was not heated. It actually felt air-conditioned, with cool breezes issuing from invisible ducts that fluttered his hair and made him shiver.

Julia Drusilla, elegant in a sleeveless white tunic, was already moving down her hallway into a living room large enough to house five or six of his entire Yorkville apartment, her bare feet soundless on black marble floors that reflected nothing and gave the place the look of an endless pit. The ceilings were high, the furniture low and surprisingly spare—white couches, small slate tables. But the most impressive part of the apartment was the view behind the glass, which ran the entire length of the living room and the terrace beyond. He caught a glimpse of a terrace dotted with evergreens and what looked like fragments of sculpture, a larger-than-life-size marble foot, half a toga-clad torso. Beyond that, the spires of Manhattan apartments, a swath of Central Park, and low-hanging clouds in an endless gray sky.

"You have a magnificent view," said Perry, taking a few steps closer.

Julia Drusilla turned her head toward the glass then back at Perry. Her pale gray eyes caught the light, startling and beautiful, but with something hard and impenetrable behind them. "I suppose," she said. "But one gets used to such things. I rarely notice."

"The sculpture— That foot . . ."

"There are a few others you can't see unless you go out there, and more at my homes in Palm Beach and Aspen, though I rarely go to either anymore." She sighed, a bony, perfectly manicured hand at her throat. "They're all Roman, late empire. The early and mid period are impossible to find; the museums have greedily scooped them up. But I'm happy with the sculptures I have. They remind me that people die but culture lives on."

"Can I borrow that for my tombstone?"

Julia Drusilla peered at him, her gray eyes narrowed. "Is that a joke?"

"Sorry," said Perry. "Not a very good one.

"No," she said, with a flicker of anger before she gazed back at the terrace. "You may go out there, if you'd like, to see the sculptures. I never do. I'm not a fan of heights."

"Then why—"

"Live in a penthouse on the twenty-fourth floor?" She smiled for a half second, translucent skin tugging away from large, capped teeth. "It was my husband's—my ex-husband's idea—and I got used to it, but . . ." She seemed lost for a moment then focused on Perry. "You're not what I expected."

"That bad, huh?"

"Another joke?"

"'Fraid so."

Julia Drusilla frowned. "You're younger and better looking. I imagined a private detective would be some sort of tough guy with a greasy little mustache and bad shoes."

Perry looked down at his old police dress shoes. They'd been good years back but not so good now, though they'd apparently passed some small test.

He glanced up and past Julia at a large abstract painting. "Pollock?"

"Yes," she said, and cast a reappraising eye at him. "You really aren't the typical private detective, are you?"

"My mother was an artist. Well, sort of."

"How nice for you," she said, brittle edging on bitter. "Mine was . . ." She shook her head and looked back at the painting. "I bought it at auction, at Sotheby's, just last week."

"Oh yes, I read about the sale." Perry couldn't remember the exact price, but it had been newsworthy. Front page. It had set a record for a Jackson Pollock painting, something astronomical, in the millions; the buyer's name undisclosed.

"You're a very observant man."

"It's my job."

"Good," she said, giving him another look, this one impossible to read. "Would you care for something, Detective, coffee or tea?"

"If you have coffee, sure. I can't seem to shake the chill."

"Oh. It's the air-conditioning. The illness raises my temperature, so I keep it on all the time. I'm afraid I hardly feel it." She waved a hand at her face as if to cool it further. "You don't mind, do you?"

"No," he said, stifling a shiver.

"So, coffee . . ." she said, a bewildered look entering her eyes. "Actually, I'm afraid my maid doesn't come in until ten, and I'm lost without her."

"No then—please don't. I'm fine."

"I don't drink it myself. How about tea? I think I can boil water."

Next thing Perry knew he was on one of the low sofas, balancing a cup of something herbal and lemony on his knee; Julia Drusilla was sitting opposite, bony fingers tapping against a china cup that looked almost, though not quite, as fragile as she was.

"That portrait, the one above your—"

"My father," she said.

"An impressive-looking man."

"Yes. He died some years ago, along with my mother, in a tragic accident."

"I'm sorry."

"Don't be. I hate it when people apologize for things that have nothing to do with them."

"I wasn't taking responsibility, merely expressing—"

She waved his explanation away. "I don't have time for niceties, Detective. I'm not a well woman."

"So you said."

"Did I?"

"Yes. But you look . . . fine."

"I look like death and know it." She made a noise in the back of her nose. "You should have seen me when I was young. I was beautiful once. Can you believe that?"

"You're still a beautiful woman," he said, and it was true, though the beauty had ossified.

"And you're a liar, but a charming one. Though you must always be truthful with me."

"I usually am."

"Except when you are flattering an older woman or trying to save someone the pain of bad news?"

"A little of both," said Perry.

"Well, don't *ever* lie to *me*. Not *ever*. I have been lied to enough in my life, and I won't tolerate it." Her gray eyes had gone cold and steely, her mouth set tight. Perry noticed her hands had balled into fists, as if getting ready to strike.

"I don't care much for lies or liars myself.

"Good," she said, the harsh glint of metal in her eyes giving way to something a bit less threatening, though Perry hadn't missed it. "Then we understand each other."

"Indeed." Perry nodded, though he allowed his stare to mimic just a bit of her rigidity before changing the subject. "So, your daughter. She disappeared from where, exactly?"

"From her father's Montauk home. According to Norman, he has not seen her for almost two weeks." Julia Drusilla was now up and pacing.

"I'll need the exact time of her disappearance."

"You can get that from Norman. I imagine you will want to speak to him."

"Yes. And your husband didn't call the police, didn't report your daughter missing?"

"No. He called *me*. Which was the right thing to do." Her voice took on strength.

"Tell me more about your daughter. Anything that will help me find her." Perry plucked a pad and pen from his pocket.

"Well, Angelina, Angel, has been living with her father, my ex-husband, since our divorce."

"Your husband got custody?" Perry tried to keep the surprise out of his voice. A father getting custody was a big deal; he knew that from experience.

"Not exactly. We determined together—my husband and I— what was better for Angel. Ours was not one of those acrimonious divorces. Angel's happiness was all that mattered." She ran one of her long fingers along the edge of her too-sharp jaw. "You're not married, are you, Detective?"

"No."

"Divorced?"

"Yes."

"Children?"

"I have a daughter," he said, wondering how this had become an interview, one he was on the wrong side of. "She lives with her mother."

"Of course she does. Always the way, isn't it? Well, almost always." She stopped pacing and sagged into one of the low couches just opposite, as if the conversation was suddenly too much for her.

Perry wondered if she was acting. Everything about her seemed theatrical.

"How old was Angel when you and your husband divorced?"

"Does that matter?"

"Maybe. I'm not sure yet."

"Fourteen. She was such a headstrong girl at the time. Of course she always was, but particularly then. Perhaps the divorce was somewhat to blame: the strain and—"

"I thought you said the divorce was amicable?"

"But I did not say it was easy. And teenagers can be difficult."

Perry nodded, though he'd give anything to have his teenage daughter around twenty-four/seven, difficult or not.

"We considered boarding school, and in retrospect I think it would have been a better choice for her."

"Why's that?"

"Because Norman is far too lenient. He spoils Angel. And he has problems."

"Such as?"

She sighed. "They're under control now."

"I need to know if—"

"I *said* they are under control." The steel was back in her eyes—and her voice.

"Mrs. Drusilla." Perry spoke quietly and chose his words carefully. "If I'm going to find your daughter, I need to know everything."

"Norman would never do anything to harm Angel. It's just that—" A short intake of breath. "He drinks. Or did. And when he does— Well, you've never seen such a personality change. It's quite"—she shook her head—"extraordinary."

"Is that the reason you two—"

"Divorced? No. It had nothing to do with *that*," she said, hard. "But he's stopped drinking. At least I think so, hope so." Then more quietly, "All I was saying is that if Norman had been tougher, Angel might not have disappeared without a word. He doesn't lay down any rules."

"What about your rules?"

"I'm afraid I have little say over what Angel does. She doesn't live here, remember?"

"But you're her mother."

"I repeat: she does not live here. I cannot be a disciplinarian from a distance, and Angel . . . well, we don't see each other very often."

"When was the last time?"

"We have not seen each other in . . ." She looked up at ceiling. "I can't say for certain but . . . probably close to a year."

"A year?"

"Yes. Give or take a few . . . weeks."

"That's a long time. Did you have a fight?"

"No. We just . . . don't get along very well. The distance is good for us." She sighed. "I'd hoped Angel would grow out of her rebellious phase—all teenage girls have issues with their mothers, don't they, Detective? Lord knows I gave my poor mother a terrible time. But Angel can't seem to get past it."

"So you *did* argue."

"In the past. But not anymore. It's hard to argue when you rarely speak."

"I see."

"No, I don't think you do, Detective." She leaned closer, her breath minty with a hint of something medicinal. "Despite our disagreements, I am her mother, and I love her very much. And I believe down deep she loves me, too. One day—soon, I hope—she will come to realize how *much* I love her." She sniffed as if she was fighting tears, but her eyes were perfectly clear, her tone clipped. "It's why I must find her. Why *you* must find her." She laid a bony hand on Perry's. It was cold and dry. "I don't have much time, and I need to make things right between us, need to . . ." Her breathing became labored, a wheezing sound, as if there was cotton wadding in her nose and throat.

"Are you all right?"

"Y-yes. Or . . . I will be once you find my daughter and bring her back to me."

Bring her back? But she was never here.

She took deep breaths, a hand to her throat. "All I know is that she is gone and no one has heard from her. I'm frightened, Detective."

Perry tried to read her face, but it was flat, expressionless. "You said that your daughter often took off, *wandered,* so there's probably no reason to suspect anything is wrong—or is there?"

She looked away, and when she turned back there was something ferocious in her eyes though she spoke calmly, "No. There's nothing. Nothing at all." She continued to stare at him, not speaking.

Perry let the quiet expand between them. Something he'd learned as a cop: let the suspect fill the uncomfortable void.

And she did. "There's something you should know, Detective. Angel will be twenty-one in less than two weeks, at which time she will come into a sizable fortune."

"I see. And Angel knows this?"

"No. At least I never told her. Of course she knew she would get money, *my* money, which is considerable, though she has a small, serviceable income of her own. I thought it best she not spend her youth knowing she would come into tremendous wealth. I did not want money to stifle her need to work, to grow as a human being. It's better to come into money later and not know about it, don't you agree, Detective?"

"Sure," said Perry. "Though I wouldn't know."

"Well, I do. Money can make one lazy, even corrupt."

Money can make people do all sorts of things, thought Perry.

"All Angel has to do is sign some papers and the money is hers. I would not have waited until the last minute, but the trust stipulates that she sign on her twenty-first birthday. Not a day earlier—or later. A ridiculous technicality, but I suppose it was put there in the event that"—she heaved a sigh—"that Angel was not alive on her twenty-first birthday. My God, what a horrid thought."

"And if she doesn't sign?"

"The trust remains entirely with me. We are meant to split what remains of my father's money, which he put in trust for his heirs."

"Let me get this straight. If Angel signs, she gets half the money."

"Yes."

"And if she doesn't, *you* get it all."

"Yes." She painted on a smile. "I see what you're thinking, Detective. That I might want to keep all of the money for myself."

"The thought did cross my mind."

"Please. I have more money than I know what to do with. And I'm dying." Her eyes locked on his. "Why would I want you to find my daughter if I wanted to keep her money?"

Perry didn't know, but he let the question sit there.

"Another two or three hundred million makes no difference to me."

"Which is it?"

"Which is *what?*" She stood up and shook out her arms, then started to pace again, her white tunic floating behind her. *She looks like a ghost,* Perry thought.

"Two or three hundred million?"

She stopped pacing and looked at him. "I'm not sure. Does it really matter?"

"We're talking about a lot of money."

"I suppose." Julia Drusilla shrugged her bony shoulders. "I just want Angel to have what is rightfully hers—to have the life she was meant to have, the freedom to do whatever she wants. Money can buy freedom, Detective." She started pacing again, tapping her bony hand against her thigh as she did.

"I can imagine," said Perry, and almost corrected himself: he could *not* imagine. He was trying to think it through: a girl about to inherit a fortune who disappears. Did she know—or didn't she?

"Is there anyone who might benefit if Angel doesn't sign those papers?"

Julia Drusilla stopped pacing again. "None who I know of."

"But there could be?"

"What do you mean?"

"You said none who you know of, but could there be someone out there you don't know of?"

"Like who?"

"What about your husband?"

"Norman? That's ridiculous. He's perfectly comfortable. His needs are well taken care of. I've seen to that."

"Two or three hundred million dollars can fulfill even more needs."

"Don't be absurd. Norman adores Angel. And he has plenty of money." Her voice went hard then softened, and she came closer, her hand on his hand again.

An air-conditioned breeze grazed the back of Perry's neck, and he shivered—or was it Julia Drusilla's touch?

"Anyone else?" he asked.

"No. No one."

"If Angel doesn't sign the papers, do you still get your half of the money?"

She let her hand drop from his. "It may take a bit longer but . . . yes."

"That must be a relief."

"I've already told you, Detective, the money means nothing to me." She stared at him, her gray eyes a mix of steely and needy that made Perry uncomfortable. "You will find her, won't you?"

"I'll need a picture." Perry glanced around the room; there wasn't a single photograph anywhere.

Julia disappeared down a hallway then reappeared with a wallet-size photo, a portrait, the girl's face filling it.

"Does she always look like this?" Perry asked.

"You mean, does it look like her?"

"Yes."

"It does."

Perry studied the photo: Angel's hair looked like gold, her eyes a startling shade of blue. There was something old-fashioned about her, too, something that brought to mind movie stars of the 1940s and '50s, her hooded eyes and the way the corners of her lips tipped up into a sly Kewpie-doll smile.

"She's a beautiful girl," he said.

"Yes," said Julia. "Very beautiful. Everybody says so." The veins in her neck stood out.

Perry took one more look at the photo then slipped it into his pocket, feeling as if he'd accepted something forbidden.

"Well then, you have everything you need," said Julia. She folded her thin arms across her chest and glanced at the hallway, his cue to leave.

He stood up, once again noticed the Jackson Pollock painting, and wondered why someone would buy a multimillion-dollar painting when she was about to die.

Julia led him toward the door.

"Your husband's address?" he asked.

"Of course." She wrote it down on a piece of lavender notepaper and placed it in his palm, her bony hand wrapping around his. "Find her, Mr. Christo. Bring my Angel back to me."

One more time, thought Perry, *it was not a question.*

You sit in the rental car you can't afford, not yet, but soon, soon, waiting outside her fancy apartment for almost an hour now, freezing, the heat switched off to save on gas, and finally he comes out in that ratty trench coat. Almost makes you laugh. I mean, Is he kidding? A private eye in a trench coat? What a fucking cliché. But this is no laughing matter.

You straighten up, concentrate on what you have to do: follow him. Not easy, following someone who is on foot, in your car, in the city, taxis and buses and people cutting ahead of you, and you don't dare use the horn and bring attention to yourself, worrying he will spot you.

Then he stops beside a parked car, fumbles keys out of his pocket, his striped scarf blowing in the wind like a banner.

You pull into a bus stop, hoping a traffic cop does not come by, and you watch from a half block away, sipping your third black coffee of the morning, holding the damn Styrofoam cup so tight it cracks and coffee leaks onto your hand and into your lap and you're trying to mop it up, cursing, and keep an eye on him at the same time, and suddenly he's driving away and you forget the damn coffee, pull out of the bus stop so fast you practically hit a taxi, the driver laying on his horn so loud you're sure the private eye can hear so you duck, keeping your head down but peering over the steering wheel, afraid you will lose him, telling yourself to be calm, to breathe, to watch, your eyes like lasers taking in the scratches on the trunk and his license plate, which you memorize, just in case, as you creep down Second Avenue, keeping a few cars between you, the way people do in the movies. But then the traffic eases and he's driving fast, weaving around cars, but no way you're going to lose him because this is the most important thing you ever did in your life so it doesn't matter if you've got hot coffee soaking your lap or that your head is aching and your eyes itch from too little sleep and your heart pounds from all the caffeine because it's finally happening: it's not just a dream anymore.

You tell yourself to relax, to be cool as you watch him steer his crummy car into the single lane that's merging into the Midtown Tunnel, your eyes on those paint scratches and license plate, repeating the numbers in your head until his car disappears into the tunnel and you follow it into the darkness with the plan in your head and murder in your heart.

2

STEPHEN L. CARTER

Perry hated Long Island. Maybe it was the traffic, maybe it was the smells, maybe it was the sense that everybody else mired in the unmoving sea of metal on the expressway was heading out to a five-million-dollar house in the Hamptons in a vehicle worth ten of the aging but faithful Datsun (which was pretty much the only thing he'd been able to salvage from the divorce). Montauk was the far end of the island, so he'd be annoyed for a while. People out that way claimed that their town had been the inspiration for *Jaws,* and Perry in his sour moments liked to imagine a two-ton great white emerging from the water to gobble up all the actors and investment bankers and their fawning acolytes.

He'd had a client a couple of years ago, an economist at Columbia who thought his boyfriend was cheating. They had a place in Southampton, and the boyfriend lived there full time, while the professor drove out on weekends. Perry must have braved the Long Island Expressway a dozen times over the course of a month. Passersby gawked at his ancient car and took him for common, which he certainly was. Finally, Perry concluded that the boyfriend was true as steel. But the client sent him back to take another look. Perry went along, because in those days he was what his father used to call *short funds*. It took

him another week to figure it out. The boyfriend was clean. It was
the professor who was cheating, and hoping to find evidence of a dal-
liance by his partner to make the breakup easier.

Clients lied. All of them, without exception. Perry pondered this
most basic rule of the business as his Northstar V8 allowed him to
accelerate past the shiny new Priuses and Audis of environmentally
conscious millionaires. Clients lied. There were the clever ones who
lied because they were proud, and the shy ones who lied because they
were ashamed. There were the mothers who lied about what they'd
done to their children, and the husbands who lied about what they'd
done to their wives. Clients lied to protect their own guilt or somebody else's innocence. Lots of the lies were innocuous. But a lot of
them weren't. Half the time, the job the client really wanted Perry to
do was a lot grubbier than the job he had supposedly been hired for.

Like his new client, Julia Drusilla. She might not have been lying,
but she certainly wasn't telling the whole truth. Perry had felt it from
the moment he walked in. She had sat there beneath that fading portrait of her father and smiled her butter-won't-melt smile and sipped
her tea and told him considerably less than half the story.

Perry didn't know yet what she was leaving out, but he could
make some educated guesses.

Take Norman, Julia's ex-husband. Whoever heard of a missing-
child case in which the mother wasn't screaming that the whole thing
was her ex's fault? And then there was the ammo. The drinking. But
all Julia had to say was that Perry should be sure to talk to him. Then
there was her sad confession that she couldn't actually remember the
last time she had clapped eyes on her daughter—an event no mother
was likely to forget. Or maybe it was her determination to keep the
investigation away from the police. Lots of clients asked for that
when the question was whether some relative had a hand in the till.
But when a family member vanished, they usually hired the Perry

Christos of the world to supplement, not to supplant, the official inquiry.

This was why he didn't like missing-persons cases: the lies were almost always central to the mystery. Once you solved the lie, the mystery ceased to mystify. Some parent or spouse was always teary, but in Perry's experience, nine times out of ten the husband or wife or child who was missing had run away voluntarily—and, most of the time, had an excellent reason for not wanting to go back. Usually the reasons involved the very person who'd hired Perry in the first place.

He wondered what Angel was running from. Julia Drusilla had spoken with relative warmth and understanding of her ex-husband, Norman. It would be interesting to learn whether those feelings were reciprocated. If Perry's own twisted life was any indication, Norman and Julia fought a lot, especially about Angel. He was even willing to bet that Norman saw less of his daughter than he would like. Perry had never met Norman Loki, but he already sympathized with him.

The expressway ended abruptly when one reached the rich part of the island, as though the denizens of the Hamptons and points east wanted to make it as hard as possible to find their weekend McMansions. In summer, the expressway would be clogged all the way to the terminus; although it was winter, and traffic light, Perry exited early by habit and was on Route 27, the Sunrise Highway, which resembled main roads in most towns in America, except that out here the luxury-car dealerships seemed to outnumber the convenience stores. But he'd miscalculated—traffic was nearly at a standstill. Directly ahead of him was a minivan with teenagers hanging out the windows, yelling at a fancier car full of equally drunk youngsters in the next lane. The cop in him knew that before the day was out somebody was going to get hurt. Perry reminded himself, with difficulty, that he was no longer on the force, and that drunk, spoiled, rich kids were no longer his problem.

His ex-wife used to accuse him of never letting his guard down, of always looking at the world with cynical cop's eyes. He would answer, stupidly but accurately, that the world had a way of living down to a cynical cop's expectations of it. On vacation Noreen would beg him to turn off his suspicion of everyone they passed for a week or at least a day, and Perry tried. Unfortunately, the hard truth was that in those days he trusted nobody but his family—and, since the divorce, nobody.

Now those cop's eyes were active again, counting off the landmarks according to their role in his working life as a PI since leaving the force: here the staid golf club where he had teased out the key clue in the Thursby investigation; there the lively garden shop where the serial killer Derace McDonald, under another name, had lived his fugitive existence. That one, he reminded himself with a shudder, had begun as a missing-persons case, too. So many of them did: it was as though America had become a vast network of lonely unhappy people so desperately seeking escape into their pasts that they were willing to spend good money to get there.

As far as Perry was concerned, it was a missing-persons case that had got him booted from the police force—although that wasn't the way *People of the State of New York v. Bayer* was filed. If you looked it up, *Bayer* had nothing to do with any missing person. It was a simple drug-possession bust, and Perry was involved because whenever his lieutenant was down on him, he wound up loaned to Narcotics, with explicit if unspoken instructions that he be assigned to forced-entry cases, preferably no later than second through the door.

And his lieutenant had been down on him a lot.

The case was in all the papers. Theo Bayer was a political firebrand and the pastor of one of the biggest churches in Harlem. Everybody running for office in Manhattan made the pilgrimage to his town house on 145th Street, until the day the Narcotics boys broke down the basement door and found enough money and drugs to put him away for twenty years. Perry wouldn't have given the case two thoughts had he not gone to dinner at the home of his uncle Jackie, by then retired from the force, who had trained the man who captained the 30th Precinct. Uncle Jackie told him that his protégé found the whole drug bust very strange. There was no narcotics activity to speak of around 145th Street, and he had never heard of a dealer of such prominence keeping a stash in his house. The drugs didn't make any sense.

Perry had been in on the bust. He assured Jackie that everything was clean and aboveboard. But he wondered. Sure, Bayer was already in plea negotiations. Sure, the brass had assured the press that one of the biggest dealers in Harlem had gone down. Still. Two of the Narcotics detectives on the scene, including the one whose informants had fingered the pastor, were men Perry had long suspected of being on the take. They made a nice side income by arresting dealers and stealing part of the stash. Not too much—always within a counting error, usually less than a tenth. So if the experts said the street value of the haul was a quarter of a million, they might bleed off ten or fifteen thousand—nothing that would ever be missed. Perry had gone to his uncle with the tale, and Jackie had laughed and told him boys will be boys. Not that he approved, the former Captain Christo hastily added. But it's a little bit like the way the factories recycle their pollution to make electricity.

Said Uncle Jackie.

But Perry couldn't leave the case alone. He'd been in plenty of drug dens, and the preacher's well-kept town house had none of the telltale signs: no reinforced interior doors, no hollowed-out mattresses, no sweet sickly smell from the drains. When a public man went down, his fans always denied his guilt, but this time the beseeching had the ring of truth. Bayer didn't live above his income. He didn't drive a fancy car. If he was dealing, nobody knew what he was doing with the money. The more time Perry spent going over the records, the more certain he was that the preacher was being framed. But he couldn't see what the crooked cops would have to gain, and he didn't know why Bayer wasn't protesting his innocence from the rooftops. On the contrary: according to what Perry heard, Bayer was in plea negotiations.

And so Perry, never one to turn away from risk, took what the lawyers called an inevitable step: he went to visit the pastor in jail.

As soon as they were alone, the first thing Bayer said was that there was no need to check on him. He was keeping his side of the deal. He would plead guilty "as promised." And when Perry asked what deal he was talking about, Bayer said he should tell the others not to worry. Then he sent for the guard and went back to his cell.

It took Perry a week and a half, mostly on his own time, to put the clues together. One informant after another had told detectives that a Harlem preacher was moving significant weight. Nobody knew the name of the pastor, but two or three said they'd heard the church was up around 160th Street.

Bayer's church was on Adam Clayton Powell Boulevard near 132nd.

And there was something else. A missing-persons report. A six-year-old black girl had vanished on her way home from school two days before the raid. Looking closer, knocking on doors, Perry discovered what nobody else seemed to know: the missing girl was Bayer's niece.

So he went to his lieutenant to report that things might not be what they seemed, that it looked as if Bayer was taking the rap for somebody else. Somewhere there was another Harlem preacher who was really dealing, and who had arranged with a couple of the

Narcotics boys for Bayer to take the fall. His lieutenant told him to sit tight and give him a chance to look into it. The next day Bayer's lawyer was on television, reporting that one of the detectives on the raid had been to visit his client in lockup, slapping him around and demanding a bribe.

The press loved it: "Rogue Cop Beats Preacher!" The way the newspapers had it figured, Perry was the bad cop, trying to cover his ass by getting Bayer to inculpate the good ones. That the story made no sense once you thought about it didn't matter to the guardians of public integrity. The brass preferred to avoid a hearing, and, on the advice of counsel but especially of his wife, so did Perry. Uncle Jackie still had a string or two to pull. Noreen pleaded with her husband to accept the offer of resignation that the department put on the table. They were seated in the television nook of their small house in Flushing. Alex Trebek was apologizing to a contestant whose points were coming off the board because he had mispronounced Bouvier.

I didn't do anything wrong, Perry had said to the one person in the world who might listen. *They knew what I'd been looking into, and they set me up.*

So what?

Perry blinked. This was the last response he had expected. He tried to keep his voice gentle, an unnatural act that he committed only in the presence of those he loved. *I'm a cop. My uncles were both cops. It's the family business. I'm good at it. I care about the force. I have to stay and fight so I can find out who really took the money.*

Noreen's face was locked against his entreaties. *If you stay and fight, there's a good chance you'll lose,* she had said.

I know that. I've given this a lot of thought, Norrie. I have friends on the force. We'll get the evidence.

She shifted ground. He had rarely known her to be so adamant. *Have you given any thought to your family? To Nicky?*

That's who I'm doing it for, honey. I don't want her to be ashamed of her father.

She's too young to understand, Perry. If you fight this—if there's a hearing—all she'll understand is that every morning when she goes to school, the other kids will ask her why her dad was on the news last night. Do you really want to put her through that?

Perry was stunned. Not by the argument, although his wife had a point. What broke his determination—and, let's be frank, his courage—was the look in Noreen's beautiful dark eyes.

His wife didn't believe him, either.

Perry had hit the Hamptons at last, but the traffic had not eased, an accident or roadwork, or both. Maybe this was the reason Julia Drusilla hardly ever saw her daughter: driving from Manhattan to the eastern-most tip of Long Island could take an eternity, and Julia was no spring chicken.

Passing an ice-cream parlor with a brace of youngsters outside, he thought again of his own precious Nicky. He knew he had no business criticizing Julia Drusilla; he was angry, really, at himself. Nicky was fifteen, and it was his own fault that he hardly ever saw her. True, he could blame her mother, and like a lot of divorced fathers, he often did. But Perry himself was the one who kept missing those rare weekends because of some case. Besides, even if Noreen used their daughter as a pawn, Perry was the one who let her get away with it. For a while their lawyers had argued, but that had been starting to cost serious money. At some point, he had stopped fighting and given in, letting Noreen control his access to his own flesh and blood.

Had Julia let her husband pull something similar?

Because for all that Perry might have been reviewing his own life in the front of his mind, out back, as he liked to think of it, the case itself had never quite left. Forget the parallels. Forget the divorce angle. Line up the facts. The fortune comes to light, and Angel, the heiress, disappears. Julia seems pretty sure that her daughter was unaware of the money, so it's not likely that she's gone into seclusion at the local convent to pray for guidance about how to spend it. Three choices: Angel hasn't vanished at all and is shacked up with a boyfriend and ignoring her mother's calls; she vanished voluntarily, for a reason having nothing to do with the money; or she vanished involuntarily, in which case a crime has been committed.

Uncle Jackie used to say at such moments that all you need is a three-sided coin.

If Angel had gone off on her own, then Perry would find her and tell her that her mother needed to see her urgently but not why. Let the girl make up her own mind what to do. If she was with her boyfriend, or her girlfriend, same deal. But if somebody disappeared her—say, to prevent her from signing the papers—well, then, he should turn the case over.

In theory.

A cacophony of horns up ahead shook him from his reverie, the obvious reason for all the traffic. Some fool in a delivery truck had tried to beat the light and wound up in the intersection, and now nothing could move in any direction. While others honked and cursed, Perry, who always had a backup plan, turned right at what looked to others like a dead end, cut through a gas station, and headed down to Hill Street, where he turned left. He would rejoin Route 27 half a mile or so up the road, the jammed intersection behind him.

The traffic snarl brought to mind a casual conversation with that Columbia economist who had hired him to investigate his boyfriend. Perry had remarked that they should widen the expressway. The professor had laughed and told him that widening roads made congestion worse: "Add more lanes and you lower the effective cost of driving. If you make a resource cheaper to consume, people take more of it, not less. The way to cut congestion, narrow the road, or add tolls. Lots of tolls. You have to make it harder, not easier. Then people will use it less."

Perry supposed that the same wisdom applied to families, too. If you want to see less of your daughter, let the other parent raise her. There, at least, Perry and Julia were in the same boat.

Passing through Southampton, he did his best to ignore the past but couldn't. It had been almost two years since his last trip to the Hamptons, and he had never expected to come back. He was half tempted to head south and join the brave tourists who, even in winter, dawdled along Meadow Lane gawking at the homes of the superrich. If you hit the water and turned right, you headed for even bigger mansions. If you turned left onto Dune Road, you'd pass the weather-beaten St. Andrew's Dune Church, and beyond the church was some of the most expensive beachfront in the country. The beach was where, on a moonless winter night two years ago, he had cornered mad Derace McDonald; and although Perry had drawn his gun many times, that was the only time in his life he'd fired at another human being.

Perry rubbed at a sudden pain in his side and drove straight ahead. The events of that night were still a blur, and he saw no reason to jog the memory.

That was the other reason he hated Long Island, at least the eastern end where the rich people lived. The last time he was in the Hamptons was the last time he got shot.

3

MARCIA CLARK

Perry squinted through his windshield, taking in the barren white dunes to his right, the rolling, black ocean to his left, and the vast, gray canopy of sky. As he shifted his gaze back to the wide two-lane highway that had finally emptied out of traffic, he was suddenly conscious of a strange, unsettled feeling.

Now that he thought about it, the feeling had begun to creep in a while ago, hovering just below consciousness. He again scanned the austere landscape searching for an answer. And found it. Openness. That's what it was. The sense of near limitless space. And quiet. No concrete canyons that echoed with eardrum-shattering horns, no teeming-humanity sidewalks. It should have been soothing. Instead, it made him anxious, scared. As though he was floating alone and untethered through space. Perry struggled to rationalize the sensation, reasoned with himself that it was just a reaction to the long stretches of lonely road, but the panic continued to surge. He was barely breathing.

He quickly rolled down the window and gulped cold, wet blasts of air. The sobering slap brought him back to earth, and he huffed with relief. But the relief brought only disgust. What kind of loser gets freaked by some empty sand dunes? A familiar lead weight sank in his chest. As usual, he'd found yet another way to despise himself. And no sooner had that feeling wormed its way to the surface than the march of Perry's parade of horribles began: his ruined career on the force, his failed marriage, a daughter he loved dearly but saw only on weekends, and sometimes not even then. He gripped the steering wheel in frustration. He didn't have time for this now. With an effort that was almost physical, Perry forced his mind to push down the lid on that treasure chest and work on the problem at hand: Julia Drusilla.

What was her angle? After years as a homicide dick, Perry accepted nothing and no one at face value (his ex-wife used to say he'd been that way long before he was a cop—he'd always tell her he doubted that). Julia Drusilla claimed she wanted the chance to reconnect with her daughter. Perry could identify with the sentiment, but that didn't mean he believed her. Yet he couldn't think of any other reason for Julia to want to find her daughter. The usual motive—money—didn't work. If Angel didn't turn up in time to sign the papers, the entire inheritance would go to Julia. So as far as Julia's financial empire went, things only looked rosier if Angel stayed gone.

On the other hand, if Julia was so bent out of shape by her estrangement from Angel, why wait a year to reach out? And why had it taken everyone two weeks to figure out that they should call in the troops to help find the girl? The pieces didn't fit. But that didn't worry him. Not yet. The jigsaw puzzle couldn't come together when all he had were pieces of sky. With a little luck, the interview he was headed for now would give him at least one central piece of the puzzle: Norman Loki, Angel's father.

The fact that Norman Loki had wound up with custody of the girl child had surprised him, no matter what Julia said. In Perry's case, his lawyer had nixed the idea of even trying for custody. Teenage daughter goes with mom, end of story. He didn't like it, but given his circumstances, he didn't have the stones to put up a fight. That didn't mean it hadn't hurt . . . badly. He'd been a good father. Hell, a great one. At least he'd tried to be. So maybe that was Julia's angle: having been knocked for a loop after losing custody—even though she denied it—she finally felt strong enough to fight for her daughter.

Perry sat with that idea for a few moments, then shook his head. That wasn't it, either. The steely crone who'd hired him didn't get "thrown" by much, if anything. And certainly not by loss of custody. When he'd met Julia, he'd been prepared for the rage and recriminations that usually swirled through these family dramas. But there'd been none of that. Julia had been as icy cool as a dry martini.

Even when it came to a discussion of her ex—a topic almost guaranteed to kick up clouds of wrath—she'd barely reacted. She'd handed him Norman Loki's information as though she were sharing her prescription for a colonoscopy. No anger, just distaste. The neutrality of her response had intrigued him enough to put in a call the moment he'd left her apartment to a source at the *Post,* who might have the dirt on their divorce. Only, surprisingly, there was none. The reporter had called him back an hour ago with the news that the divorce had been fairly civilized. No trial, no hearings, but most important, no custody battle. Just a rapid settlement with the bare minimum in court appearances. Lord knew, if anyone had the means to tear into a fight over who gets "baby," it was Julia Drusilla.

No, whatever was driving Julia's current zeal to find her daughter, it wasn't hurt feelings over custody.

The shoreline up to that point had been narrow and rocky, uninviting. But now, a sizable stretch of white sand beach came into view, the kind where you see handsome couples strolling hand in hand as if in a Viagra commercial. And signs of civilization were beginning to appear. Homes—okay, mansions—but informal, ranch-style mansions, with wraparound porches and grounds filled with hardy shrubs and squat wild-looking trees, dotted both sides of the highway. As dialed down as these manses were, Perry knew the smallest of them cost at least a few million. And the limited number that occupied the bluffs overlooking the ocean went for a great deal more. Norman Loki had scored one of them.

Perry spotted the road that led up to Loki's place just ahead. He pulled off the highway and followed a private lane until it stopped in front of a five-car garage. *Only* five cars. Nice to know the rich could rough it when they had to. Perry didn't see any security gates or cameras. But he guessed that made sense. Why would burglars make the trek out to the edge of the world when there was a whole city's worth of conveniently located marks within walking distance?

Looking for a place to park, Perry noticed a weather-beaten Jeep whose scarred and pitted paint said it had habitually been left out in the cold. Thinking that Jeep would make good company for his ancient Datsun with its dangling exhaust pipe, Perry parked alongside it. He climbed out and started to lock the doors then looked from the Jeep to the Datsun. He put the keys back in his pocket.

Out here on the bluff, the wind cut into Perry like an icy blade. He wrapped Nicky's scarf around his neck and dipped his head to spare his face but willfully left his trench coat open (a wardrobe choice he freely admitted was a bit on the nose, but he liked the zip-out lining feature—currently zipped in).

The ranch-style house looked to be about ten thousand square feet, judging from the size of its bleached-white facade. Like the other houses in the area, it had a generous veranda that wrapped around the entire perimeter and several large shuttered windows. Just beyond the house, Perry spotted the pool. He climbed the steps to the front door, then stopped and turned to enjoy the view for a moment. The sky and ocean blended to form a vast, seamless gray expanse that made Perry feel smaller than a grain of sand. Oddly, the thought relaxed him.

Through the door, he heard Jimi Hendrix crooning his mournful version of "Hey Joe." Perry let his hand hover over the doorbell to listen for a moment. When he finally pushed the button, it played some tune, something sweet and syrupy. Was it "The Impossible Dream," of all things? *Jesus.* Luckily, it played for only a few seconds and he got another full minute to listen to Hendrix's guitar solo. He had just raised his hand to try knocking when he heard a man call out, "Yeah, I'm coming, gimme a sec."

Perry instinctively reached for his badge and gun, preparing to bang the door open, then stopped himself. Shook his head. Old habits died hard. Whatever this guy was hiding—and it was a fair assumption he was hiding *something*—it was unlikely to have anything to do with Angel.

Thirty seconds later, a man Perry presumed was Norman Loki stood in the doorway.

In spite of the near-freezing temperature, Loki's feet were bare. And very well-tended feet they were. At a glance, the rest of him looked equally as well groomed. But his wardrobe choices were a strange, almost dissonant counterpoint. His jeans were holed out and ripped, but they were neatly rolled to a precise few inches above shapely golden, and seemingly hairless ankles. His T-shirt (bearing the bull's skull logo that even Perry—no big fan of the group—recognized as that of the Grateful Dead, circa 1970s) was thin and faded, but sparkling clean. A silver skull pendant hung from a leather cord around his neck, and an engraved leather cuff snapped around his wrist. Hippie-esque threads on a country-club body just starting to lose its battle against time.

Perry would've tagged Norman's age at no more than mid-to-late forties had he stopped at the neck, but the face edged his estimate up by about twenty years. Though still blondly handsome, time—and no doubt sun—had leached the bounce from his cheeks, turned the few remaining wisps of hair to straw, and left deep creases in the skin around his large, age-paled blue eyes. Still, there was a gap between body and face that seemed to be commonplace among baby boomers. Perry guessed that meant his own nascent paunch, despite hours spent at the gym, showed he was part of the younger generation. Nice to know all those beer and pizza dinners were good for something.

Behind Loki, an impressive stack of wood was burning fast and high in a large, brick fireplace. The heat rolling out of it gave Perry welcome relief from the stinging cold wind that whipped behind him.

Loki peered at him cautiously. "You the PI?"

"Yep." Perry held up his ID. "You Norman Loki?"

"Yeah. Come on in, man. It's a bitch out there."

Julia Drusilla had obviously called ahead to announce his arrival.

Perry walked into what he imagined the interior decorators called a "great room," and he had to admit, it earned its name. Three thousand square feet of gleaming wood floors, thick Oriental rugs, and overstuffed, comfy-looking furniture for sitting, lounging, sleeping, and "hanging." The high, wood-beamed ceilings gave a sense of spaciousness but also warmth.

"Get you something to drink?" Loki offered. "Warm you up a little."

"Thanks, no," Perry said, with regret. It would've been nice to kick back with a shot of whiskey in front of that blazing fire on a day like this. He supposed he could opt for something wimpy, like tea, but that would only make him miss the whiskey more. "I'm good."

He recalled Julia's comment about her ex-husband: *He drinks . . . or did . . . and when he does . . . But he's stopped drinking . . . at least I think so.*

Norman took his coat and directed him to a pair of matching leather lounge-style chairs with ottomans near the fireplace. Perry sat and immediately found himself sinking back into the down-filled cushions. If he'd been alone, he would've been asleep in seconds. He pulled himself up and perched on the edge of the chair. Loki settled into the lounger opposite him and swung his feet up onto the ottoman in one elegant movement. On the wall behind Loki, Perry noticed a framed diploma from Harvard Law School.

"You still practice?" Perry asked, nodding at the diploma.

"Ah . . . no, not really. Not anymore." Loki smiled. "And don't worry, I never did criminal defense." His smile twisted with a shrewd look. "Bet you hated those guys."

Either Julia Drusilla's heads-up phone call to Loki had been a lot newsier than she had let on, or he had done a little quick digging into Perry's bona fides on his own. Perry suspected the former. Loki didn't seem like the digging type. Unless it was for clams. Perry shrugged. "Most of 'em were okay. They had their jobs; I had mine. So what was your game?"

"I had a civil rights practice."

"Which means?" Perry asked, though knew very well.

"Employment discrimination, an occasional wrongful death, that sort of thing. I loved it. Cases I could believe in, where I could do some good for the little guy."

Perry nodded, but his bullshit meter was ringing. "But you quit because . . . ?"

Loki sighed. "Because the big corporate lobbies brought in tort reform. Killed my entire practice. Basically shut down the courtrooms for everyone but their cronies."

"Gee, that's a bitch. But I've got to hand it to you—those employment discrimination cases are tough. You ever go up against any of the bigs, like IBM or Mercedes-Benz?"

Loki's stricken expression told Perry he'd rightly guessed that Loki's experience went no further than the noble, well-rehearsed speech he'd just given. Unfortunately for him, Perry knew something about the field. When Perry got shamed out of his uniform, a real civil rights lawyer had lobbied hard to get him to file suit against the department. She was convinced he'd been framed and was gung ho to prove it. Perry had thought about it, had wanted to get the chance to go public with the truth. It didn't bother him that it would be an ugly street brawl of a trial. What did was the knowledge that he couldn't win—on any level. The fix was in, the truth didn't matter, and it probably would never even be known, given the kind of press coverage he'd get. So ultimately, he'd declined. But in the process, he'd learned a few things about employment discrimination cases—as the man squirming across from him had just found out the hard way.

Loki licked his lips and rubbed his hands on his thighs. "Uh . . . no, not really. I guess you could say I handled the less . . . complicated cases."

Or, Perry thought, *you could say that Loki is a bald-faced liar.* But Loki's nervous retreat made it clear he knew he'd been busted. All to the good. Nothing like a little shaming to inspire honesty. "How'd you and Julia cross paths?"

Loki's eyes darted anxiously around the room, managing to hit everywhere but the place where Perry was sitting. "A dinner for new associates. I started out at Schilling, Stearns and Castleman."

Perry recognized the name. It was a high-power, multinational corporate firm. The kind only Harvard Law grads with big connects got into. The kind that represented those Goliath corporations Loki had just declaimed.

"So you met Julia shortly after you passed the bar?"

Loki took a deep breath and stretched his legs. "Yep. Married for thirty-two glorious, fun-filled years." Though Loki said it with a tinge of irony, his voice held no rancor. In fact, Perry thought, his tone seemed a little wistful.

"Whose idea was it, the divorce?"

Loki turned toward the fire. Without meeting Perry's eyes, he replied, "It was what you might call a mutually agreed upon parting of the ways."

Should Perry pursue the issue? Loki and Julia Drusilla's relationship might be relevant to Angel's disappearance, but then again, it might not. Before he could make up his mind, Loki leaned forward, his face tight. "Look, you're not, like, a real cop anymore, right?"

Perry tried not to wince. The admission still had the power to wound. "No."

"It's just that, this whole situation . . . it's got me kind of stressed out. I really need to power down, man."

"Have at it," Perry said. Relaxed meant talkative. Fine by him.

Loki moved to the fireplace and reached under a framed photo of the Beatles (autographed by all four) walking barefoot at Abbey Road. It swung open to reveal a safelike cavity. Only there were no stock certificates or bundles of cash. There was just a large-size zip-lock baggie of weed, an assortment of pipes, and one multicolored, blown-glass bong. Loki took out a small brass pipe and held up the baggie in silent invitation.

Apparently Norman Loki had exchanged the booze for the bong.

Perry'd always hated the stuff. It made him paranoid. And slow. And it stank. "No, thanks. But by all means . . ."

After three long, loving tokes, Loki slid back in his chair and put his feet up. His eyes were red but a lot less darty. "Now where were we?"

"We were just chatting about what caused your divorce."

"Oh, right." That wistful tone again. "Let's just say we found we had one too many things in common."

Perry waited, hoping the old trick of silence would make Loki jump in to fill the gap. But Loki wasn't jumping anywhere. His gaze drifted complacently over Perry's right shoulder and out through the

window to the dark ocean. Perry sighed. Note to self: next time a witness says he needs to relax, hum something by Enya.

"I understand Angel's been missing for two weeks?"

"Yeah." Loki pulled his attention back with an effort. "Last time I
saw her, she said she was going up to Hartford to see a showing with
Lilith."

"Does Lilith have a last name?"

"Bates. She's Angel's latest BFF."

Perry would follow up on that shortly. "And what was the showing of?"

"Art. Something modern, I think. Lilith is an artist." Loki's
mouth curved in a smirk. "'She don't look back.'" He glanced at
Perry. "That's—"

"Bob Dylan, yeah, I know. Did Angel tell you where they were
staying up there?"

Loki's expression sobered. "I know where she *said* they were staying. The Sheraton. But when I couldn't reach her on her cell, I called
the hotel, and they said no one by that name had ever checked in."

"I assume you also checked under Lilith's name."

Loki gave Perry a look that said he was stoned, not a stoned idiot.

"Have you been able to reach Lilith?"

"I called her right after I called the hotel. She said she hadn't gone
to Hartford, didn't know of any art showing, and didn't recall Angel
ever saying she was going there. Said she hadn't seen Angel since . . . I
guess it would be the day I last saw her."

"So Lilith and Angel are close? How long have they known each
other?"

Loki squinted. "A year? Probably less." Loki shook his head.
"Angel goes through BFFs the way Limbaugh goes through oxy. Always has. I give their little 'womance' six months tops before Angel
gets tired of her."

Pretty tough talk for a dad whose daughter was missing. But it was probably the most honest answer he'd given so far.

"You think Angel might be a little . . . flighty?" Perry asked.

Loki sighed. "In all fairness, probably no more than any other spoiled rich girl would be in her situation. But to just disappear this way . . ." Loki's mouth turned down.

"Has she ever done this before?"

"Not for this long. She'd fall off the radar for a day, maybe three days. But never more than that."

"When was the last time?"

Loki stared off until Perry was ready to knock on his head to see if anyone was home, but finally, he continued. "About a year ago. She was supposed to go to her cousin's wedding in Boston. Instead, she wound up in Woodstock. Never even made it to the reception. No heads-up, no apologies."

"How'd you find her?"

"She eventually called. But it took a while, which worried me because I'd been leaving messages on her cell and she never turns it off. Keeps that thing glued to her side twenty-four/seven. Every time I called, it went straight to voice mail. Three days after the wedding, she finally got in touch. Said she couldn't call before because there was no signal where they were staying."

"Did you believe her?"

Loki shrugged. "Why would she make something like that up?"

Perry thought, *Because sliding up to Woodstock and missing her cousin's wedding might have been the least of it?* But it was a year too late for that talk.

"Woodstock," Perry said. "Does she usually go in for retro, hippie stuff like that?" Perry watched the other man for a grin, a raised eyebrow, some sign of recognition about apples and their proximity to the trees they fall from. *Nada.*

"Not necessarily. Angel's just . . . adventuresome."

"Does she go to school?"

Loki's face brightened. "Sure did. She went to Vassar. Graduated in three years. With honors." He stood up. "I'm parched. You sure you don't want anything to drink? Water?"

"Sure, water's fine."

When Loki returned with two large crystal glasses of water, Perry asked, "Graduated in three years with honors? That's quite a feat." Especially for the girl Loki had just described.

Loki settled back into his chair, took a long swallow of water, and nodded. "She's definitely got brains. And obviously discipline, too—when it suits her." An edge of disappointment slid under the pride in his voice.

"But?"

"But it turned out the only thing she really cared about was getting done with school as soon as possible. She kept her grades up because she knew that if she didn't, she'd get hell from me."

"Not from her mother?"

"They rarely spoke."

Loki glanced at the side table where he'd set down his pipe. Perry knew if he picked it up, their interview was over. He was about to knock his glass of water onto the floor to distract him, but Loki left the pipe alone and continued.

"Ever since she graduated last year, it's been one long party." Loki paused, shook his head.

The irony of Loki making a remark like that almost made Perry laugh out loud. He stifled the impulse by taking a long drink of water, then asked his next question. "And Angel doesn't have any real expenses, right? She doesn't pay rent here?"

"No."

"So who does?"

Loki's shoulders dropped, and he stared into the fire. "I have some investments . . ."

"Might some folks call those investments 'child support'?"

Loki shot a look at Perry out of the corner of his eye, then turned to stare into the flames. Busted—again—he didn't even try to argue.

For a few moments, the only sounds were the *crackle* and *pop* of the wood. A log rolled off the top, and Loki picked up a poker and shoved it back away from the screen.

When he sat down, he dropped his head into his hands. "Having to call Julia last week and tell her that I'd basically lost our daughter was one of the worst days of my life." When he finally met Perry's gaze, his face was haggard. "Look, I know I wasn't the best dad, but I wasn't the worst, either. I may have been a little too permissive. But one thing I can say for sure: Angel always knew I loved her, which was a lot more than Julia—" Loki stopped abruptly.

"So there never was any love lost between those two?"

Loki pressed his lips together. "Honestly, I don't know. The dynamic between mothers and daughters . . . it's always complicated, isn't it? You have kids?"

"I do. But my daughter isn't about to inherit a fortune."

Loki's eyes widened. "What are you talking about?"

Perry studied him for a long moment. "You don't know that Angel gets access to a sizable trust fund on her twenty-first birthday?"

Loki sat forward. "This is the first I've ever heard of it."

Perry's bullshit meter was ringing again, though he wasn't sure why the man would bother to lie. Maybe he was pretending to be shocked so no one would think he'd been Mr. Cool, Permissive Dad all those years in order to curry favor with his soon-to-be-stinkin'-rich daughter. Or, on a more sinister note, maybe there was something in it for Norman Loki if Angel didn't claim her share of the inheritance. Perry was going to have to drill down on the exact terms of that trust fund. Loki's reaction didn't ring true. It seemed a little . . . forced, over the top. Perry waited, hoping silence would lure him into saying something he'd regret. Frequently, silence was the best interrogator. But after several moments went by without a word, Perry was forced to concede it wasn't working this time.

Perry replied, "That's actually part of the reason Julia wants Angel to be found right away. Angel has to sign the papers on her twenty-first birthday to get that money."

Loki broke into a laugh. And not a little chuckle, either. A big, hefty, belly shaking, "Ha-ha-ha."

"I take it you don't believe that," Perry said. "According to Julia, she doesn't need Angel's share of the money."

When his laughter had scaled down to a few stray chortles, Loki responded. "Oh, no doubt *that's* true. Julia's got more money than the Vatican. I just find it difficult to believe in this sudden . . . well, never mind."

Perry didn't want to never mind, but Loki had made it clear he wouldn't share any more than he had to about his ex-wife. His protective attitude toward her was puzzling . . . or maybe it wasn't. Maybe it was just a wise decision not to bite the hand that fed him. And was probably still feeding him.

"I'll need Angel's cell phone number—" Perry said.

"Of course. I'll write it down for you." Loki stood.

"And while you're at it, I'll need Lilith's information, too."

Loki nodded. "Good idea." Loki went over to a small writing desk against the wall, wrote down the information.

He gave Perry the piece of paper, then held out his hand. "Thank you, Mr. Christo—"

Perry shook his hand. "Call me Perry."

"Perry. Whatever you may think of . . . all this, I am extremely worried about Angel."

At that moment, the doorbell chimed its absurd little tune. "That'll be my trainer." Loki retrieved Perry's coat from the couch and handed it to him. "Whatever you need, please feel free to call me."

"Thanks, I will."

Loki opened the door to reveal one of the few men Perry had ever seen who truly deserved to be described as an Adonis. Well over six feet tall, with wavy, shoulder-length blond hair and pecs so large they showed through his waffle shirt. The warm smile he'd aimed at Loki turned to puzzlement when he saw Perry.

Loki quickly introduced them, and the man recovered his one-hundred-watt smile. After enduring his bone-crushing handshake, Perry bid them farewell. The moment the door closed, he wiggled his fingers to work out the kinks from that death grip.

As Perry turned to go, he heard the two men laughing. He slowly walked down the porch steps then stopped. It seemed odd that a worried father would have a trainer come out at a time like this. Odder still that he'd be in the mood to laugh. About anything.

As he drove down the private road back toward the highway, Perry mentally replayed his interview with Loki, the aging, dependently wealthy hipster. A bit of a poser, a big doper, but a kidnapper? A killer? Hard to believe. Then again, how could a lawyer not know about his own daughter's inheritance? And if he did know, why lie about it?

Perry sighed as he turned onto the empty highway. The interview that was supposed to give him a central piece of the puzzle had instead only delivered more questions. The scream of a lone seagull pierced the sky above him. Perry looked up and nodded. "Yeah, I'm with you, buddy."

You don't have to drive down the road to find out why the private eye has come here and who he's come to see because you know exactly who he is talking to.

You wait by the side of the road, car under the trees, hidden in the shadows, trying to imagine their conversation while you gnaw on a PowerBar to keep up your energy. You've got a whole bag of them, plus apples and juice boxes. You're prepared.

You think about all those mansions you've passed, the way these people live, and you're going to have it, too, because you deserve it, and you don't care who gets hurt. Somebody always gets hurt, but not you, not this time.

You're trying to picture it, your new life, when the PIs junk heap of a car comes rattling back down the private lane and he's so damn preoccupied he doesn't even look your way, just turns onto the main road, and you wait a couple of minutes so as not to arouse suspicion then turn the key in the ignition and follow under a sky with low dark clouds like filthy rags and feel a kind of electricity coursing through your body, hands tingling on the steering wheel because this is what you've been waiting for.

4

It didn't take Perry long to reach his next destination.

The afternoon sky over the Hamptons was darker now, an icy rain just beginning as he headed down the long drive.

The minute Perry Christo walked into Lilith Bates's studio, one thought came into his mind.

Wannabe.

She had made the third floor of her lavish East Hampton mansion into her work space, and it appeared that she had worked hard to create the image of the artistic recluse; canvases were everywhere. She'd studied the studios of others, and she'd had the house revamped to create magnificent, floor-to-ceiling windows and skylights for her work. She had all the proper utensils for her craft, palettes of oils and watercolors, cabinets with half-opened drawers spilling over with brushes, paint thinners, pens, pencils—every artistic supply an artist could ever want.

Trust-fund baby turned artist!

The Bates's butler had walked him up, and he knew that she was expecting him, even though she pretended to have completely forgotten he was coming.

One thing he would say for her—Lilith was beautiful.

She was dressed in a form-hugging tank top and knit pants; a white smock blouse— artfully splashed with paint—was carelessly worn over her clothing. She was slender—it seemed that being slender was a requisite in the area. But she also had curves, and the black tank and knit pants revealed that the woman didn't seem to have an ounce of fat or extra skin—surely carbs never passed her full, well-formed lips.

She was, he believed, thirty-plus, and maybe plus, but whatever plastic surgery she had endured had been done with greater artistry than that seen on any of her canvases.

She looked up from her current work in progress as the butler led him in.

"Mr. Perry Christo, mum," the butler announced. The butler had already made Perry feel as if he had stepped into an old black-and-white English film on the aristocracy. He was dead straight, didn't crack a smile, and wore an impeccable tux. Maybe that was what butlers really did—walk around in impeccable tuxes and look good and stiff.

Hmm. If the guy *were* a stiff, he might not look much different.

"Oh, dear! That was fast. You just called."

"I did say fifteen or twenty minutes, didn't I?"

"It seemed like only a moment ago. I'm a mess."

She is anything but, thought Perry.

Lilith seemed disconcerted as she set her brush on the palette, rose from the chair she'd been sitting in before her canvas, and walked— no, sailed, and quite regally—over to him. She extended a hand—a perfectly manicured, soft hand—and smiled.

"How do you do, Mr. Christo. It is *Mr.,* right? It's my understanding you're a private investigator, and not a detective? I seldom see people, but you did sound as if you had such passion when you called!"

The way she smiled at him—like a grinning bobcat about to pounce—he wondered if she had looked him up, if *she* knew about his past, too.

"Yes, it's Mr. Christo. But please, call me Perry," he said.

Her smiled deepened. She assessed him as he stood there. He felt a little like a cut of meat at a butcher's shop. But maybe it was important. He took some of his frustrations and his anger—mostly at himself—out on gym equipment. That might stand him well today.

Though at the moment, the way she was looking at him, he felt like some male escort. Clearly, she had deigned to see him because she was curious.

"Call me Lilith," she told him. "Jeeves, we'll take champagne, please," she said to the butler, not bothering to look his way.

The butler's name is really Jeeves?

"None for me, thank you," Perry said.

"Oh, Mr. Christo—Perry!" she said. "Indulge me. Obviously you're here because you want something from me. That does mean that you should humor all my whims."

He didn't say yes or no; the butler with the improbable name silently turned and disappeared.

"Do come on in, Perry," Lilith said with a broad sweep of her hand. At the one end of her studio was a settee with a small table before it. She indicated that he should sit.

As he walked toward the settee, he looked at her work. Lilith took the concept of "abstract" to the extreme. Splotches of color adorned most of the canvases.

"What do you think?" she asked him.

He smiled. "I once went to a showing at the Guggenheim," he told her.

"And?"

"They had just spent an incredible sum on a painting called *Black*."

"And does my work remind you of that priceless piece of art?" she asked.

He shrugged. "It was black."

"Ah, but art is in the texture, in the subtext! What was the artist saying?" she asked.

"That he'd gotten a lot of black paint?"

She waved a hand in the air. "Well, of course, you were a cop. You were, right, at one time?" she asked, her smile dazzling. Her lips were generous and well formed, rich. Her eyes were a brilliant blue, and they set in her perfectly chiseled face like twin beacons of mischief. One of her elegant ringed hands moved in the air with an expression of patience. "One doesn't expect someone unschooled in the arts to understand."

He blinked, willing himself to keep his face impassive, and quickly put himself in check; he wanted information out of this woman, and despite his inclination, he smiled and said, "Actually, I was lucky. My mother was an illustrator for a series of children's books. She loved art—she would have loved to see your work. You're exactly right; great art is usually in the subtext.

"And Lilith, you are following along the lines of some magnificent work in the Hamptons. Why, two of the finest leaders of abstract expressionism—*action painting*—lived, worked, and even died here. Willem de Kooning moved to the Springs section of East Hampton in 1963 and died there at the ripe old age of ninety-two. His wife, Elaine, who did JFK's official painting, came and went, living with him sometimes even after they divorced. Then there was Jackson Pollock. He moved here to the Springs, and, we know, poor devil died in a car crash. His wife, Lee Krasner, was an artist, too. You're in the perfect place." He quietly thanked his mother for his art education.

"My, my, my—Perry. You *do* know something—about the Hamptons, and about art," she said, slipping her arm through his. She pressed close. He could feel the rise of her breasts against his upper arm.

He paused by one of her paintings, hoping he didn't choke on his words. "This . . . this is magnificent. The blues . . . I can't claim to know everything, but in the drip of the paint, in the sweep of the colors, I see something of Dalí. I'm seeing the ocean merge into the sky. And the dots . . . people, like ants, moving about and never seeing that they're all part of something grand. They're far too busy in their little lives to realize that earth and sky meet, and yet there . . . your lone voyeur—she sees it all, and she sees herself melting into earth and sky sadly, so aware that she's but a speck of sand or a grain of salt in the ocean."

Lilith looked at him and then at her painting. "You do have a deep soul, Perry. I'm so glad you like my work."

"It's brilliant," he lied. Quite frankly, the painting looked like smudges of blue and green with some black dots sprinkled throughout.

"You've voiced my work with greater empathy than I might have managed myself," she murmured.

Of course he had. She'd had no idea of what she'd been painting. And neither did he.

"Do sit down, please, and tell me why you've come, why you wanted to see me."

She led him to the settee. He sat at one end. She draped herself at the other but in a way that brought her leaning close to him.

Jeeves cleared his throat and tapped at the door. He carried a silver tray with a silver ice bucket and crystal champagne flutes.

"Shall I pour, mum?"

"Yes, please do, Jeeves," Lilith said. She had one arm leaned on the back of the settee. Her legs were half curled beneath her. She wore the white shirt open, and the mounds of her breasts generously spilled above the scoop of her tank top.

She still didn't look at Jeeves; her eyes were on Perry, and that secretive smile curved her lips. Jeeves slipped her champagne flute into her hand. "Thank you," she said briefly.

Perry reached for his own glass and nodded his thanks to the butler. He couldn't help but think of the movie *Clue.*

What do butlers do?

They butle, of course.

"Will that be all, mum?" Jeeves asked.

"Yes, please, and see that we're not disturbed. Mr. Christo and I have a matter of some importance to discuss," Lilith said.

Jeeves left them, closing the door to the studio behind him.

Lilith took a sip of her champagne and paused to enjoy the taste. "Do drink up, Perry. Once a bottle of champagne is opened . . . well, you know."

Not exactly—at least, not in the case of Lilith Bates.

"So," she asked, and her tone was like warm honey, "just what is the matter of importance we need to discuss?"

"Angelina Loki," he said.

He didn't think that he really took her by surprise, but he was astounded by the knife's edge glitter that came into her eyes.

"Oh?"

Everything about her that had been relaxed, sensual, and sinuous as a cat seemed to change.

"She's one of your best friends, isn't she?" he asked.

"Of course," she said quickly. Too quickly.

"She's disappeared."

"Oh, I doubt that she's disappeared; I mean, people don't just disappear, do they? Of course, you may be using that word in an abstract way . . . rather like abstract art. What you see is that she's disappeared, but of course, she hasn't really," Lilith said.

"So you know where she is?" he asked.

"Me? No! Goodness, no!" She'd sipped her champagne so delicately before; now she chugged the contents of the flute.

"Have I upset you?" he asked her.

"No, I mean, I'm quite certain the little minx is just fine, it's just that—well, as you said. She is one of my dearest friends."

She rose—rather she unwound herself—in full grace again and walked a few feet into the room, her empty glass forgotten in her hand. "Why are you looking for her?"

"Her mother is distraught; she needs to find her."

Lilith laughed. It was a dry and brittle sound. She spun on him. "That battle-ax? The only thing that causes her distress is discovering a new wrinkle! Trust me: if that woman is trying to find Angel, Angel's better off wherever she may be."

"Ah. I take it you don't much like her."

Moving more like a wooden figure, stiff and disjointed, Lilith reached into the ice bucket for the bottle and poured herself more champagne.

"No, I don't much like her. And that family's money is wound up into more trusts than you could ever imagine."

"And you know this from Angel?"

"She may have mentioned it. I just, well, I just assume in a wealthy family like that . . ."

"That there are financial trusts. Did Angel have one?"

"I . . . assume so. She never seemed to worry about money."

"And she'll have more coming after her mother dies?"

"I suppose. But I wouldn't know about that. How would I?"

"So Angel never said anything to that effect?"

"No." Lilith's lips tightened around the word, as if she were lying.

"I see."

"Julia Drusilla is a gorgon. She has the mothering instincts of a cub-eating papa bear." She stopped speaking and spun on him. "Oh,

I see—private eye. You're being paid to find her for that witch who calls herself a mother."

"I'd never bring harm to Angel," he said.

Lilith sniffed and turned away from him. He saw that there was a wavering mirror that reflected one of her canvases.

She was looking at her own image in it.

"Could you tell me how well you do know the family?" he asked her.

"We run in the same social circles," she said, as if that should explain all.

"So you don't really know her?" he asked.

Lilith moved slightly, arching her back as if she had a crick in it. She was gaining control; once again, her movement as sensual and sinuous as that of a cat.

"Angel came to one of my art showings. She loved my work; she bought a painting. We began to talk about art . . . music . . . life. Then she called me a few weeks later. Poor dear, she loves both her parents, of course, the way children always do, but her father has freed himself from that dreadful woman. You must understand: Angel is a child of beauty—a child of nature. She's young, impetuous . . ."

"Young and beautiful," Perry agreed.

Lilith brought her free hand to her face as she studied her skewed image in the mirror.

Beautiful. Young *and beautiful.*

He thought then that as rich and beautiful as Lilith was herself, she saw her own youth slipping away. She had everything she wanted, perhaps, except for the youth that might make Angel more desirable than she was herself. He couldn't really judge her age, but he believed she was in her mid-thirties.

She was still young, but she was, he realized, one of those women who wanted to be the most beautiful, who thrived on the adulation of men.

And needed it. Any little slip in her hold on her perfection would be painful, and in comparison to a young woman just at the first flush of legal adulthood . . .

She spun around again. "I'm sorry, you'll have to forgive me. Julia Drusilla has donated large sums of money to many charities I'm associated with over the years."

"So you *do* know her."

"Like I said, we have, at times, moved in similar circles, but *know* her, not really." Lilith forced a smile. "She provided for Angel—all the right things. The right clothing, the right schools . . . so much *right* that she never saw the person her daughter was becoming. She wanted to make a Mini Me out of Angel, and that's just not Angel."

"Tell me about her?" Perry asked quietly.

Lilith set her glass on the table and moved—sailed—across the floor to a bank of wall electronics. "Tell me, Perry—do you dance?"

The strains of something Latin came on the air.

"I move my feet to music," he said. "I'm not so sure about what you're playing."

She smiled. "Ah, Perry, it's just a rumba. Back, side, forward, side, back. The dance, of course, is all in the foot and hip movements. So many people hear Latin music and want to sway their shoulders all over. It's a sensual dance . . . all about the subtlety of music. You're not very subtle are you, Perry?"

"I try to be straightforward."

"Come dance with me."

He stood, feeling a little awkward. His illustrator mother had taught him a great deal about art, though she hadn't been a dancer.

"Come to me, Perry, please, come to me."

She stretched out her hands to him, closing her eyes. She began to move to the music herself. Her shoulders did not move, but her hips swayed evocatively with each step.

She could be, he was convinced, his path to Angel.

He stepped forward.

"Now, take me in your arms, Perry. A man always leads in such a dance, but you're learning, so I will back lead you. You don't grip a woman as if she were a fence, Perry. You are firm in your hold; gentle and yet forceful as you move so that a woman understands just what it is you want her to do."

He tried not to step on her feet. The basic step was easy; he got it quickly enough. She was extremely correct in her stance but didn't seem to care that her partner was not so majestic.

"Will you help me?" he asked, her perfume in his nose. "Please. I won't let any harm come to Angel; I just need to speak with her myself."

She'd held her head away from him at an angle—as was proper with the dance, he was certain. A slight smile curled the marble beauty of her face.

"Did you think I was hiding her here somewhere, Perry?"

"No, but I think you could tell me where to find her. I'm afraid for her, Lilith. She's missing, and no one seems to know where—"

"Lift your arm just so on the back step, and I can turn . . ." Lilith said.

"Please," he said.

"Angel is, as you said, young and beautiful," she told him.

"Did you hear me? I'm afraid she may be a victim, that she may be in trouble, that . . ."

She paused for a minute, drawing back. A look of real concern tugged at her features.

"Dead?" she whispered.

"I don't know and won't—not until I've searched everywhere." Perry tried not to think it. He tightened his grip on Lilith's thin waist.

"Young and beautiful means men," Lilith told him.

"A particular man?" he asked.

Spinning in his arms, Lilith came to a dramatic pause with her back against him. His chin rested on her head. She inhaled, waiting for the next count of music, and when it came seemed to move again with regret.

"She could have her pick of men," Lilith said.

"But was there one special man?" he asked. To his amazement, he was getting the hang of it. They weren't going to be calling from *Dancing with the Stars* anytime too soon, but he could at least move as she wanted and concentrate on his questions at the same time.

"So, she was seeing many men?"

"She went through men with total disdain and absolute ease," Lilith said. She moved her head close to his in a calculated dance movement. "In fact, quite bluntly, she went through men like toilet paper."

"Then, she might have angered someone?" he asked.

Again, Lilith spun around, stopping right in front of him. "No, not really. They would always drool after her, hoping that she would come back."

"What kind of men?" he asked.

She grinned. "Oh, the very rich kind. Some, mere boys. Most, high-powered. Stockbrokers, doctors, lawyers, an actor or two." She moved against him, looking up at him. "Most," she said in a silken whisper, "were a lot like you. Tall, well built . . . muscular." Her fingers trailed down his arm.

"Can you give me some names?" he asked, fighting an involuntary chill.

She stopped moving. The music seemed to go on, out of sync.

She looked at him hard and seemed to tire of her game. But she was judging him again. And he was grateful to see, she seemed to judge him well.

"What about you, Perry?" she asked.

"Pardon?"

"Let's see . . . a man like you. Well . . ."

"Did Norman Loki call you about me?"

"No. After you called me, well, forgive me but I googled you and skimmed a few articles. Is that such a bad thing?" She smiled. "I see you made some mistakes in your misspent youth. You lost the woman you loved, did you not? You probably didn't appreciate her when you had her and now . . . You have a child, yes? You look back at the past, and you believe if you run hard enough, you'll find a future."

"I've been bad places," he told her. "I don't know where I'm running to now."

"You're honest. I like that."

"Will you help me? Is Angel really your friend?"

She turned away from him and walked back to the table, elegantly picking up her champagne glass and studying its contents, as if it would give her answers.

"Yes, I really consider Angel a friend," she said after a moment. She looked his way again. The music ended.

Outside, the winter wind suddenly seemed to buffet against the glass of the studio windows; a skeletal branch slapped against the wall.

"Winter," she said. "So cold and bitter. I like summer much better, you know. Of course, I could spend winter in the city. Or Barbados," she mused.

At the moment, Perry wished to hell he was in Barbados, too.

"Maybe Angel has opted for a warmer climate," she said.

"Tell me about Angel's men, Lilith."

"There's one," she said.

"Yes?"

"I always warned her to be careful," Lilith said, walking to the window to look out at the cold gray day. "I told her to be careful about whom she was meeting, and that, even if she was just going to be amused and then toss them away, she should make sure others knew about them. Oh, I loved to hear her talk! She would tell me about this one or that one . . ." She paused, looked at him, and flashed a smile. "It sounded sometimes like we were in a men's gym room, her language could be so graphic. 'He has huge feet . . . but never go by that old wives' tale!' she told me about Larry, the yacht broker. And 'Big things come in small packages—sometimes!' That was in reference to James, the cyber heir her father wanted her to date. Sadly, she said he had the stamina of a dead dog. I warned her . . . so often . . . you must understand. She's *passionate*. She's a true Renaissance woman. She is Bohemian. She will do what she wants when she chooses, and, of course . . . that's hard on her blue-nosed mama. And her father . . . Norman!"

It sounded almost as if she spit out the last.

"Ah. So you don't care much for Norman Loki, either?" he asked.

"Maybe Angel uses men because she saw how her father used everyone," Lilith said. "As far as I'm concerned, Norman Loki is a prick who believes that he can use anyone. The poor child . . . on the one hand, her bone-thin mama bear, and on the other, Norman the snake."

"But her father claims to have no knowledge of her whereabouts. He seems as distressed as her mother."

Lilith sniffed.

Perry waited and then asked, "Do you believe that Angel might be with Larry, the yacht broker, or James, the cyber heir?"

"No, they were safe. They were the kind of men she *should* have been playing with," Lilith said. She spun on him. "Don't judge her. You have to understand the beauty of her soul. Men have done what they will through the ages. Angel . . . she doesn't hurt them, she gives. She allows them to entertain her; she gives them the pleasure of her company."

Perry stood his ground and fought for patience.

"So?"

"You know, I would never speak to the police like this," she told him.

"I'm grateful, truly grateful, that you're speaking to me. But help me, please, Lilith." Perry spoke softly, his eyes on her, trying hard to keep her engaged and on his side.

Lilith sighed. She walked over to the stereo control again. This time she played a very slow Sinatra number.

"Dance with me again. Let me lie against your chest. I'll tell you what you want to know."

He really felt like a male escort then. But if that's what it took.

He walked over to her and took her in his arms. She eased her head against his chest as he held her and they moved slowly, doing little more than just shuffling their feet.

"This is nice," Lilith said. She arched her body against his. The scent of her perfume was subtle; the tease of her hair against his chin was both evocative and oddly sad.

He pulled away from her slightly. "You're Lilith Bates," he said quietly. "Talented. Beautiful. You can have anyone you want. You don't need to try to prostitute a private eye who is trying to help your friend."

"Ah, so you'll go only so far!" she said, breaking away from him.

"Lilith—"

She sat down on the settee, glaring at him. "Yes, I can get many men myself," she told him.

"But?"

"But they're not real," she said softly. "Oh, they're flesh and blood, but they're always playing a game. Who is in the paper, who has made the most money, who is in the midst of scandal! Where lies the promise for the royalty of the future!" She smiled at him. "Don't answer me—I'm not looking for an answer. Sit down and I'll tell you what I know."

He came over to join her and sat at one end of the settee. He could see that, outside, an icy rain was falling again. It seemed ominous.

"It's the tattoo boy, that's who it is!" she said, though she seemed sorry the moment she'd said it, a hand to her mouth and her eyes looking away from him.

"The tattoo boy?"

"Oh, yes, Angel could have anyone. And you know what happens when you can have anyone?"

"What?"

Her lips curled in that bittersweet smile of hers. She picked up her glass of champagne and refilled it. "Drink!" she told him.

Obediently, he drained his glass. He watched her as she refilled it.

"Don't worry, Perry Christo. I am not seducing you. I prefer not to drink alone—though, certainly, I will do so."

He sipped his champagne, watching her.

"When you can get whoever you want, you want that one person out of a million who plays hard to get."

"And in Angel's case, that was this tattoo boy?"

Lilith nodded. It was clear now that she couldn't stop talking. "He's really a no-good grease monkey. A mechanic, can you imagine!"

Well, he could, actually, but he understood that Lilith couldn't, her remark so biting it seemed almost personal.

"So Angel fell for a mechanic . . . who wanted nothing to do with her?" Perry asked, fishing.

"Oh, I didn't say he wanted nothing to do with her. The two had an affair—a love affair—a passion that ran hot and deep, and was carnal and sweaty and . . . quite wonderful, I'm sure." She smiled, but it was forced, and her eyes weren't smiling at all. "She told me about his tattoos—*all* of his tattoos. And his body is quite extensively covered in art, if you know what I mean."

So Angel had been dating a hot sweaty mechanic who provided amazing sex.

"Did he leave her?" Perry asked.

"Well, of course, he couldn't really leave her, because he was never really with her. He could infuriate her—she'd go to see him, and he'd want to spend a night with his hot, dirty friends, drinking at the dive bar on the very wrong side of town and picking up loose one-hour stands. Well, fifteen-minute stands, from what I understand. Angel would go away furious, swearing she'd never see him again. Then she'd go back to his wretched garage and he'd see her, walk over to her, just about throw her up against a car . . . and she would be all over him again."

"This tattoo guy have a name?" Perry asked.

"Randy Hyde," Lilith said, a frown immediately replaced by a leering smile. "He's tall; he's built like a brick; and he's handsome, rough and tough. Ill-mannered and ill-tempered. I mean, I wouldn't even glance the man's way—not even for great hot, sweaty sex." She turned away again, wrapped her arms around her chest. Then back, her voice tougher. "He's . . . uncouth! I wouldn't let Angel bring him here—ever. I mean, don't let Jeeves fool you; if I say someone should be thrown out on his ass, it will happen!"

"So you met him," Perry said.

A moment's hesitation then she nodded. "We were going to the club—my yacht club. I made the mistake of letting her drive. I mean, it was just supposed to be the two of us for lunch. What Monsieur DeVeau—the chef at my club—can do with a foie gras is quite amazing. But Angel claimed that there was something wrong with her car and that we just had to stop and get it fixed. So we went by the garage, and there he was—tattooed, tall and muscled, arms gleaming since he wore one of those ridiculous wife-beater shirts even in the cold! She seemed to melt in the car seat."

"And what then? Did he ignore her, disdain her . . . ?"

"No. He came swaggering over and ignored me and planted a totally graphic kiss right on her lips."

"And then?"

"And then it turned out that her car was just fine and I was driving off to lunch on my own and Angel was staying behind, sitting up on some kind of a mechanical thing, just waiting for her wretched grease monkey to be done with work—and done being a tough guy around his greasy friends—so that they could go off to *fornicate* wherever it is that the two of them go," Lilith said. She repeated the word. "*Fornicate*. It does really sound dreadful, doesn't it? Nothing like *making love*. But then, there is just a difference, don't you think?"

"But you said that she was passionate."

Lilith nodded. "Still, one should bathe, don't you think?"

Perry lowered his head, escaping the question. "Lilith, this fellow's name is Hyde. Randy Hyde, right? Can you tell me where to find him?"

"I can tell you where to find the garage—I'm sure you'll find him there." She stood up and walked over to one of her cabinets, drew out a piece of paper and a pen, and scratched down an address. Perry noticed that her hand was shaking.

"This is what you need, Mr. Christo. Angel is my friend. If she's with any man—or if any man has held her . . . harmed her in any way—this is the one you want. He's the only one she cared enough about to look for if she was in any kind of trouble. And as greasy and sweaty and rude and crass as he could be . . . there was something about her that made him keep coming back, too. I can't believe that he'd hurt her—I won't believe that he'd hurt her. But if anyone knows anything, and it isn't me . . . you'll want to talk to Randy Hyde."

She handed him the paper.

He rose. "Thank you, Lilith."

She nodded.

He walked to the door.

She called him back. "Perry?"

"Yes?"

"You are a beautiful man, Perry. Good luck. You may call upon me again, if you wish."

He thanked her again.

Downstairs, without blinking an eye, Jeeves bid him "Good day" and saw him out of the house.

As he left the rich stone mansion, he looked up. Lilith stood in the window. The glass was frosted, making her image a bit askew, as it had been in the mirror.

She was still a beautiful woman.

And yet, even as he hurried to his car, raising his collar against the blustering sea wind and pouring rain, he couldn't help but feel that he'd just escaped a scene from *Sunset Boulevard*.

A butler. A goddamn butler! You almost laugh it's so damn funny, so damn corny, the man standing there in the entranceway, in his tux.

You imagine yourself knocking on the door and the guy opening it and saying something like, 'Good day, old chap,' and you just smile as you get your hands around his neck and squeeze and squeeze while the woman screams and screams, all of it like some old black-and-white movie that your mind is spinning as you wait and wait, telling yourself it's okay because it's all going as planned and because you've waited so long that it feels right to be waiting a little longer, like you have been on some long winding road that you need to follow to get to the pot of gold, like you are about to win the goddamn lottery.

So you sit shivering in the damn rental car, eyes closed, envisioning all the great things you are going to have.

But then the pictures start: all the stuff you don't want to see, don't want to remember, your mind spinning again and you can't control it, shivering so bad and it's not because of the cold.

You tell yourself to stop. You squeeze your eyes so tight against the ugliness and pain, but you know the only possibility of stopping it, of surviving, is to do this, to make others suffer as you have, and to make them pay.

5

CHARLAINE HARRIS

Gil's Gas & Auto office windows were shining through the pelting cold rain. The garage bay doors were down, but that wasn't surprising on a day as miserable as this one. Perry saw lights coming from the narrow windows in the bay doors, too. There were two trucks parked to the right of the building, and a Lincoln in one of the customer slots. Perry pulled the collar of his trench up, flung open his car door, and dashed to the entrance. A bell rang as he pushed open the door and practically jumped into the office.

Like every garage in the world, this place smelled of oil and metal and rubber, and it was none too clean. The coffee in the pot was past stewed, the Formica on the service counter was chipped, and the middle-aged woman leaning against it was equally past her prime. But she didn't like to think so. She was retrieving the keys to the Lincoln from the extended hand of a man half her age, a tall and brawny stud in mechanic's overalls.

The woman and the stud both turned startled faces toward Perry, whose trench coat was dripping copious amounts of rainwater onto the floor. The water could only improve the dirty linoleum, Perry figured. It was obvious from the woman's body language and the way the mechanic was smiling as he handed over her keys that the two had been in deep flirtation. The woman's seductive slouch vanished like a raindrop in the desert as she turned to look at Perry. The mechanic's face went completely blank. There was a moment of silence, broken only by the drip of the water from Perry's coat.

Finally, the fortyish woman broke the little silence. Turning to the stud, she said, "Randy, when you get the part for the car, give me call. I'll bring the car in myself." She did everything but write her phone number on his hand.

"No chauffeur?" Randy asked. His overalls were tight, dark blue, and his name was stitched on his chest in red. He looked good in them, and he knew it. Even in the chilly weather, his sleeves were rolled up to exhibit muscular arms, tattooed with dark pseudo Japanese patterns.

"No chauffeur," she said, looking at him in a very meaningful way. "I'll come . . . in person."

"I'll call you," Randy said, grinning. "That part should be here in a couple of days."

"I'll look forward to it," she said, fluttering her fingers, and passed Perry in a waft of Blu. She picked up a Burberry umbrella propped by the door and, stepping out and snapping it open in one practiced move, she hurried to the Lincoln.

"Can I help you?" the mechanic asked. "I'm a little short-handed today. Our girl's out, and we're closing soon."

Perry approached the counter. He could see now that there was a space heater on by the desk behind the counter. The office felt warm and cozy. To Randy's right, a door was open into the service-bay area. A car was up on a lift, and there was another Gil's Auto employee under it, looking up into the car's workings. He was older and thicker than Randy Hyde, his hair graying. He was what Randy would be in fifteen or twenty years.

"I hope so," Perry said. "I'm Perry Christo. I'm a private detective, and I'm looking for a woman."

"Aren't we all?" Randy laughed. "But I haven't got a spare one. Only car parts." Randy was handsome as well as brawny, which was maybe the answer to what Angel, a girl with money, was doing with a guy like this. The mechanic was blessed with absolutely regular white teeth, thick wheat-colored hair, and a jaw and nose like a Greek god's. There was no denying that Randy exuded vitality. But his hands and nails were embedded with dark lines of grease that all the scrubbing in the world wouldn't remove.

"Like I said," Perry repeated, "I'm looking for a woman. A specific woman. If you're Randy Hyde, I've heard you know her very well."

Randy pointed to the embroidered name on his chest. "I'm the only Randy here. Like I said, I ain't got a woman in the shop at the moment, but I do know a lot of women. And I know plenty of them *very* well."

"I'm sure you do, but I'm trying to ascertain the present whereabouts of only one: Angelina Loki," he said flatly.

The humor went out of Randy's face, and he raised the flap to come out from behind the counter. The space suddenly seemed much smaller as the two men confronted one another.

"What makes you think I might know where Angel is?" Randy asked. He was close enough for Perry to see golden stubble on his cheeks. Perry was rooted to his spot on the floor.

"A little bird told me," Perry said.

"I bet it was a little canary," Randy snarled. "And I bet she's named Lilith Bates."

Perry shrugged. "Does it make any difference? I need to talk to Angel."

"Why?"

"Not your business, grease monkey." Perry tossed out the insult, hoping to get a rise out of the guy.

"Grease monkey—really? You want something from me, and this is the shit I get from you? Some detective." Randy was sneering, but there was something else in his face. Maybe a trace of genuine hurt. But it was gone as fast as it had surfaced, and now Randy's face showed only anger. It was clear Perry had touched the right nerve.

"Okay, I was out of line," Perry said. "But I do have to find her. There are legal issues involved—I can tell you that much. And I understand that Angel and you have hooked up in the past."

"Maybe we have before, and maybe we did two weeks ago," Randy said. "But I haven't seen her in a week. I can't help you."

"You can't help me, or you won't help me? I'm not looking to screw her up. This is all to her advantage."

"Easy for you to say. How do I know what you want? You're not from around here—I don't know you. And Angel would have called if she'd wanted me to tell you anything. So unless your car's thrown a rod, leave."

"Not without your answering some questions. Angel hasn't called anyone. She's vanished off the face of the earth, as far as her family knows. That's why I'm looking for her, and I need your help."

Randy seemed to think about his next move for a minute. "Hey, Uncle Dirk," Randy called, and the other mechanic ambled into the office from the bay. He brought a gust of machine smell with him. He closed the office door behind him and leaned on the counter. Up close, it was apparent he was even bigger than Randy, and had maybe two inches on Perry. He had a long scar around his neck, and a small, tight beard. His hair had once been as blond as Randy's. The two men were obviously fish out of the same gene pool.

"You the owner?" Perry asked.

"That would be Gil, and he ain't here. I'm the manager." He angled his chin at Perry but spoke to Randy. "What's this guy want? He don't look like our usual clientele," Dirk said, looking at the visitor with cold blue eyes. Dirk was tattooed, too, but his tats were probably prison ink. "Our customers can afford something better than that heap out front."

"He's looking for Angel; he says she's missing," Randy said. "How long's it been since she called me?"

"That blond bitch with the legs?" Dirk said.

Randy nodded.

"She called you about two weeks ago, am I right? From that no-tell Memory Motel. You couldn't figure out what she was doing in a place like that, no matter how famous it is."

"See?" Randy turned to Perry. "She called me. I didn't go looking for her."

Perry didn't understand why Randy thought that cleared him of any wrongdoing, but he appeared to believe if Angel had sought him out, he couldn't be accused of harming her. "Did you join her?" The detective did his best to sound neutral, but the thought of the delicate girl in the picture in his wallet in a liaison with this sex machine in a jumpsuit . . . it made him sick.

"Sure." Randy shrugged, a big movement from his broad shoulders. "I needed my chain pulled, you know?" He smirked at the two other men. "I didn't go back to my place for a week, at least. That Angel knows tricks most pros don't know."

Perry's fists clenched, a reaction that didn't go unnoticed by Uncle Dirk or Randy. But his voice came out calm enough when he asked, "So all you did was have sex, for a week?"

Randy shrugged. His hand played down the front zipper of his overalls. "What can I say, Mr. Detective? I'd bang her in the morning, come to work, go to the motel for lunch, bang her again, and after we ate some dinner at night we went another couple of rounds. I got stamina, and I got assets." Uncle Dirk laughed and reached for a rag to wipe his hands.

"Did she get any phone calls that you can remember? Mention any plans?"

Those questions seemed to sober Randy. The facile braggadocio slipped away. "She really missing?" he asked.

"Yeah, she's really missing."

"She got some phone calls, sure. But she didn't tell me who she's talking to, and I didn't ask. That's her private shit. I know Lilith called her a couple of times, though, because Angel told Lilith what we were doing when the phone rang. She put in a lot of details. She wanted Lilith to be jealous." His smile returned.

"You and Lilith . . . ?" Was Randy lying? Or was Lilith? Perhaps the woman had protested just a bit too much.

"Every now and then she needs her oil changed," Randy said. "She gives me a call. We do quality work here at Gil's Auto." His leer was automatic.

Uncle Dirk said suddenly, "You going to tell this guy what happened? Her running out?" He seemed to take a malicious pleasure in that.

Randy swung to face him, and the warm, oily air in the shop office became tense for a few moments. Then Randy relaxed. And so did Perry, who'd been holding his breath without being aware he was doing so.

Randy turned away from his uncle and spoke to Perry. "Yeah, okay. If you're really sure that Angel's in trouble."

Perry felt a frisson of excitement. Maybe now he'd get a piece of information that would lead to discovering the missing heiress.

"The last night we were together at the motel, a week ago," Randy began. "She'd picked me up here at work. My truck was running rough, but Uncle Dirk and me didn't have time to work on it—we were too busy with jobs that paid."

Dirk had poured himself a mug of coffee and was sipping it cautiously. He nodded, as if he was letting Perry know he confirmed Randy's narrative. He still looked amused. Randy said, "About midnight, she got a phone call. We'd just gotten to sleep, so I didn't catch everything she said. She went into the bathroom, left the door open just a crack. She sounded really upset."

"Do you know who she was talking to?" Perry leaned on the counter, fighting a wave of weariness.

"Nope," Randy said. "All I heard was some mumbling, and then she threw her clothes on and left."

"When she came back, did she tell you what had happened?"

"She never came back."

There was an uneasy silence until Uncle Dirk said, "And that's the whole story."

"Did you hear from her again?" Perry's sleepiness had vanished. He was alert now, and more worried about Angelina Loki than he'd been before.

"Not exactly. After work that day, I went back to the motel and found out she'd gotten all her stuff. Or someone had. When I talked to the asshole who runs it, he said my girlfriend must have been pretty disappointed, to run out on me that way. And I owed him a night's pay on the room." That had rankled—it was obvious.

"You sure you didn't drive her somewhere yourself that night?" Perry was skeptical about the story's details. "Or maybe follow her to see what she was up to?"

"If I'd driven her somewhere, I'd have had to walk back to the damn motel in below-freezing weather. I could have gone home just as easy. Why would I stay there? And I didn't follow her, either. I fell back asleep."

"Why didn't you take Angel to your house in the first place?" It
was the first time Perry had thought to ask this obvious question, and
he realized he needed some rest more than he'd thought.

Randy flushed. "She didn't want to stay at my place," he said.
"I told her she could stay at the house; I got a little place on Oyster
Street. But she said people were looking for her, and she needed to
be somewhere she could just walk out of. I guess she was right . . .
because that's what she did."

"You haven't heard from her since?"

"Not a word." Unexpectedly, Randy kicked the counter. The violence of the motion and the resounding thud of his boot hitting the
old wood caused the other two men to jump. Uncle Dirk said, "Shit,
Randy!"

"I'm worried about Angel," Randy said. "She's here, then she's
not. It's not like we see each other steady, or anything. But she's never
done something like that before. I was half asleep when she left that
night, but I did ask her if she wanted me to go with her."

"What did she say?"

"She kind of laughed and said she wasn't scared, and she'd be
back the next morning in time to take me to work."

"He called me at seven thirty," Uncle Dirk said. He'd finished
his coffee and was ready to get back to work. He stood in the doorway, shifting from side to side. "I picked him up, brought him here,
watched him answer the phone all day hoping it would be her." The
older man shook his head, maybe disgusted that Randy had been
blown off by a woman.

"You were worried," Perry said.

"Hell, yes, I was worried." Randy looked angry, embarrassed, and
resentful all at the same time. "I shoulda gotten up to go with her, or
made her stay. I shoulda . . . I don't know what I shoulda done. Something."

"Did the motel desk clerk say that Angel herself had come back to get her things?"

"No. When I went straight to the room, I found out it was locked, and her car wasn't there. I went to the office to see if she'd checked out."

"Had she?"

"He told me after he left the office for a second to go to the john, he came back and found the key on the counter. The maid told him the room had been cleaned out when she went in to make the bed."

"That car isn't fixing itself," Uncle Dirk said abruptly. Apparently, he was tired of Angel and her problems, or maybe Perry's disruption of the shop routine. He went out into the bay after shooting a pointed glance at his nephew.

"Yeah," Randy said, "I gotta get to work. Listen, I hope you find Angel. She's world class in the sack, and I . . . yeah, I feel kind of bad about her going out into the night like that. At the time I didn't think anything of it," he said, changing his tune, "just mysterious rich-people shit. But now . . ." He shrugged again.

"Thanks for your help," Perry said.

"Yeah, right," Randy said heavily, and went back to work.

Perry hunched down into his trench coat again for the short sprint to his car. The rain was still pelting down, and Perry felt cold to his bones. He sat in thought for a moment, then pulled out his cell phone to call Henry Watson. When he'd been on the force, he and Henry had been close, and after Perry had become a private eye they'd cautiously maintained a friendship.

"Watson," said a gruff voice. In the background, there was a lot of noise. With the pounding of the rain on the car at his end, Perry could barely make out what Henry was saying.

"You got a minute?" Perry said loudly.

"Let me get out of this," Henry said, and a moment later the noise abated to a tolerable level. "I was on the street," Henry explained. "I'm in a lobby now."

Perry said, "I need a favor, and I'll tell you why." As briefly as possible, he explained the situation to the cop.

"So you want me to run a check on this Randy Hyde?"

"Yeah, if you can. I'll owe you the best bottle of Scotch you can find."

"I can find a pretty good bottle."

"I'm counting on it. This Randy, he seems genuinely concerned about Angel, but on the other hand, he's quick with the kicks and punches. Lots of room for something bad to have happened. And can you run her mother and father? Julia Drusilla and Norman Loki? I can't imagine them having records, except maybe Loki for pot, but the minute you don't check—"

"Yeah, it'll come back to bite you on the ass," Henry said. "Okay. In my copious spare time."

They chatted for a minute more, Perry asking after Henry's new kid and new wife, Henry admitting they were all doing great and trying not to sound as proud as he was of his wife's career and his kid's being gifted. Just as the conversation was winding down, Henry said, "Wait a minute! I know a local out there, on the force. We were together at a gunshot-wound seminar. His name's Arthur Gawain, and he's a strange bird. But I think he's a good cop. Give him a call. He should definitely know where the bodies are buried in East Hampton."

"Thanks," Perry said. Some local insight could be a big help. The area cops always knew plenty of stories that never made it into a courtroom. Perry had gotten tight with a couple of cops in Southampton when he was on the Derace McDonald case, but Southampton was not East Hampton, and that case had been two years ago. He was thankful for the new contact. "Got his number?"

He scribbled it down as Henry read it off. "Thanks, Henry, and give my love to Maria," he said.

When he'd hung up, he sat in the car for a moment. Through the small windows in the doors of the service bay, he could see movement, and he knew Randy and Dirk were back at work. As he himself should be. With a sigh, he raised his phone and dialed Detective Arthur Gawain.

6

SARAH WEINMAN

Perry Cristo mentally kicked himself as he got back onto Route 27. Here he'd just spent the past thirty minutes at an auto shop and it had slipped his mind to check the needle on the gas gauge. It was at the three-quarter line, enough to get him to the motel, and maybe fifty miles after that, but not much more. Normally he wouldn't care where he filled up the car, but February in Montauk was more damp and bone chilling than in the city, which was saying something. And the light disappeared early enough to make the prospect of freezing his ass off to fill the gas tank that much more unpleasant.

But this was the Hamptons, and there wouldn't be another gas station for ten miles. *Fuck it,* Perry thought, *might as well get to the motel and figure things out from there.* That strategy had worked for him in the past, as a cop, and it worked still as a detective without the badge. He'd only had a vague sense of what to ask Randy Hyde at the auto shop, and the kid had still told him something important. They almost always did, no matter how hard they tried to hide things. Sometimes it took a little extra cajoling, a longer beat of silence they couldn't bear to leave unfilled, but inevitably something spilled out. Even the smallest nuggets paid off in the most unexpected ways.

Now, thanks to Randy, Perry was on his way to a place he'd never visited but had certainly heard of before. The Memory Motel. He wondered if Angel was a Stones fan, too, if their song had lodged in the back of her memory, or if she and Randy had shacked up in a room there because it was convenient. There was no point in asking Randy about it; the kid, once he'd spilled the info to Perry, had nothing else to give. It had been the same, even more so, with Lilith, the artist. Now there was a piece of work. He still heard her smooth-talking seduction in his head. For someone who chose to live the artist's isolated life, Lilith had gone out of her way to be memorable. Plus, she'd lied to his face about not knowing Randy Hyde when she knew him in the way that counted most. Then again, maybe Randy had been lying about fucking her. Everyone lied. Why did it always come down to that?

Perry looked down at the GPS he'd installed to make sure he hadn't missed the turnoff. He didn't like to rely on the device's artificial voice. Too prim, too proper, too grating, and since he liked long drives to work through the thorny knots that cases always presented him, hearing words with a robotic sound pissed him off even more. And more often than not, the voice was wrong, and "recalculating" was really code for "where the fuck are we."

Perry saw he had another three miles to go. But as he looked down, he felt something whisper up his spine. He glanced in the rearview mirror, but there was nothing behind him. No cars ahead, either. He'd had that feeling before, and it was never good. The case was already starting to move away from simple math to more complicated algebra, but he wasn't ready to admit there might be a darker force lurking. And if there was, he hoped he could at least fill up the gas tank.

The turnoff arrived—as always, a hair sooner than Perry anticipated—and he skidded a bit before hitting his mark. And there it was, the Memory Motel, the joint where Mick Jagger sang about hanging with Hannah baby, of curved nose and teeth. Then Perry's mind drifted to a very different memory, of his ex-wife's nose curving above her laughing mouth. He shook his head to make the image disappear. Not the time, not the place.

This place, though, didn't live up to the song. It was trying too hard to be respectable. The old gaudy sign was gone, replaced by some upscale piece of crap that pretended toward upward mobility. Two statues stood on either side of the door, and when Perry went up close he won the bet with himself: they were gargoyles, the ugliest kind. He'd heard the Memory had been sold a couple of years ago to one of those tech billionaires who claimed he was going to do something "major" with it. But those plans had been cut off at some point. The outside was in dire need of a paint job, and the lobby walls were covered in a greenish tinge that couldn't be anything else but moss.

Perry was alone in the lobby. He sniffed at the air, a stale mix of booze and cigarettes. As he did so a voice from behind him said, "What are you, a health inspector?"

Perry turned. The man's voice was "Long-Guyland," but the face was a generation and a half younger, at least, than he'd expected. Tattoos covered both of the man's arms, and while Perry hoped to hell never to see underneath the all-black garb, he was sure there was more ink on the guy's torso and legs.

"Nope. Just a visitor. You responsible for the smell?"

The man folded his arms and glowered. It would have been pitiful because of the other man's babyish, fine-boned face framed by wispy blond hair, but Perry knew better. He'd been young once, too, with a few bar fights under his belt. He'd made sure not to get his ass kicked much, but the one time he hadn't been able to avoid it was because of a guy like this one, barely suppressed rage ready to boil over at the next possible customer.

"You could say that. So what can I do for you?" he asked with undisguised hostility.

Perry took a long breath. There was no sense in being anything other than calm. "I'm going to take something out of my pocket. Are you the kind of guy who flinches when someone does that, or will you stay quiet?"

As he'd expected, the tattooed man flinched at the question. How much time he'd done and where, Perry wasn't about to ask.

"I'll stay quiet," the other man said, the hostility ebbing a little.

"Good." Perry took out his PI license. On this guy, using expired NYPD credentials, like he had for other cases in the past, wouldn't work. He let the other man take his time examining the laminated card. "I'm tracking the movements of a girl named Angelina Loki. Know her?"

"It's my business to know," the tattooed man said. "I manage the place." The man extended his hand and let out a hearty chuckle. "Elisha Hook. Man, I never thought I'd meet a guy with a more ridiculous first name than mine. *Pericles?*"

"Yeah, and that was reserved for only one person: my mother. Everyone else calls me Perry. Anyway, how long have you been the manager here?"

"Three years. Took over from my dad, who took it over from *his* dad. Otherwise, the new owners would have tossed me out with the trash, like they did with so much shit around here."

"The sign?"

"The sign. The chandeliers. The railings. You name it. They said they wanted to make it a classier joint. Instead, a week doesn't go by before some asshole declares himself cock of the walk in the bar and we have to boot him out. Last Saturday was terrible. This one spic fills himself up with Jägermeister and throws a roundhouse on the black guy sitting next to him. For no reason. We never used to need bouncers around here. Now the economy's made everybody more crazy." For extra emphasis, Hook circled his temple with his left index finger.

Perry didn't tune out Elisha Hook, but his little speech was useless. Now Perry knew Hook would ramble on unchecked if he didn't steer the conversation in the direction he wanted. When Hook took a breath, Perry found his opening.

"But back to Angel Loki."

"Yeah, what about her?" Hook's face changed, pupils widening with anticipation.

"So you do know her?"

The light in Hook's eyes dimmed, and he shifted uncomfortably. "Depends on what you mean by knowing."

"Well, she was here at the Memory?"

Hook paused, as if he didn't know how to phrase what he was going to say next. Perry's ears pricked up, but Hook didn't break the silence.

"She was here, then?" Perry asked. "For how long?"

"Couple of weeks, on and off. Mostly off," Hook said, his voice dropping to nearly nothing.

"Sounds like she made an impression on you."

"You seen her?" Hook upped his volume. "Photos don't do that girl justice. She has . . . not sure how to describe it exactly, but she has *something*. So many celebrity big shots come and go around here, and so I know how to spot it."

"Star quality, you mean?"

"Sure," said Hook, "if that's how you want to put it. That girl, she had it. She could walk into a room, stay for thirty seconds, tops, and everyone would remember. I saw it happen in the bar a couple of nights. Guys and gals alike, they all wanted to know who she was and she wasn't talking to any of 'em." Hook's face scrunched up like he was trying to stave off a bad memory.

"So she didn't talk to you, then," said Perry. His voice had softened, too, not by design, but because the situation seemed to call for it. Something about Hook didn't quite sit right, and as the other man launched into an embellishment of what was clearly an incidental encounter—beautiful woman, clearly unavailable and unattainable, only speaks when she needs to check in, check out, or call up for room service—Perry realized what it was: Hook had the appearance, and the first initial presentation, of a man who'd done violence, but he didn't have the physical bearing, that weird pheromone all hyped-up types give off, of a true offender. It was as if he pretended to a rap sheet of felonies when he was lucky to have third-degree misdemeanors, at best. Perry figured Hook had been dealing with this disconnect his whole life.

"I see," Perry said, fighting off a creeping discomfort. "When did she leave?"

Hook did a double take. "Oh, right. Really early in the morning. Like she was just waiting for the sun to come up to get out of town. Which was weird. She was more the type to show up in the bar at the tail end of last call."

"When everyone would look at her but she wouldn't give them the time of day," said Perry.

"Something like that."

"How did she seem when she left? In a hurry? Scared? Happy?"

"Definitely in a hurry," Hook said. "Scared? Nah, I wouldn't say that, but she wasn't calm, either. Maybe she was on something. I don't know, and I don't check. But that early, hers was the only car zooming off onto the highway. Hell of a motor on it, too."

"That's the Memory Motel policy: to keep clear but watch everybody?"

Hook laughed without any trace of humor. "Is that it?" The question offered a single response. Perry went for it because there was no other choice.

"For now, but I may be in touch." Perry fished out a business card and put it on the desk. Hook didn't take it, his arms folded, as they were when they first started talking. "Thank you for your time."

But to Perry's surprise, the other man hesitated, his face growing sheepish. Perry waited a beat. "Don't tell anyone what I told you, okay?" Hook muttered.

"Why's that?"

Now Hook was blushing full-on. "I, ah, might have let on something else to the guys. You know, after she left. When it was late, in the bar."

Perry did everything in his power not to burst into a grin. "I won't tell a soul," he said.

Hook wasn't done. "I mean it. It took a hell of a lot of work for me to build my reputation back up in this part of town. Everyone thought I was some kind of pussy. It never mattered what I did." He held out his arms, showing off the elaborate art on it as he rotated his forearms. "It never mattered what I inked. My old man gave me the business, but if he'd found any other way, he would have. There's nobody else to run this motel. Just me. And now that things are starting to fall apart, who's going to take my place?"

Then the man shifted again, like he was snapping out of a trance. His eyes zeroed in on Perry's, and the PI knew an exit line when he saw it approach like a ninety-mile-an-hour fastball.

Perry mumbled good-bye and left Hook to his fantasies of manhood and thwarted romance. Sometimes that's all a man ever gets.

But as he got back into his car and found his way back to the Montauk Highway, Perry wondered if he had played the scene right. By his reckoning, Elisha Hook was the last guy to see Angel. He'd corroborated Randy's story of the on-and-off timetable, but no one else saw Angel leave. For good measure Cristo had peeked into the adjacent bar, to see if he might question one of the bartenders, but it wasn't set to open for another hour.

•   •   •

The rain was still pissing down and the temperature had dropped an-other five degrees at least while Perry was talking to Hook, and he reached down to crank up the car's heater to the max. As he did he caught a glimpse of headlights in his rearview mirror. His spine tingled again, but he had no place to stop the car. Perry drove another mile down the highway before he was sure there was a car behind him, keeping pace several lengths back, but conspicuous enough to indicate this was more of an announcement, not a stealth job.

Why follow him?

Perry peered into the mirror to see if he could make out anything about his new friend. The car was way too far away and the rain coming down too hard for him to discern any numbers on the plates, but the car was clearly boxy and black.

At the next turnoff, for East Hampton, Perry veered a hard left and then another sharp right around Aboff's paint store. He did so again. The car kept pace, though it dropped back a few more feet. But before then Perry saw it was, indeed, a black car. Midsize, a Toyota like one he rented for a job a few years back. There was mud on the plate, too. Intentional? Had to be. What the fuck? He'd only started looking for Angel this morning and already someone was on him. Well, whoever it was, Perry would have the last laugh. His car-evasion skills were legend, dating all the way back to his academy days.

Here we go, he thought.

Left, right, turns at the very last minute, rolling stops. Perry had to give the Toyota's driver credit for keeping up, especially in the pouring rain, but he couldn't be experienced at it—and definitely wouldn't relish the expensive bill that would come due when the suspension blew out. Perry sighed. He could give another ten minutes to this crap—that was it.

On 27, the other driver got cocky, narrowing the distance between his car and Perry's. When Perry sped up, now close to eighty, hoping his Datsun could handle it, the other driver did, too. Perry wasn't worried, but he didn't feel like getting into some bullshit mano a mano thing with an unknown driver.

At the next turnoff, Perry slowed down and took it more normally. Another three lefts and a couple of rights to the precinct, but he decided to reverse it and come back to see if he could trap the other driver. For the first part, the car did as Perry wanted. But when he doubled back and wound up in front of the precinct sooner than he thought, there was no black car. *Just as well,* Perry thought.

Later on, when things were knee-deep in hell, he'd wonder if that was another move he hadn't exactly played right.

"You got a room?" Perry asked.

Elisha Hook was surprised to see him again. And Perry was surprised to be back at the Memory Motel. But Arthur Gawain had been called away. It was cheaper to spring for a night in the Hamptons, see Gawain in the morning, and leave for Manhattan afterward instead of driving back and forth and wasting gas. The rain was supposed to clear out in the morning, too.

"Guess you didn't want to leave town without staying in our famous digs?" Hook's face crinkled into something approximating a grin. "You're in luck. Mick's old room is free."

"Sure, sure," Perry said. He doubted the motel manager had any idea where Mick Jagger had ever slept.

Hook slid a key across the counter, and Perry filled out the guest card.

"Can I get something to eat in there?" He angled his thumb toward the bar.

"Sure. It just opened up a few minutes ago. We usually got live music, too, but not tonight. A shame."

Perry said nothing. Live music was not what he needed right now.

Inside the bar, he took a seat at the farthest left, away from the handful of locals who acted like the place was their living room. The bartender, with his weathered face and taciturn expression, looked a little old for the job, hovering around fifty, if Perry was any judge. The PI ordered a Driftwood Ale and a turkey sandwich, then slid Angel's photo across the mahogany surface.

The bartender studied the photo. "She was here, couple of weeks ago, with a real bruiser. At least he wanted to think so."

"Why? He start trouble?"

The bartender shook his head. "I just didn't like him. Thought he was God's gift to everyone, especially women. The girl, though"—he tapped Angel's photo—"she didn't mind."

"What makes you say that?"

"Just that he had his hands all over her, and she seemed to like it fine."

"You see them often?" Perry wanted to know.

"They came in for drinks and snacks a couple of nights. I didn't spend much time with them. The place gets crowded." The bartender shrugged. "But she was a real looker, hard to miss." Something at the other side of the bar caught the man's eye. "If you'll excuse me," he said, leaving Perry to his beer and food.

Three swigs later, a man of about forty, in black jeans and a hooded sweatshirt over a green sports shirt, took the barstool beside Perry's. "Nasty night," he said, signaling for a drink.

Perry scooped up the photo of Angel but not before the other guy got a good glimpse. "Pretty," he said.

"Uh-huh." Perry said, downing the rest of his beer. The bartender returned with two more Driftwoods. *What the hell,* Perry thought. Since the guy was clearly interested in Angel's photo, it was worth asking a few questions.

"You're staying here?"

The other man shook his head. "Nah, just passing through. I thought the Led Zeppelin cover band was playing tonight, but I got the dates mixed up. They're supposed to be really something else." His eyes brightened. "You know this place was voted the best bar in the Hamptons a few years back? That's why I had to stop by. I didn't want to miss it. I've already missed too many things."

Perry wondered what the hell that was supposed to mean but said nothing. The guy continued. "My mother always says I'm too dramatic . . ." He trailed off into a half chuckle. "So what's your deal? You staying here?"

"Just for the night. Had a meeting that got pushed back a day," Perry said. "Plus, I'm looking for information about the girl. Know anything?"

"Never seen her," the man said, running a hand through his hair. "But I know my mother would have a lot to say about someone that pretty."

Perry let the comment slide. Some guys, they dress like adults but stay children forever, their best girls always their mothers.

He felt a rustle to his right, turned to find a blowsy blonde smiling up at him. "Well hello, sailor." She was eager, buxom, and Botoxed.

Perry wanted to roll his eyes, the urge he always had with women trying too hard. "Hey," he said.

"What are you drinking?"

"I'm good."

She laughed. "Your bottle is empty." She signaled the bartender for another round. "What brings you to the Memory?" she cooed.

Perry slid over Angel's photo. "Her."

The woman frowned. "What about her?" she asked, her voice sharp as glass.

"She was here a while ago. Now she's gone. Know anything?"

The drinks arrived, but the woman pretended not to notice. "Why would I know anything? Am I supposed to know something about every person who ever walks into this dumb joint?"

"Well, I'm not sure—" Perry started, feeling off-balance. Was this woman bipolar? First she was hitting on him; now she was insulted.

"Oh, forget it," she said, grabbing her bottle and sliding off the barstool. "You're a real stinker."

As she stalked off, leaving Perry bewildered at the whole exchange, he looked back to his left. The man in the sweatshirt was gone. And Perry was stuck with the tab.

Ten minutes later, still discombobulated from the whole bar business, Perry found his Datsun in the still-pouring rain and parked it in front of room twelve. He bolted the few feet, slammed the door behind him, and took stock of the room. A little dingy, a little musty, with a haphazardly made bed and some weird Painter of Light shit hanging on the wall, but it would do. It was a stopgap kind of place, perfect for Perry's current state of mind: in suspended animation, needing a better read on where Angel might be.

He lay on his back on the paisley bedspread and took out her photo again. Just as before, he sensed he was missing something about her. About the case. But before Perry could ruminate further, exhaustion won the night.

The rain pounds against the glass and you try to stay calm, tamp down your adrenaline as you stare through the windshield of your parked car, lights off, just one more vehicle in a parking lot of vehicles, concealed by darkness and veiled by the weather.

The neon sign casts wavy colors into the night, and across the parking lot puddles like a psychedelic light show.

You watch him get out of his car, collar up against the downpour, dash to the motel door.

You imagine him stripping off his wet clothes, plodding naked to the bathroom, standing under a hot shower—that scene from *Psycho* suddenly playing in your mind, along with the piercing sound track of harsh and distorted strings and screeching violins. But this time it's you—you're in it!—opening the bathroom door, about to tear back the shower curtain and then, then— But how can this be? It's not him but you in the shower and the kitchen knife is stabbing you, piercing your flesh over and over, blood spurting and mixing with the shower water, and you can't clear your head or stop the movie.

You gasp for breath, press the heels of your palms against your eyes until everything goes black.

It's the drink. You know you're not supposed to—not with the meds—but you couldn't help it.

You open the car window and lean out. Rainwater spills over your face. It feels good, like a baptism, like you are with Him, your Maker, and your mind starts to ease and your breath to slow because you know He is there for you, just for you, on your side, and everything is going to work out just fine.

7

BRYAN GRULEY

The next morning it was gray. Perry had had his fill of the gray, his fill of the Hamptons. He just wanted to get back to the city. Then he spotted the car in his rearview mirror. The same car. Again. Like the gray.

"Enough," he said. He sped down the road, then swerved onto the shoulder, his car crunching to a gravel halt. As the car neared, he saw it wasn't the Toyota but a Mercedes. It slowed, the driver perhaps considering a U-turn that would have been a giveaway, though at this point, Perry wasn't sure of what. He waited. He had stopped on a stretch with some distance between cross streets so the Mercedes wouldn't be able to duck away easily.

He caught a quick glimpse of a woman at the wheel, a brunette in aviator shades, and her license plate. He grabbed his notebook off of the passenger seat and jotted the number down. *Ten bucks says it's Upper East Side,* he thought. Only Upper East Side brunettes wore sunglasses in this weather. He checked his rearview once more before pulling back onto the road.

Waiting in a windowless conference room at East Hampton Police Headquarters, Perry smelled something cooking. He realized he was hungry. He'd bought a bagel from a deli near the motel but hadn't been able to eat it. He'd swiped off half the cream cheese before taking a bite and had gotten some on his pants. He glanced down now at the white streak between his zipper and right pocket. *Jesus,* he thought, *anywhere but there.* A cop seeing it might think he'd had a hooker in his passenger seat. Of course, he'd made it worse by trying to wipe it away. Why did they have to slather on so much cream cheese anyway? Was there a surplus they had to bring down? He'd thrown the bagel away after two bites.

At first, Perry thought the room looked like any other cop-shop meeting room. But he saw no coffee cup rings on the long oaken table. He scanned the beige carpeting. It could have been cleaned the day before. It took him back two years to the Southampton PD, something he wanted to forget. Then there were the framed photos lining the wall facing him, all of various East Hampton chiefs squinting against sun in grip-and-grins with celebrities: Donald Trump, Wendi Murdoch, Dennis Franz. Perry thought of Franz in his *NYPD Blue* heyday. What would *he* do to find Angelina Loki? Round up a suspect or two, slap the truth out of them between commercials for beer and tampons?

A door to Perry's left swung open, and an officer entered in full uniform: hat perched on head, navy tie knotted and clasped, pistol on hip, handcuffs dangling from belt. Perry couldn't help but think of Barney Fife. A brass nameplate over the officer's right breast read GAWAIN. Perry stood, offering his hand and a tentative smile.

"This isn't a round table," he said.

Gawain had heard the joke, such as it was. "Guh-VAN," he said, giving Perry's hand a perfunctory shake.

"Pardon?"

"It's not GAH-wayne."

"Sorry," Perry said "You're not from around here."

"Neither are you."

"No. The city. Though I spent a few years in Detroit after college. Does that count?"

"Not bad hockey there."

Perry heard HAW-key. "You're from Mass, right?"

"Hingham."

"BPD?"

"Statie."

"That how you knew Henry?"

"Henry?"

"Watson. NYPD."

Perry was hoping Gawain would sit, but he stood there, Fife-like, with his hands still on his hips and his hat still on his head. His cheeks sagged a little on a thin face decorated with a salt-and-pepper goatee.

"We worked on a case once."

"Ugly?"

Perry had read about it in old *Boston Globe* clips. The New York cops were hounding a drug dealer who'd survived the Mexico wars and left a bloody mess in Harlem before skating up to Boston on his way to Canada. When the Boston cops rousted him from a crack house in Dorchester, he'd shot an old lady while stealing her car. The cops ran him down on the interstate. The Mexican took a fatal bullet to the head, then four more that disintegrated the left side of his face. After the Mexican embassy got involved, the shooter—a state cop—was relegated to desk duty and soon found work elsewhere. Elsewhere being East Hampton.

"Depends on your perspective," Gawain said.

"I suppose."

"You were a cop, weren't you, Pete?"

"Perry. Yep."

"Henry said." Gawain removed his hat, revealing a feathery widow's peak. He set the hat on the table. "Sometimes you're just doing what they told you to do, and next thing you know, they forgot they told you to do it. You know?"

"Sure do."

"You interested in some breakfast?"

"That sounds very good."

"Got some chowder here."

"For breakfast?"

Gawain managed a smile. "You'd eat this chowder for your last meal. We get it from Jeanne's down the street. She's from Yarmouth. Back in a minute."

Butter shimmered golden on the surface of the scallop chowder. *Such good things come in foam cups,* Perry thought. He wanted another bag of oyster crackers, but he and Detective Gawain were into Angel Loki now, and he didn't want to interrupt.

He'd told Gawain about his assignment, about Julia Drusilla, about the family millions, about his trip to Montauk, about Angel's cloying so-called friend Lilith, about Angel supposedly taking off with her alleged boyfriend, one Randy Hyde of East Hampton. Perry had slid the snapshot of Angel across the table to Gawain, who'd given the photo a long look before sliding it back.

"Pretty," Gawain said.

"Lots of pretties around here, though, eh?"

"That's correct. Has she been officially declared missing?"

"Not yet."

"And she dumped Hyde?"

Perry nodded. "We think so."

"It wouldn't bother us if he was dumped for good."

"He's a problem?"

"A tick."

Gawain recited as he dug the last sweet bits of scallop out of his cup. "Hyde, Randall Carter. Date of birth: seven/fifteen/eighty-three. Six feet two, one hundred ninety-five pounds. Eyes blue, hair blond. Drunk and disorderly. Assault and battery. Driving on the beach. Bike too loud. Car too loud. Telling cops to eat shit. You know."

"But the ladies love him."

Gawain pushed his cup aside and dabbed at his mouth with a restaurant napkin. "You seem surprised," he said.

"No. But you really think a girl from her side of the tracks would go for a grease monkey?"

"Why wouldn't a guy with big muscles and a big bike and a big attitude make some smart rich kid think she could change him for the better? Isn't that the way of the world? Besides, you ever watch those reality shows? Greasers are all the rage now."

"I don't watch TV."

"And, oh, rumor has it—though I have not personally confirmed this—that Mr. Hyde has quite a torque wrench between his legs."

"Ah."

"Not that that or money or good looks are of any importance to women." He stared into the table for a moment, then looked up at Perry, as if appealing to him. "They really just want men of good character, right?"

"Right." Perry glanced at Gawain's ring finger. It was bare. "Did Randy Hyde by chance ever go around with some of the, shall we say, older ladies who summer out here?" Perry pretty much knew the answer but hoped to get it confirmed.

"Let me put it this way," Gawain said. "We have yet to find sufficient evidence to charge him with prostitution."

"Got it. And he's never been busted for sexual assault?"

"Nope," Gawain said. "I mean, Randy Hyde is a total loser, and I wouldn't want him near any daughter of mine, but he doesn't strike me as the kind who goes for that sort of thing."

"What about his business? That in decent shape?"

"It wasn't—it isn't his. A guy named Gil Stone owns it. I have to say I've heard old Hyde's actually pretty good at keeping a car running, which can be lucrative around here. Not a lot of Jiffy Lubes out this way."

Perry had to wonder again if Hyde knew about the pot of money awaiting Angel. Or if he had ever encountered Julia Drusilla. She seemed like the kind of older woman who might be inclined to sample his goods. He stifled a shudder and said, "Anything else?"

"I wish," Gawain said. He stood, picked up his hat. "The truth is, we can't do a lot until this Angel girl is declared missing."

"Right." Perry stood. "Thanks for the soup."

"*Chowder*," Gawain said. "Look, I'd like—we'd like to be helpful. Henry's a good cop. And we can do without Mr. Hyde, even if the women can't."

"Ah—reminds me," Perry said. He snatched his notebook from a pocket, tore a page out, and handed it to Gawain. "Brunette followed me from Montauk. Didn't get much of a look at her. But can you run the plate?"

"Can do," Gawain said. "We'll get back to you."

The lonely water flew past Perry on both sides of the one-lane as he pushed toward the city. He told himself his trip to Long Island hadn't been a waste of time. He added up what he thought he knew: Julia Drusilla wasn't telling the whole truth. Someone in the Hamptons didn't like Angel. Randy Hyde was and had a big dick. And Angelina Loki might never be found. Might be dead.

He saw the hazard lights blinking from half a mile. A car sat on the right shoulder. He could make out a figure leaning against the passenger side. *No way,* Perry thought. He grinned and tapped the brakes.

The brunette glanced at him as he pulled up behind her Mercedes. Then she turned away. She was smoking a cigarette, still behind the aviator shades. Steam swirled up from the hood behind her. Perry killed the ignition and pocketed the keys. No telling what might happen next.

"Need a hand, ma'am?"

She kept her stare fixed on the water, silent. Perry stopped walking eight feet away. "Or are you just waiting for me to pass so you can resume following me?"

"Who the hell are you?" she asked, without looking at him.

"Come on. You know who I am."

She turned toward him and, with her cigarette hand, lowered her shades briefly. Perry saw her brittle blue eyes. Then they were behind the shades again. She turned back to the water. "A tow truck's on its way," she said. "Move along. I'm fine."

"How are you, Lilith?"

"Ms. Bates to you."

"Really? After all that . . . dancing?" Perry stepped closer. Her perfume floated off of her shoulder-length hair.

She turned slowly. "How dare you."

"You were following me. I want to know why."

She reached into a vest pocket and snapped out a cell phone. "I'm calling the police."

"Fine. Just be sure to say it guh-VAN, not GAH-wayne. Hopefully he's run your plate by now, so he knows exactly who you are, *Ms.* Bates."

She whipped off her sunglass and took a step toward him. "What the hell do you want?"

"Why would you follow me?

She shook her head, seemingly incredulous, and came another

two hard steps closer. "I was on your tail because you drive like an old lady."

"Come now, Lilith. You can do better than that. You really should take your car in for a checkup before you tail someone. Hey—maybe Randy Hyde can take a look, huh? Is that who's coming to save you? Got ol' Randy's number on your phone there?"

That stopped her. She took off her sunglasses, then dropped her cigarette on the shoulder and crushed it beneath the toe of one of her rubber-toed duck shoes.

"You've been to see Randy?" she asked. "Did he . . . mention me?"

Bingo, Perry thought. "In fact, he did."

"What . . . what did he say?"

"That he knew you. Biblically speaking."

Lilith took a deep breath and let it out slowly.

Perry saw her eyes drift past him. A black SUV, big as a city bus, windows tinted charcoal, rolled past. Perry was looking at it, think- ing, *How many cars can possibly be following me,* when he felt some- thing slam into his chest. It was the heel of Lilith Bates's right hand. "Whoa," he said, falling back a step as she kept coming. He ducked a roundhouse, sidestepped right, grabbed her by a bicep, and twisted the arm around behind her. She flung a leg back and got him on the knee. "Jesus, stop."

"I'm not just an artist. I take tae kwon do."

He pulled her closer and bent her arm a little farther, hoping he wouldn't actually hurt her. "Your teacher sucks," he said.

"Let me go."

"No more dancing?" he asked.

She was screaming now. Perry looked down the road to see if whoever was in the SUV might be watching. It was gone. "I'll let you go when— Ouch!"

She'd stamped her heel on his right foot. He loosed his grip enough that she wriggled free. She spun around to face him and took what Perry could only assume was a tae kwon do stance. She slipped her phone out again. "Now I'm calling," she said.

"Call away," he said. "But look, you were following me, and you know it. But you seem pretty harmless—"

"Fuck you."

"Okay, okay, you're not harmless. But really—"

"Fuck you."

"We might be able to help each other."

"Forget it, we're not—"

"Listen, damn it. Randy Hyde. I want the truth."

She backed away. She was breathing hard. Perry smelled perfume and sweat. He liked it.

"I'll ask again: You and Randy Hyde?"

Lilith straightened, pulled some hair out of her eyes. She considered a moment, then said, "Randall and I . . ."

Randall, huh, Perry thought.

"We met. On occasion. It was nothing serious."

"And you weren't jealous of his relationship with Angel?"

"Are you serious? A man like that. I would never—"

"But you did."

"It was just . . . fucking, Mr. Christo. Can you understand that? Or have you forgotten what that is?"

"Careful who you bed down with, Lilith."

"I hope you'll be a gentleman and keep this to yourself. A woman in my position—" Lilith glanced at the water. "Randall took off a week or so ago."

"With Angel?"

She shrugged. "Could be. He loved her, after all."

Christo thought he heard more than a tinge of jealousy in her voice. "I hear Randall loved a lot of women," he said. "Including you."

"I really wouldn't know about that."

"Tell me about *Randall*. Where he goes, who he sees?"

She chuckled to herself. "Randy never went anywhere but Sammy's Bar, his garage, and the bedroom of whoever would let him in."

Yellow flashers were blinking down the road. "There's your truck," Perry said. "I'll wait."

He left Lilith with the tow truck after she'd sworn up and down that she had no idea where Angel was, that she'd only been tailing him to find out if Randy Hyde had blown her cover. She was embarrassed and worried about her precious reputation. *Maybe she'll be helpful down the line,* he thought. And she really was a looker. He had to admit that he kind of liked the way she said "fucking." Maybe the trip had been more productive than he'd thought.

Veering off 27 toward the LIE, Perry saw a state cop pull someone over and found himself thinking again of Gawain. Barney Fife had shot the face off of a bad guy. Perry felt certain then that Gawain had his own ex-wife. But it was about the only thing Perry felt certain about after a confusing morning. That and the delicious chowder. He chose, for now, to believe Lilith Bates, and her reason for tailing him. But what about that Toyota? That wasn't so easily explained.

A restless sleep, your body still aching from the cramped confines of sleeping in the car in that damn motel parking lot. But you stayed on his trail to the local precinct, then saw that crazy woman having a fight with him on the side of the road before the long ride back to the city tailing his beat-up Datsun through Nassau and Queens and finally the Manhattan streets, driving around until he found a parking space that was good for a few hours, the PI too cheap to put his junk heap in a lot. Then you followed him to his lousy brownstone and waited, sitting in the rental until he came out and then it starts all over again—following, watching, waiting. But you do it because it's what you have been dreaming of and waiting for. It's your future and it's so close you can almost touch it, almost taste it.

8

ALAFAIR BURKE

Perry felt hungover from not enough sleep. All night, his mind had been running through the case: from meeting Julia Drusilla to the drive out east to see Angel's not-so-grieving father to speaking to Randy Hyde and Lilith Bates, and checking out the Memory Motel. At some point he had managed to make himself interesting enough to explain why that crazy Lilith Bates had been following him. Now, after meeting with Arthur Gawain, he was back in the city to meet his old friend at the 19th Precinct.

Located on East Sixty-seventh on the Upper East Side of Manhattan, the 19th Precinct serves one of the most densely populated neighborhoods in the country. More than 217,000 people packed into approximately 1.75 square miles. Nearly twelve hundred per city block.

All things being equal, more people means more policing. But not all populations are created equal. This one also happened to be one of the richest in the nation—the chosen locale for foreign consulates and ambassadors, the city's most elite prep schools, and the kind of New Yorkers who believed that jeans were for south of Twenty-third Street. The only kind of "spree" going down in the 19th on a usual weekday morning would be of the shopping variety, committed on

Madison Avenue by ladies in coats that cost more than Perry made in half a year.

But just as not all populations are created equal, not every weekday morning was the usual. Perry had been on the job long enough to read the energy of a station. This morning, the house was hopping.

Bumper-to-bumper squad cars lined the south side of Sixty-seventh Street, red lights flashing from the tops of the RMPs. Uniformed officers poured from the station to take their places behind the wheels of their radio motor patrol units. Others stayed busy filling the backs of two flatbed trucks with metal crowd-control barricades.

Where was Watson? They were supposed to meet outside so Perry could skip the always-pleasant experience of announcing his always-memorable name at the front desk of his old precinct—not that he cared.

He started to take in the action from the front of the neighboring building until he noticed the sign at the entrance: KENNEDY CHILD STUDY CENTER. Man alone outside a day care. Way to blend. He moved west and leaned against the side of the precinct's brick exterior, pretending to fiddle with his phone like any other multitasking pedestrian.

The experienced officers looked put out by whatever mission they were on, but comments shared among the rookies revealed their eagerness.

Perry spotted Henry Watson hop out of an unmarked fleet car halfway down the block, easy to spot since Henry was a good head taller than everyone else. As he walked, Watson popped a white square of gum from a foil packet in his pocket.

Perry called out to his friend. "And they said you couldn't walk and chew gum at the same time."

Watson caught Perry's gaze and smiled, then flashed him five fingers as he pulled one of the uniformed officers aside. He needed five minutes.

As Perry continued to listen in on the action, he started to piece together the reason for all the activity outside the precinct. *For once, a protest that actually makes some sense.* Protest scheduled for noon. Ninety-first Street outside the Russian Consulate. Hunter College sophomore. Body found in "the guy's" bed last weekend. He's some kind of attaché. *Like a briefcase?* No, numbskull—it's some kind of diplomat thing. GHB, the date-rape drug, in her system. *We can't touch him.*

Only four syllables, but each one dripped from the young officer with anger. *We can't touch him.* Perry knew the feeling. He'd felt it on the job more times than he should have, including on the case that first brought Watson and him together. Watson was working homicide in the Bronx, Perry in downtown Manhattan. Two different boroughs, two missing girls, two sets of grieving families. No reason to make the connection.

The girls had been missing for more than six years when Perry got word: police in Portland, Oregon, had cleared four unsolved murders with a DNA hit. Now the defendant was ready to give up more names and dates. Girls in six states across the country—totaling either sixteen or eighteen. He wasn't certain, but he knew it was an even number. He liked to kill in pairs.

Among the names the suspect was dangling were Kerry Lighton, a struggling artist who painted by day and stripped by night, and Tonya Barton, a for-hire "escort" who dreamed of becoming a nurse once she kicked her heroin habit. Perry was the detective on Lighton's case; Henry Watson was the detective on Barton's.

All those dead women. Six states, but not one of them with an active death penalty. The killer was already serving four consecutive life sentences without parole. So the district attorneys in the five remaining states cut a deal: life sentences to run concurrently with Oregon's in exchange for information about the location of the bodies. It would bring the families "closure," they explained.

We can't touch him. Perry and Watson drank together for six hours after the sentencing hearing.

Four minutes after he'd flashed five fingers, Perry's old friend, Watson, waved him into the precinct, patting him on the back as he entered. It was all the greeting they needed.

"Is that Nicorette I saw you chewing?" Perry had recognized the packaging when Watson first popped the gum on the street. He realized it had been too long since the two men had talked.

"Feel like an eleven-year-old girl, all the gum I'm gnawing these days," Watson said. "Maria didn't want me smoking around the baby. I mean, don't get me wrong. I know she's right but, man, I've tried everything. The patch. The electric cigarette. Acupuncture. Meditation. Self-help recordings. All kinds of crap Maria brings home from the natural-food store. Hypnosis." He lowered his voice for that last one. "I got newfound empathy for all those junkies I pulled in over the years."

"Right. Because when I think of Henry Watson, that's what I think of—empathy for the hard-lived and downtrodden. You have any contact with this Hunter College thing I'm hearing about?"

Watson shook his head and sighed. In context, he was answering in the affirmative. "Bad guy's got diplomatic immunity. He claims she OD'd, but we say he dosed her. Turns out it doesn't matter, because his country won't waive. That's what I was talking to the grunt about. Poor girl's parents are getting hounded by the media. Figured this convoy to babysit the protestors could spare one car to keep watch at the family's front door."

"It's not easy working those cases," Perry said. "Especially now that you've got a daughter."

"Tell me about it. I was holding Anna's little hand last night and found myself wanting to microchip her. One tiny GPS tracker under her soft, pale skin, and maybe I'd never have to worry about her again."

There was a time when Perry had been the young married father, and Watson had been out every night collecting numbers scrawled on matchbooks. Now the tables had turned. Except Perry's form of bachelordom wasn't holding up its end of the swap.

Watson fell hard into the chair at his desk. "Jesus. I've turned into frickin' Jabba the Hutt."

Perry noticed for the first time that Watson had added a good fifteen pounds to his already large frame. "Having kids will do that to you. I remember with Nicky."

Watson waved off the comment, and Perry knew his friend was saving him from the funk that would come from talking about the old days with the family. "Listen to us talking about weight gain and babies and health regimens. Like a couple hausfraus on *Dr. Phil*. Not what you came here for."

He gestured for Perry to take a seat in the wooden chair next to his desk and removed a file folder from the top drawer. "I ran all the names you gave me. In no particular order, we've got Randall, aka Randy, Hyde."

Perry took the printout Watson handed him.

"We've got juvie pops for a residential daytime burg and starting a brawl at a multiplex. Turns out when you're fifteen, you're young enough to take a girl to see a cartoon movie about talking cars, but old enough to bean the head of a kid three rows in front of you with a popcorn bucket for talking smack about said girl. Seven teenage boys kicking the crap out of each other by the time it was over."

"Who said chivalry was dead?" Perry scanned the rap sheet. "Nothing as a grown-up?"

"Nada. Next on your list are Julia Drusilla and Norman *Lawkey* or *Lowkey*."

"Loki," Perry said, spelling it: "L-o-k-i."

"Whatever. I found him." Another two printouts. "I swear, I

thought you made up these names to screw with me until I got hits on them. No criminal history, but they were in the system as complainants."

Perry was still scanning the documents. "Anything recent?"

"Norman Loki had a Rolex swiped last summer, a break-in. Description of the suspect was white male, twentyish. Never turned up."

"What about Julia Drusilla? You said she also turns up as a complainant?"

"Nothing quite as exciting as Mr. Loki's break-in, I'm afraid. Her parents died in a car accident a decade ago, and the reconstruction investigators for the New York State Police questioned her for background. Nothing came of it, though."

"Why an investigation?" Perry asked. "Was the accident considered suspicious?"

Watson shrugged. "Seven o'clock at night. Dad driving, mom in the passenger seat. Car swerved into the wrong side of the road on I-684. T-boned into an eighteen-wheeler. No drugs or alcohol in either tox screen."

"So why'd they talk to Julia Drusilla?" Julia had told Perry that her parents died in a car accident, but never mentioned an investigation or being questioned by State Police.

"You'd have to ask them," Watson said. "My gut? You've got two dead bodies with a Park Avenue penthouse address in a three-hundred-thousand Maybach."

"What's a Maybach?"

"If you gotta ask . . ." Watson grinned. "A *car*. German. Started before the war, after the war, I'm not sure. But a real status symbol. They just stopped making them—too expensive—soon to be collector's items."

Perry got the picture.

"Rich couple like that, State Police are going to cross the *t*'s, dot the *i*'s, and whatnot. They called around. Tried to see if they were missing anything. The daughter—what's her name, Julia—was upset but wasn't able to offer any relevant information. They figured the old man fell asleep. So what gives on these people?"

"Hmm?" Perry was still thinking about the death of Julia's parents and didn't register his friend's question.

"When I was running the names, I was reminded of those tests back in school: How do these three things go together? A thug like Hyde; a socialite like Julia Drusilla; and this Norman Loki, out at the beach. What ties these three together?"

Perry told Watson about the disappearance of Angelina Loki and her relationship to each of the three people Perry had asked Watson to run through the system. "If I find her by her twenty-first birthday, she stands to inherit a big chunk of her grandfather's estate."

"Grandfather, as in the dead guy in the Maybach?"

Perry nodded.

Watson let out a whistle. "Major bank. Seems like a good reason for the girl to want to be found."

"If only I were so lucky."

Perry had looked into the source of Julia's family's money. Her father, Antonio, had come from modest beginnings, the son of a father who worked as a dressmaker in the Garment District and a mother who taught piano in their Forest Hills apartment. But Antonio had more ambitious plans. Thanks to his first marriage to an heiress more than twice his age, by thirty-five years old, he was a widower in control of a $100-million inheritance. Through leveraged buyouts and other investments, he managed to turn that comfortable little sum into a fortune that landed him on *Forbes* magazine's annual list of billionaires for more than the last decade of his life.

"Well, good luck with the case, man. It's really great to see you. Been way too long."

"I don't want to press my luck," Perry said, "but any chance I can hit you up for one more favor? That deadline of Angel's twenty-first birthday is almost here, and it's not looking good. Plus, I think someone tried to follow me back from Long Island last night, so I'm starting to think she could be in real trouble. Any chance you can track her cell phone for me?"

Perry still marveled at how much more information law enforcement could gather now than when he was on the job. Thanks to technology, police could find out what Web sites people frequented, who they e-mailed, and what books they bought, usually without even having to get a search warrant. By pulling a few strings with Angel's cell phone company, Watson would be able to determine not only whether Angel was receiving or making phone calls, but also her possible location. A phone's pings to cell phone towers for service used to give police an area of a few square miles to narrow down a search. Now, with the proliferation of towers and a little bit of luck, cell phone tracking could put you within a city block of the person you were looking for—or at least of her phone.

"Careful, Watson. You do a friend like that a little favor, and the next thing you know, you're on IAB's shit list."

Perry turned toward the intruding voice. It was from a short-haired, pink-faced man in a dress shirt that stretched across his belly. He was no looker, but the Donald Duck tie suggested that even he managed to have a kid in his life. Perry didn't recognize the man, but the man obviously recognized him.

It was also obvious the man wasn't done making noise. "Doesn't matter how many years go by, Christo. You walk into a house, someone's gonna notice."

Perry felt his fists clench on impulse. Did this smart-ass think he was the first self-righteous cop to make a wisecrack about the Internal Affairs Bureau at Perry's expense? Did he believe that his jabs were any kind of penalty compared to the price Perry had already paid? The job. His wife. His daughter, Nicky.

How many times had Perry seen the dirty looks and heard the snide comments? He'd lost count, but every single time, he found himself wondering the same thing: Did these high-minded cops sit in judgment over Perry for what he supposedly did, or for getting caught supposedly doing it? Invariably, the ones who were loudest in their disdain for him were the ones who used racial epithets, joked about domestic violence, and referred to bribes as "consulting fees." Perry always suspected that their sole reason for casting dispersions was to mask their true approach to doing the job.

And Perry had learned from experience that there was no point in offering a retort. Instead, he turned his back to the man, like he always did. But today, Perry wasn't alone to hear the gibes.

He saw something in his friend Watson's face that was unfamiliar. Embarrassment. Sympathy. Pity.

"I'm sorry, man," Watson offered. "We should've met at a diner or something. But don't mind that hump, okay? Dude's one flask away from a liver transplant."

Perry started to tell Watson not to worry about it. That it wasn't the first time and it wouldn't be the last. That he was almost used to it after all these years.

But sensing Watson's guilt, he did something else instead. He flashed a smile, patted his friend on the back, and said, "So about Angel's cell phone. Let me write down that number for you."

9

JOHN CONNOLLY

T here is, thought Perry, *nothing like progress.* With Watson on his side, the possibility of finding Angel had at least taken a step from the shadows of improbability without yet emerging, blinking, into the light. This sudden surge of optimism made him glance back at the 19th Precinct, with its blue window frames and terra-cotta trimmings. It looked almost festive when considered in the right frame of mind, at which point he decided that he was getting carried away, and that pretty soon he'd be looking at half-empty glasses in a whole new way.

This part of the Upper East Side had always boasted a dual nature: in a sense, Perry encompassed it in himself through his lineage. At the end of the nineteenth century, the western edges had housed the city's cigar makers in the new tenements. The tenements doubled as factories, with the cigar manufacturers buying or renting whole blocks and subletting them to the cigar makers and their families. It was, effectively, the industrialization of a process that had been ongoing for years, ever since cigar makers paid to the manufacturers a deposit of double the value of the tobacco supplied before taking their stock home and rolling the cigars in their rooms.

His great-grandfather had been one of those men, although he had died of tuberculosis long before Perry was born. Perry's grandfather used to joke that his old man smoked so much tobacco it was a wonder anyone else ever got to try his product. He had been a union organizer, and had been instrumental in pressuring the union to accept women as members in 1867, one of only two national unions to have done so at the time. Perry suspected that his great-grandfather had probably been a hard man: back then, union organizers had had their skulls broken, and had broken skulls in turn. These days they were the whipping boys for everything that was wrong with the economy, as though the days of child labor and dismissal without cause had never happened.

Meanwhile, his great-grandfather's brother Petros had found less gainful employment in the precinct's eastern extremes, where the gangs congregated among shanties built among the rocks in the river and made their living from theft and, occasionally, murder. Family lore, possibly sanitized for general consumption, took the view that Petros had never actually killed anyone, although it stopped short of canonizing him as some kind of Robin Hood figure, as Petros had never limited his acts of larceny to the rich, and any redistribution of wealth occurred within his own gang. Perry had found the name of Petros among the old records, and the sole charges leveled against him had been those of pickpocketing and vagrancy, but he had run with a crowd that wasn't slow to use a blade, and the only photo Perry could find of Petros showed a dead-eyed figure with outsize hands. Petros Christo might not have had a murder charge against his name, but he had the look of a dangerous man.

Perry found it amusing that his apartment in Yorkville was closer to the old stomping ground of Petros Christo than it was to the tenement of Petros's worthy, left-leaning brother. Those who had hounded Perry from the department probably felt that the link to Petros Christo was not only one of geography but also of character.

He would never be able to convince them otherwise, but it was enough that cops like Watson still believed in him. It also made his job a little easier, particularly when it came to missing persons. The police had access to resources that were beyond the reach of private operatives like Perry, and it paid to have a handful of cops on his side. If nothing else, he hoped they saw in Perry a way of spiting the suits in the department, and the hated Internal Affairs in particular.

Now, as he walked, he thought of Angel. She certainly got around for a twenty-year-old girl, although Perry's experience of twenty-year-old girls was necessarily limited, and had been even when he was a twenty-year-old boy. At least she seemed happy to spread her favors widely across the social divide, according to Lilith Bates: from rich boys to mechanics. His great-grandfather would have approved, but it didn't suggest a balanced personality. Had his own daughter behaved in such a manner, Perry would have—

Would have what? He had enough trouble getting Nicky to talk about anything more than Internet memes and the last movies she'd seen. She'd been smart enough to deny him access to her Facebook page as well. Admittedly, she was a good deal younger than Angel, but he sometimes wondered if it might have been more productive to follow his daughter around instead of chasing after the specter of a girl he didn't even know.

The sky was still overcast, and Perry longed for the sun, for that glorious New York City winter blue. Now there were more heavy clouds overhead, and the forecast was for icy rain, maybe even snow. Perhaps it was his awareness of the impending change in the weather, or the associations he had made between a missing girl and his own beloved child, but he felt a growing sense of unease.

He took his cell phone from his pocket and checked his messages, even though he knew that he had none waiting. It gave him the opportunity to lean against a wall and take in the situation around him.

His gaze danced casually over businesspeople and stray tourists, over deliverymen and mothers pushing carriages, but the only person who seemed to be paying undue attention to anything on the block was himself. Still, it was there: a prickling of the skin on the back of his neck, as though something were slowly crawling up his back. He had long ago learned not to ignore the sensation. In the past it had presaged the impact of a brick on the sidewalk beside him, and once the *snick* of a blade that might otherwise have gutted him had he not responded to the goading of his fear by taking a step backward instead of forward. And it had been there that fateful night when he was tailing Derace McDonald, but not strongly enough to avoid a bullet. He had felt it, too, seconds before the shadow of IAB had fallen across him, although in that case no amount of fancy footwork could have saved him from the touch of its knife.

Nothing. He scanned windows and doors, seeking any hint of surveillance, but none revealed itself. He paused again at St. Catherine's Park on Sixty-eighth and watched a group of young guys shoot hoops despite the frigid weather, while kids who would have been floored by the impact of the basketball played on the jungle gym. For a moment, he thought that he saw a pair of eyes alight on him and remain there for just an instant too long, features indistinct beneath the hood of a sweatshirt, body hidden beneath layers of winter clothing, but then a crowd swallowed the figure up. Had it been a man or a woman? A boy or a girl? Did she look like Angel? He had no idea— it had all happened too quickly.

I'm not just jumping at shadows, thought Perry. *I'm jumping at the* hope *of shadows.*

He moved on, but took a circuitous route back to his apartment, making a long loop onto First Avenue to buy milk that he didn't need. The prickling went away, but the memory of it did not. He entered his building and waited until he was certain that the door had closed properly before he turned his back on it, and the stairway to his fifth-floor walk-up seemed darker than before. When he opened the door to his apartment, he paused for a moment before entering, but if there was anyone hiding in there, he wished them luck: his apartment was so small a game of hide and seek would have lasted about two seconds. There was a bedroom with just enough room for a bed, a kitchenette with just enough room for a stove and half-size fridge, and the living area crowded with all his PI equipment.

What it did have was shelving: lots and lots of shelving. It was what had attracted Perry to it in the first place. With a little work, he was able to create spaces for his collection of vinyl and his books. He had an iPod that he had loaded with music from the CDs that were now in storage, but he rarely used it. He preferred vinyl, and not because of the difference in sound, although he had read about a study in which music played on vinyl had calmed mentally disturbed patients while music played through a computer had made them angrier, which didn't surprise him in the least. No, what Perry liked was the ritual involved in listening to vinyl. With an iPod, you could press a button and listen to music for days, but the problem was that you could also do lots of other stuff at the same time: laundry, cooking, answering e-mail, dozing off. But vinyl demanded your attention: you had to put the record on the turntable, make sure the surface and the needle were clean, and then wait until the needle found the groove. After that you only had twenty minutes of music, so you might as well sit down and listen because pretty soon you'd be back on your feet again to change the side. Your focus became the record and, by extension, what you were hearing. Perry didn't like music as a background. Either you immersed yourself in it or you didn't listen to it at all. Jazz, classical, country, folk, rock: it was all the same to him. If you liked it enough not just to buy it but also to keep it, then the least that it deserved was your attention.

He kicked off his shoes and put on the latest Sun Kil Moon album, bought from the band's Web site. He looked around his apartment as the music played, Mark Kozelek's voice almost as deep as his own, as though he had found a way to put his own sense of dislocation to music. Those first years outside the department had been the hardest: he had lost not one family because of what had occurred, but two. The NYPD had been as much a part of his life as the woman and child who shared his home. Now both families were gone, but he was still here: he had survived the loss of both, even though he would have sworn years before that such a thing would not be possible.

And although he could not have said that he loved what he did— the insurance cases, the missing persons, the casework for lawyers seeking to get clients off the hook regardless of their innocence or guilt—it suited something deep in his nature. Perhaps he had always been more inclined to a solitary existence than he might have wanted to believe, although he continued to fight it. Women passed through his life, or he passed through theirs: sometimes, he wasn't sure which was the truth. He lived alone; his ex-wife had a new man in her life; his daughter was growing up too fast—but he kept trying, as much for Nicky's sake as for his own. He tried never to miss his scheduled calls with her, though it happened, and he paid his child support even when it left him broke for the rest of the month. He gave his ex, Noreen, no cause to complain because he was desperate to hold on to his daughter.

The thought brought him back to Julia Drusilla. Despite all that she had said about her daughter, there had been a disconnection between what was spoken and what was felt. Until now, Perry had struggled to grasp the source of his dissatisfaction with the woman, but thinking about his daughter in the solitude of his apartment had made it clear to him: there was not enough pain. For Perry, the absence of his daughter in his day-to-day life was like an open wound, an emptiness in his being that erupted in agony with even the softest touch of memory. Maybe the fact of Julia Drusilla's own impending mortality had dulled the loss of her daughter, but then why the need for a deathbed reunion? Yes, there had been a sense of urgency to Drusilla's desire to have her daughter back, but was it to fill a hole in her being or a hole in her wallet? But Julia Drusilla was rich, so what need did she have for the money? She was also dying, which made the need for money even less pressing, unless she planned to be buried with it.

He stopped thinking, and started listening. He closed his eyes and let the music wash over him as he imagined his daughter sitting next to him, her hand in his, sharing silence in music.

The needle rose. The telephone rang. The timing could not have been more perfect. He picked up the phone and for a single second expected to hear his daughter's voice. Instead, Arthur Gawain from the East Hampton Police Department spoke.

"We've found Angel's car," he said.

"And Angel?"

"If we'd found her, do you think I'd have started off with the car?"

"Anything I should know?"

"The car looked as if it had been abandoned, that's all. No sign of anything else."

"I'm coming out there," said Perry, thinking if he left now he could be there before dark. He hung up before Gawain could say no.

Before he left, he replaced the record in its sleeve.

You had to be careful with fragile things.

So much easier to follow the PI on foot than by car.

You leave just enough distance between you, and there are plenty of people on the street for distraction. But damn, it's cold, and you've been following him since morning, first to the police station, waiting outside, standing around trying to look innocent in front of a police station, almost funny, all those cops going in and out and no one giving you a second glance. You try to imagine who the PI is here to see, someone who will hopefully help him and help you at the same time.

You walk up and down the block trying to keep warm, your hands going numb, damn gloves left behind in the car, and then, just as you're passing in front of the precinct entrance, the PI comes out and you practically jump but he doesn't notice, he's so preoccupied, and you slide behind a group of uniforms, using them as a shield.

You let him get a half block ahead then catch up walking slowly but purposely until he stops and you duck under the awning of an apartment building and watch as he gets his cell phone out and scrolls through messages, half looking at his phone and half surveying the area, and you wonder if he's aware of you at all.

He starts walking again and you do, too, slower now, cautious, and when he stops beside a church, you turn around and pretend to buy something at a newspaper stand until he's moving again, heading home, you think, though his route is different so you're not sure, wondering if he's learned something important and if he's heading somewhere else, so you move a little quicker, afraid you might lose him, following around a corner and onto First Avenue, the wind in your face, an icy chill off the river. And when he goes into a deli, you speed up, a daring part of you wanting to tease the situation even more than you already have and so you follow him in, watch him take a carton of milk to the counter, the two of you only six, seven feet apart, your hood up so he can't see your face, and you're nervous but excited, your whole body electric.

Then he looks over and you feel his eyes on you and you know he's thinking: Is this someone I should look at, is this someone I know? But you don't dare look up. You just reach for a box of Oreos acting casual, normal, waiting until when he's paid for his milk and then he's out of the store and you buy the cookies and wait again to make sure he's not going to come back. Then you head out, stop in the doorway, peer up and down the street, spot him a half block ahead, and wait another minute until you see him turn the corner.

You catch up in time to see him go into his apartment building. Then you slide into the rental car and eat the Oreos one by one, splitting them open and licking the cream with the tip of your tongue, the whole time staring up at the PI's fifth floor, waiting.

10

JAMES GRADY

Another trek out to the Hamptons. It was almost three when Perry finally pulled into the garage. He needed to see and hear what Randy had to say about Angel's car. Thought if he was smart, he'd have ol' Randy check out his Datsun, too, all the miles he was putting on it with this case.

"You don't belong here."

The woman behind the counter who snarled those words at Perry as he entered the office of Gil's Gas & Auto wore too much makeup that did too little to cover the hard miles that had plunked her here in this Long Island garage. Her twentieth high school reunion had come and gone, but local gossips often noted she was "still" pretty. Her perfume, white blouse, and dark slacks cost more than necessary for working this auto shop's computer, credit card reader, cash register, and customer counter. She kept coffin eyes on Perry, shook a cigarette out of the pack on her desk, flicked a blue flame from a lighter.

Swirling cigarette smoke carried Perry's eyes to the gas station wall, hung with five framed photos faded by sunlight and weighted by dust. He hadn't noticed them last time, but now he took them in.

Perry saw the five photos were all of the same man as he aged through life, from a high school football player to a soldier in two photos of American soldiers in desert camo fatigues. Soldiers in one photo held a banner: LONG ISLAND NATIONAL GUARD MECH. DIV. ZULU—OPERATION IRAQI FREEDOM. The fourth photo showed the same man, but older and looking lost. The fifth photo showed him even older and standing beside the thirtysomething ghost of the woman smoking at the desk. The ghost clutched a bouquet, wore a workday dress and the brave smile of some last best hope.

Perry nodded to the photos. "So that's Gil."

"Like you care," said the woman. "I got told what you look like. You're not supposed to be here."

Perry shrugged. "Free country."

"Since when."

"I'm here to see Randy."

"He doesn't want to see you again." She sucked on the cigarette. Made its ember burn traffic-light orange. "He told me. You got nothing for him. Nothing on him."

"It's heartening to see a boss who cares so much about her employees."

She billowed a cloud of smoke toward Perry. "I'm not the boss."

Perry nodded. "Sure."

Left her with her smoldering cancer stick and walked into the garage bay.

"Randy!" she yelled past him. "If you need me, I'm here! I'm here!"

Perry found Angel's ex-*whatever* Randy standing beside a car lift that held a luxury sedan suspended above their heads.

A gray work shirt hid Randy Hyde's tattoos, but not the bulge of his muscles. His empty hands flexed with the ambition of fists.

Perry stopped beside an overturned fuel drum covered with tools.

Randy said: "We're done talking."

"We're done with your bullshit, but we're not done with talking about Angel."

Randy drew his lips back over his teeth. "So, guess you're just another hotshot wannabe hooked by that blond cunt."

That brutally degrading term keyed Perry's cop savvy of how much multilayered malice could trigger the word. Beyond that alarm, he felt as if an affront had splattered him or someone he loved—someone not like his ex-wife and certainly not like his daughter but . . . He felt himself shimmer from *smart* to *street*.

Perry said: "So, if that's what she is, guess now you're just a worthless dick."

The mechanic lunged like a barroom brawler.

Perry grabbed a two-foot steel pry bar from the oil barrel's pile of tools and police-baton rammed it into his attacker's guts.

Randy gasped, shoved Perry under the suspended vehicle. Randy stumbled with him, wrestling for the steel bar. A twist of Randy's hands flung it from their grasp.

The steel pry bar clanged off the lift control wand hung on a wall hook, hit the wand's green button marked Lower.

A black steel cloud sank toward the two fighting men.

Perry fired his fist into the mechanic's ribs. Randy's head bumped the transmission shaft of the car sliding down from heaven. Perry dodged a knee strike, pulled Randy into the police academy's *ogoshi* hip throw. Randy's legs swept up off the oil-stained concrete but hit the undercarriage of the sliding-down car. That collision sprawled the two men in a heap on the garage-bay floor.

An arm yoked under Perry's chin. Death smelled like oiled cement as he saw the black car sinking closer. Perry gouged Randy's eye. Randy yelled.

Perry rolled out from under the sinking steel sky, hesitated—grabbed the mechanic's flailing arm and pulled the top half of the pain-blinded man out from under the car seconds before the touched-down tires took the weight of that luxury machine.

They sat side by side on the floor, their legs splayed under the low-ered car, their faces reflected in the polished black steel doors.

Perry slammed Randy's face into the car.

Caught him as he rebounded, his eye bloodshot, his nose bleeding.

The woman from the office loomed by the car's trunk: *"Randy! What did you do to him? I'm calling the cops . . . ambulance—"*

"I pulled him out from being crushed under that car—I fucking saved his life!" said Perry. "If you call the cops now, you throw him into trouble!"

The woman froze.

"*Wha*-what?" said Randy.

The woman said: "Whatever he—"

"Nora!" yelled Randy. "I got this. Go back to where you're sup-posed to be."

"Where's that?" she muttered.

Left two men sitting on the cement floor with their legs under a rich man's car.

Slammed her office door.

A radio in the office abruptly blared an old rock song in sound-muffling defiance.

On their feet, Perry splayed Randy against the car for a police stop pat down.

The growl in Randy's ear said: "What did Angel see in you?"

"I . . . I'm . . ."

"You're a punk-ass nobody in the last of your glory days."

A shove bounced Randy off the car. Perry didn't let him turn around.

"She . . . she needed me . . . and wanted me."

"Maybe, but you led with *needed,* so that's the heart of what's be-tween you."

Randy wiped goo streaming from his gouged eye.

"Why did she need you?"

"I protected her."

"From what? Who?"

"Whoever I could. I told you she was scared. But she was always spooked. Like somebody was going to find her or some secret and . . . I don't know. Get her."

"Did she ever say who?"

"No. Just . . . She said she got weird phone calls."

"From who?"

"I don't know, man! Who wouldn't call her! Ask her!"

"I can't. She's missing. Remember?"

"Still?"

"You think I drove all the way back here from Manhattan because I'm hooked on some woman I've never met?"

Randy shrugged. "If it's Angel, makes sense to me."

"I'm not you," said Perry. "An East Hampton cop called me this morning, a badge named Arthur Gawain who said they found her car abandoned. But no Angel."

"Where is she? Is she okay? I got to—"

"You got to be able to sell your story to the cops."

"You don't have to sell the truth!"

"What planet do you live on?" Perry frowned. "If you were her protection, why'd she break it off, why'd she leave you behind at the motel?"

The private eye saw the shoulders shrug on the man who stood before him facing a car he could never afford and the radio-filled office that signed his paychecks.

"Guys like me didn't dare bother her 'cause of me. And big-bucks boys from Wall Street, Harvard princes come up here for two weeks of summer—they figured the score when she walked with me, though they never stopped trying."

"Tell me what changed," said Perry. "The woman who dumped you is missing. I'm the only guy who cares about finding her and the truth. You need me to help sell whatever that is to cops, who only care about easy answers."

Randy's words came out hard: "She found somebody who's more."

"More what? More protection?"

"That's all bullshit. Nobody's protected. Not from everything."

"But this new guy's closer to some *everything*?"

"He's got money. Power. Politics." The back of Randy's hand wiped his bloody nose. "Married, but a woman like Angel makes that not matter."

"How do you know about him and her?"

"After her *'I need more'* talk . . . I followed her one day. Saw them." Randy leered at Perry: "You want to see a picture?"

"I have one."

"Here's another." The bloody mechanic got his cell phone off a workbench, handed it over.

The photo had been stalker-snapped from behind a pine tree by a parking lot. Randy had already zoomed the image as large as his phone allowed so the figures filled the screen in Perry's hand.

Angel. Her face cupped by a beefy sandy-haired man. His hands made her look up at him. Perry thought: *He's older than me*.

"Who is he?"

"A state assemblyman. Might be other guys, but he's who I caught her with."

"They know that you know?"

"I e-mailed her the photos to show her I wasn't no fool."

Photos.

Perry had owned this same phone two upgrades ago. He finger-swiped the photo to the next stored shot. The beefy politician was bent over kissing Angel. She stood with her hands at her sides. A third photo showed the same kiss, only now Mr. State Assemblyman pawed Angel's breast.

Randy said: "That's all I got of them— *Hey!*"

Perry swiped to the next photo. The phone in his hand trembled.

Angel. Naked. Standing in a steamy shower facing the clouded glass door. Blond hair blurred like golden light. Closed eyes. Her arms bent and vanished behind her head. The clouded glass made her wide mouth a blur of pink. Revealed epic, natural, handful breasts. Angel had a narrow waist. The photo ended where a bikini would have begun.

She didn't know the asshole was taking this, thought Perry.

He finger-swiped to the next photo: her laughing at the camera, at Randy.

All the other photos were of cars or auto work, except for one taken by a person who'd grabbed the phone to put her portrait in it: office Nora.

"Give me my cell!"

"After I fix it so it's not rare enough to kill you for."

Perry e-mailed the photos of Angel and the political animal to his own phone. He sent her laughing portrait. Then the image of her naked behind clouded glass. Each e-mail vibrated the iPhone on his belt. He deleted the naked shot from Randy's phone. Let Randy keep the others: *Preserve your chain of evidence and back up what you got.*

"What's his name?"

"Tweed."

"Tweed who?"

"Tweed is his last name."

"You've gotta be shitting me."

"What's funny about that shit? He's Cyrus Tweed, some state legislature guy, got an office here in town. His name is his name."

Perry tossed the phone back to its owner. "Remember *my*

name—Perry Christo. I programmed my number in there. You hear *from, of,* or *about* Angel, call me first, call me fast. Don't make me figure you for a fall."

"I got enough trouble."

They both stared at the garage office where the closed door vibrated from a radio.

Perry said: "That Nora being older and married wouldn't stop a guy like you."

"You think I'm stupid?" Randy didn't wait for Perry's answer. "I know what I know. Gil's war hollow. Just stands around their house. She thinks I got what she needs—that's more than *you know*—and she lets me know what's waiting for me. I hunger bad. But I do that, come later when she realizes who I'm not, my ass is tossed out the door. Or worse. I don't dare even hint about *if Gil was gone*. What she might do then scares the shit out of me. She's driving me crazy."

"There are other jobs."

"What planet are *you* from."

"Does she know about you and Angel?"

"Nora figures my anybody else's don't count. Figures she's where I'll end up."

Perry shook his head: "Do your own math."

He walked away from that brick gas station/garage that felt like the 1940s, smelled of rubber, old gas, expensive perfume, cancer smoke. The chill of the gray-skied afternoon and the smell of the sea reclaimed him to here and now.

The private detective unwound his woolen scarf, sat behind the steering wheel of his car. Worked his iPhone like his professional predecessors had worked the soles of their shoes. Google searches showed him New York State Assemblyman Cyrus Tweed's gerrymandered legislative district twisted like a rattlesnake on Long Island but covered only a slice of this town. Perry found pictures of Mrs. Cyrus Tweed holding the hands of their two children. She was a pretty woman who knew how and when to smile.

Cyrus Tweed's legislature Web site listed his district office address on the other end of Main Street. Google Street View showed him its picture: a two-story brick building, offices above yet another trendy coffee shop.

His investigator's bones made Perry google the address for that building.

Save Our Beaches listed its headquarters at that address. So did the Long Island Jobs Coalition Crew, Liberals United for Victory, Conservatives for American Values Endeavors, Cultural Preservation and Protection League, Congressional Reform Action Program, the Montauk Medical Charities Foundation. Other groups with more vaguely purposed names. All at that land address, but each with a different "suite" number, so any search engine "exact match" profile of one group would not link them.

Fourteen organizations plus a coffee shop and Tweed's official state office.

All at one address.

Perry rechecked the Google Street View: a few rooms above a coffee shop.

As long as he had his phone in his hand, he looked at the e-mail of Tweed trapping Angel's face in his hands. Tweed mauling her. Angel laughing. The shower photo where her blue eyes were closed.

He clipped his phone onto his belt, started the car. Hit Seek on the FM radio and landed on the local station's slogan singing "the place to be since 1963," back when we murdered presidents and Perry's parents were teenagers. He was sure this same oldies sound had blared back in that gas station. Not his music. But something about the beat, the rhythm, the dark urgency of what wasn't being said in that song from yesterdays he'd never known captured Perry's mood. He drove down Main Street. Traffic was scarce, parking places plentiful, and he just knew he could handle any nor'easter from the climate change monster hiding in the late afternoon's heavy gray sky.

Vibrations rumbled his right hip where once he'd holstered his 9 millimeter.

Cell phone: e-mail or text message. Illegal to check while driving.

He coasted the car into a parking place in front of a white wooden storefront with a display window painted with ornate script: BETTER DAZE BOOKSHOPPE—NEW & ANTIQUE COLLECTIBLES.

No cynical laugh came from him. This emporium fit with other shops and boutiques on this Main Street. Some stores were closed behind SEE YOU NEXT SEASON! notices. Other sported signs that read: SALE. The "bookshoppe" where he parked had two coffee table books in the window under a SPECIAL DISCOUNT LIMITED EDITIONS sign: photography collections, one a colorful-jacketed volume called *Sand Sea Sky* by Tria Giovan, and the other a black-jacketed volume called *Out of the Sixties* by iconic dead Hollywood actor Dennis Hopper, who'd of course been "a close personal friend" to oh so many of the town's seasonal residents.

The cell phone buzz was a pro forma e-mail update from a Manhattan law firm whose client Perry'd helped shelter from a federal corruption probe of Wall Street.

Nothing about Angel.

Two quaint coin-operated newspaper kiosks stood outside the "bookshoppe," a blue kiosk for *New York Times* traditionalists, a yellow kiosk for a local weekly paper.

Perry fed the yellow metal kiosk quarters for last week's local news.

A bell dinged as an old woman left the bookstore. She seemed too small for her red-and-black-checked wool coat. Her bird hands tied the strap of a clear plastic rain cap under her chin as she told no one in particular: "I hate it when the weather gets like this. Feels like a whole lot of lonely."

The cold wind blew her down Main Street.

He drove to the far edge of town.

The two-story building fit its googled image. Perry circled the block, spotted the pine trees he thought Randy had hidden behind when he took those rear parking lot pictures of a creep and Angel, wanted to check the photos to be sure, but didn't. Christo didn't look at any of the photos. Then. He parked on Samadi Street, where he could see the front of the building. Surveilled its door to upstairs and the front windows of the espresso café.

Ten minutes came and went without anyone entering the expensive coffee shop. The café windows showed him three bored employees and no customers.

No one used the door to the upstairs rooms where lights shone in the windows.

He drove his car to the rear lot, walked around to the Main Street front. The doorknob to the upstairs suites turned in his hand and put Perry in a yellow-walled vestibule with brown wooden stairs. A sign tacked on the vestibule wall read: NO HANDICAP ACCESS—SORRY! A label that read NEWSPAPERS was stuck on a wicker basket on the vestibule floor.

That means the door probably stays unlocked. Anybody could drop something in the wicker basket any time of the day or night. Or into the steel box the size of an airplane carry-on suitcase bolted to the vestibule wall. The box lid had a flap big enough for a coffee table book to be dropped through and a built-in lock plus a padlock. The sign on the flap read: MAIL SLOT FOR ALL SUITES IN BUILDING.

Perry climbed the shadowed wooden stairs. Smelled radiator heat and lemon floor polish. He reached the top landing, let the air and quiet settle around him.

Four doors waited, two on each side of the dimly lit hall.

Words on the two doors at the far end of the hall were readable. The solid door on the left held a handmade sign: COFFEEHOUSE OF-FICE. Blue paint formed the word SUPPLIES on the also solid wooden door across the hall.

The two doors closest to the stairs were glass.

The glass door on the right held black lettering: DISTRICT ASSEMBLY FIELD OFFICE.

Gilt lettering on the glass door across the hall read: CYRUS TWEED.

Perry glanced into the government "district" office: low-bid desk and computer setup, gray file cabinets, colorful posters for Long Island, New York City, New York State. Three steel chairs waited in a line for someone to come sit behind the big desk.

The "Cyrus Tweed" door showed a woman sitting on the desk, her dress high on sleekly stockinged legs as she straightened the hair of the beefy man in the big chair.

Perry's blitz entrance startled them. The beefy man jerked back in his chair as the woman whirled to scan the intruder. She wore hennaed hair to her jaw, red lipstick to match, makeup that triumphed rather than hid her forty-some years. The rusty-haired woman beamed seasoned sensuality.

Perry flashed on Angel in a steamy shower.

As the redhead slid to her well-shod feet, the beefy guy behind the desk bellowed: "Hey, we're about to close up shop for the day, but how are you?"

"Here," said Perry.

The woman said: "I'll check on those constituent issues."

She swayed past Christo on her way across the hall, gave him a crimson smile and the scent of musk.

The door closed behind her as Perry watched Cyrus Tweed watch her go.

The politician felt the stranger's eyes on him, shot out his right hand: "Call me Cy, Cy Tweed. Cyrus sounds too—"

"Whatever," Perry said as he claimed the visitor's chair.

The mahogany desk matched the wood paneling hung with oil paintings, plaques, and spotless framed photographs of Cy playing golf *with* and sunset beach partying *with* and backstage rock concerting *with* and black-tie events *with* Hollywood stars and billionaires. One photo showed his colleagues on the floor of the state assembly applauding Cy. Portraits of him shaking hands with the current and other-partied former president of the United States hung on his wall. So did a photo of his wife and children.

Cy said: "And you are . . . ?"

Guy like this, thought Perry, *his every breath is a lie.* Hit him hard, fast, straight.

The private eye said: "Angel."

The politician peered around the man sitting in front of his desk to look through the glass of his closed office door and across the hall into the public official's office where the redhead had gone, told his visitor: "I . . . I'm not sure what you mean."

"But you know who I'm talking about."

"Did she send you?"

"I work for people who care about her."

"Whoever they are, it isn't *her* they care about. Me, I—"

"You're a busy man. Your wife and kids. Your 'whoever she is' across the hall."

"Gwen is . . . a really public-spirited citizen. Volunteers to run my local office."

"You mean your office across the hall," said Perry.

The vision rose in him and came out like the narration of a movie:

"You're the fixer. All those groups who get mail here—left wing, right wing, Wall Street, union lovers, tree huggers, developers: all the groups are shells run by you and your *volunteer*. Gwen's probably on what books they keep. You take money from *whoever* and funnel it to *wherever*—for a handling percentage, *sure,* that's only fair, because you're the guy who buys results without fingerprints. Sometimes it's good: a Hollywood star wants to save the planet, so he gives the group you run a check and you pass most of it along to save the whales. Sometimes it's a big-money boy who sends you a couple hundred thou' to launder to the national groups who anyway barely need to explain the millions they spend to buy presidential campaigns.

"Plus the cash that gets dropped in that steel box. The real dirty money you wash. Say from a Mexican cartel giving you dollars to support tough-drug-law candidates so the illegal market stays intact."

Cy said: "I never do nothing for guys like that!"

"Good to know you've got lines. Or at least a price that hasn't been met yet."

Perry shook his head. "I almost forgot about the coffee shop! No customers, but I bet it bangs out business on the books. Who owns it? Some corporate name? Just like who owns this building where the taxpayers and those political groups pay rent? Your own campaign always has the most dollars, plus you arrange contributions for other officials who do you favors you charge the big boys for. You get it coming and going."

"You've got nothing on me!"

"Don't make me try . . . What about Angel?"

"You can't tell anybody about her! Is this about the pictures?"

"Have you seen them?"

"She said they were out there. I just wanted her to . . ."

"What does she want?"

"She . . . She wanted more from me. For me to . . . to do more."

"You mean . . . marry her?"

"I don't— *No*. She said I was blowing a chance to do and be some-body important. Hell, here, like this, I'm bigger than anybody thinks. I am somebody!"

"And you have the thanks of a grateful nation."

"Who are you? What do you want?"

Perry tossed his card on the desk, watched as it was scanned then scooped out of sight.

Cy said: "Those pictures . . ." Again he peered toward the office across the hall. Said: "They can't get out!"

"You're not worried about your wife—you're worried about your partner, that it?"

"Either one could ruin me. If one does, the other will, too." Cy shrugged. "Alone, my wife would just force a quiet settlement."

"But your *volunteer* . . ."

"Gwen." The elected state official shook his head. "Gwen has to believe—*know*—that she's my . . . that she and I . . . If she knew about Angel, she'd burn down the house. She accepts my wife: that's a . . . a carrying cost. But Angel . . ."

"If you dump Gwen, she could cut a deal and send you to jail—"

"What I do is essentially legal!"

"Or just take the empire from you, make you her puppet instead of a partner."

"She loves me enough to do worse than that. I've got to keep it that way. Those pictures, even though Angel left me—"

"When did Angel leave you?"

"When the clocks stopped." He shrugged. "A week or so ago. Right after she figured out . . . what you figured out."

Perry laughed.

"What's so funny?"

"I just left a man who doesn't dare fuck the woman he has, and now I'm with a man who doesn't dare *not* fuck the woman he has."

"Is that other guy tied to Angel?" Cy smiled. "She doesn't like amateurs." He leaned across the desk to whisper: "Where is she?"

Perry leaned forward until their faces were barely a kiss away. "Missing."

Cy paled under his tan. "How . . . . What happened?"

"The cops found her empty car but not her."

"Cops? Do they know about— I can squeeze the sheriff. Or State Police, locals."

Don't give him Gawain's name! Perry said: "As far as I know, no badges know about you and Angel."

Cy stared into lost time.

The private detective said: "Where would she go? Who is she afraid of?"

"I don't know. She wouldn't tell me. She was . . . too disappointed."

"If she gets in touch, surprise her and do the smart thing: call me."

"When you find her . . . Tell her I'm still here for her."

Perry frowned. "You want her back even though she's big trouble?"

"She's worth all that. More."

Perry left that office. Looked through another door's glass and caught the redheaded woman sitting behind a cheap government desk staring back at him. He felt the weight of his cell phone on his hip. Envisioned the picture of Angel caught by a creep who saw and wanted and tried to capture the redeeming essence beyond her mere physical beauty, her sensual hunger. A creep like that, that strong of emotion, people killed for less. And the redheaded woman staring at him now, Perry'd seen that kind of jealousy paid out in too many corpses, just like he'd seen the deaths caused by the tangle of desperations embodied in the politician named Tweed who could have found his courage in an explosion of violence in some curtained room. *But she can't be dead, not Angel, not someone that vibrant. Not before I . . .*

Don't finish that thought. Any of those thoughts.

He walked down the long dark stairs into the dying light of the day.

Walking through that town has made you excited and furious and frustrated all at once, and it's not just the waiting and following, but the feelings you've stored up like a hive of bees buzzing in your brain.

But you're cool, no one can tell, walking slow, acting normal, smiling when people pass, some smiling back, no idea of the murderous thoughts that are going through your mind, thinking how you will do whatever you need to do, how you will not let anyone get in the way, the whole time tamping down the feeling that you are going to explode.

You watched the PI go to that garage again and then to see that politician, and you wondered what that could be about and if it will help you get closer to your destination—to your destiny. But you just get back into the rental car and drive down the lonely stretch of highway, driving as the sun sets and you hold on, clinging to the idea that soon, soon you will have it all.

11

KEN BRUEN

Perry cursed. Damn if he wasn't in a foul mood, all this driving, all these unanswered questions and not any closer to finding Angel.

The East Hampton cop was still unavailable, so he'd decided to pay Norman Loki a surprise visit, tell him they'd found his daughter's car but not his daughter. Not exactly good news.

Growing dark now as he drove back up to the Montauk house. His car seemed embarrassed to be asked to appear in such surroundings. A PI's car that harked back to the glory days of Rockford.

Save Perry was no Jim Garner. Not even close. Past forty, he felt it, the driving, the garage brawl, the past two days of interviews had drained him, dealing with liars and, yeah, scum.

Scum like Randy Hyde. And now that politico creep, Tweed.

Would test the best of men.

Perry was not even close to his best, whatever that was. This acidic line of thought always led to the shame, the dismissal from the force and all the other cluster fucks of his life.

Being a cop, straight out, he'd freaking loved it. Was *proud* to carry the shield. His ex, Noreen, used to accuse, "You don't bend Perry, you're too . . . *rigid*."

Not the first time he heard that. But it enraged him even now, like being honest was a crime. Fuck it, maybe he'd been *too* honest.

His buddies on the sheet, taking firstly nickel-and-dime crap, moving on up, and *fast,* to serious shit, serious dirt.

A *dirty* cop.

Hung that on him, Jesus H. Christ, not as much as a damn burger on the lam and Internal sneering:

"Count yer blessings, pal, you ain't doing time."

Doing time?!

Like having that jacket for the rest of his woebegone life, like that wasn't a sentence?

His ex. Believe this? Saying to his daughter, who was all of nine years old then, "Daddy's a crook." Okay, not exactly Noreen's words, but close enough.

You wanna talk criminal?

Yeah, her goddamn lawyer, that's who.

Perry could feel it, all the bile and self-pity and, yes, fury he always tried so damn hard to keep under wraps rising. Damn, he was tired.

And now he had to deal with this damn lawyer with his damn house on the beach, and, like, did the guy even give a toss about his daughter? He hardly seemed upset last time he'd been out here.

Perry mentally composed himself, willed steel into his eyes, thought *Today, buddy—trust me—today you are going to give a damn!*

But hell, was he just thinking about himself, about the fact that he'd lost his daughter and his wife along with his shield and still wasn't over it, never would be?

He looked up at the house, even on this drab, cold, February eve, the house seemed to whisper, *Yo, dipshit, this ain't never . . . ever going to be your abode.*

Right on the bluff overlooking the beach, and, fuck, a pool. You had the whole goddamn ocean—you needed a pool?

Perry parked and walked over to have a look. Something floating on the water's surface . . . Jesus, couldn't be . . . used condoms? Like, wouldn't they . . . sink? What the hell sort of pool parties was Norman Loki throwing?

Shook himself, *Get straight*. Forget the damn pool. Forget your own bitterness. Stick to the case.

Perry looked up. Saw a face at the window.

Loki?

Last visit, Loki had been alone. Except for the Adonis trainer.

But hell, why did he feel like this was a goddamn contest? Just 'cause the guy didn't seem to care, didn't make him guilty. Or did it? Maybe Perry just wanted to fight with a man, a father, who had it all and didn't seem to give a shit.

This time, Perry had ammunition: the interview with the politician, finding Angel's car, the shifty mechanic part-time boyfriend—oh yeah, different ball game this time. Okay, not exactly ammo, but info. And information was power, isn't that what they said? Whoever *they* were. He needed to feed it all back to Loki, see and hear how the man reacted.

Before he rang the bell, he tried to smooth the wrinkles of his slacks, his beat-up trench, get that tough no-shit vibe going. He looked down at his old dress shoes, damp and scuffed. Not so dressy anymore.

Physically shook himself, muttered, "Christo, goddamn it, get a grip. This isn't about you."

Pushed the bell and was once again treated to a few bars of "The Impossible Dream."

Fuck on a pretentious bike.

He heard footsteps, slow, no hurry there then, the door eased open.

Norman, drink in hand, in shorts, garish maroon number, bare feet, and, worse, a bare chest. He said, "Salesmen to the back door."

Perry said, "There have been some developments."

Norman continued to look at him, like, *Who the fuck are you, dude?* And nervously glanced toward the back of the house. Something was off, Perry felt it.

He asked, "May I come in, sir?" Managing to leak a bit of edge on the *sir*.

Norman waved him in, peering closely at him, then said, "Got it, you're the private dick."

"How soon we forget." Perry sighed, asked, "If you could maybe put a shirt on?"

"Whoa, Shamus, take a chill pill, life's a beach, man." Loki laughed.

The guy was even more stoned than last time. Perry wanted to slug him, hard and often, bring him back to reality. He knew he was taking something out on Loki that he wanted to take out on Randy Hyde or Cyrus Tweed or maybe even himself. But still.

Norman ambled off to grab a shirt, said, "Grab a pew, pilgrim."

He'd affected some sort of stoner accent that slipped among, maybe, six different tones.

Perry sank into a leather sofa, and as it creaked and groaned, got up, moved to a hard wicker job. He could hear muted voices from the back and an angry buzz building. He took out his notebook, the police-issue one, a futile link to his glory days, if glory meant a job you relished.

Then Norman was back, a T-shirt with a faded logo of Jerry Garcia and the words BE GRATEFUL, DEAD.

He moved to a bar in the corner, asked, "What's your poison?"

Jesus. Perry said, "Some water would be good."

Norman turned, a highball glass in his hand, pushed. "No Long Island Tea? Rock your mundane world—you ain't lived until you've got on the other side of ol' Norm's LIT . . . get it, LIT?"

Not just stoned, bombed. On booze.

Julia Drusilla's words played again: *He drinks. Or did. And when he does . . . you've never seen such a personality change.*

"Put the glass down," Perry said.

Norman gave him an inebriated stare.

Time to rein him in. Perry said, "We found Angel's car."

Norman didn't seem to hear him, fixed a lethal amount of some colored mess, drank deep, shuddered, said, "*We?* Or Five–O did, and you're, like, grabbing the headline?"

Perry said, "The normal response would be to ask if she was in it."

"What?" Norman gulped more booze, barked off a short laugh, said, "And where the be-jaysus would be the mystery in that?" This said in a very bad Irish lilt. He drained the glass. Then said, "You accusing me of something?" but didn't wait for an answer, already adding more alcohol to his drink.

Perry really needed to get this schmuck's attention and snapped, "Do I have to say it again? In a few days, Angel will come into a sizable inheritance; it's vital she's around to sign the document. You forget that, or you too stoned to remember?"

He let that simmer, hoping he'd shot a nice barb into Mr. Unruffleable, see him wiggle out of that.

Norman sucked on an ice cube noisily. "You think you've scored some sort of *points* with that revelation. Hey, news flash, I *wrote* the fucking document, drew up the whole gig."

"I see," Perry said. It looked like the booze was working in his favor. Last time Loki had denied any knowledge of the trust. "So, uh, you wrote Angel's trust."

"Just said, didn't I?"

"So you did." Loki really was out of control. *Right now, a good thing,* thought Perry.

Loki took another gulp of his drink. He shook his head. "Julia, my ex, she must have loved you, just flat out fucking loved you. She flashes her boobs, which I paid for during my stint as her loving husband, no matter what *she* says, and you swallow anything she dishes out as gospel. No wonder you had to quit the force."

Perry was cool. Let the drunken fool ramble on. Maybe he'd say something else he shouldn't. "Your wife—your ex-wife—flashed nothing. She's worried about her daughter."

Something flared in Loki's eyes, sadness or disbelief or weariness, but it didn't last long. Then a sound from the back diverted him, and he quickly added, "But hey, don't feel bad. I figure you talked to that local politico my little girl is hanging with these days?"

"So you know about that?"

"A little birdie told me."

"A little bird named Lilith?"

"Lilith?" Norman laughed. "She hates me. Tried to turn my daughter against me."

Wouldn't take much, thought Perry.

"She pretends to be Angel's friend . . ."

"And she's not?"

Norman swigged the last of his drink.

Perry injected steel in his voice, said, as Norman began to build another lethal drink, "I need you to pay attention, sir."

Norm whirled round, fire in his drink-fueled eyes, spat, "Pay attention to *what?*"

Perry's hands balled into fists.

Another sound came from the back bedroom, like . . . a giggle?

Perry asked, "Am I interrupting something?" Then a thought

occurred. "Is Angel here?" On his feet as he asked, his whole body poised for confrontation.

"What? No way." Norman handed Perry a cut-glass tumbler, the water close to the brim, said, "Galway crystal, from the home country, make you feel right at home, Paddy."

Perry put the glass down, had to count to ten. Was this jerk trying to avert him from all sorts of stuff? Was this drunk act maybe just that, an act? He said, "I really need you to focus."

Norman did an exaggerated eye tightening, said, "Finding Angel's car is no big deal. I know my daughter. Six years that girl lived with me—if I'd a hot nickel for every time she left that car, I'd be building an extension to this beach paradise. She's fine."

"How can you be so sure?" Did he know where she was?

Norman shook his head, and for another brief moment there was something on his face other than a boozy grin. Sadness? Anxiety? Perry wasn't sure.

Perry said, "I took meetings with her former boyfriends, the mechanic and—"

Norman shook his head, all traces of sadness gone, butted in. "The grease monkey, now you want a suspect. *Jesus,* hello, did you see *the state of his nails?* I mean, *come on*! So okay, we can't all afford manicures but a little pride, is that too much to ask, I mean, *is* it?" And he looked, pointedly, at Perry's nails, which were chewed, and emitted a "hmph": the words *I rest my case* hovering over their heads.

Perry's fury was close to exploding. "If you have reason to believe any of those persons of interest might—"

He was cut off again by a roar of contemptuous laughter. Norman said, "Persons of *interest?* I mean, did you actually speak to them, *interest?* They've got to be two of the dreariest muthah's on the planet; man, if you think they are *of interest,* I'd hate to meet who the fuck you think is boring." And paused, reeling a bit. Then said, "Don't take it too personal, some of us are born to serve." He fixed his eyes on Perry, and for a moment, the cool lawyer of old was present. He said, "You come barging in here as if you know something. Boy-friends? What do you think they're going to tell you?"

Before Perry could answer, Norman continued. "Angel's mother, my ex, she started a big brouhaha, dragging you in. Damn that Julia, had to go and—"

Perry tried to see what the guy was hiding. "The other day you—"

"Look, if I know my Angel, she's out having herself a time, and that's all. Being her daddy, ain't no day at the Mardi Gras—you get some kin of your own someday, you'll be feeling me," he drunkenly sneered. The condescension hovering like napalm, the whole gig of parent vs. the poor childless bollix at play.

Perry snarled back, "I have a daughter, she's fifteen years old, so, you know, I can *feel* you."

"Yeah? Is she missing?"

Loaded. Norman had surely been looking into his past.

Perry, a straight shooter, even when it was to his detriment, said, "She's with her mom."

Norman sneered, "*Her mom,* what? You couldn't keep it in your pants, that it?"

Perry had a second of darkness, then he had Norman by the T-shirt, hissed, "You listen to me, I'm trying to find your daughter, try-ing to empathize here, and you . . ." He had to gasp for air. "I don't know if you're so stoned and drunk you can't think straight but you had better start—"

"What?" Loki trying to stare him down with bloodshot eyes.

"You put on this, this act, mincing around like your daughter's absence is some cosmic joke." Perry managed to pull it back a notch, let go of Norman, then reached for his water, gulped it down, tried to speak calmly. "How many times must I say it: I need you to pay attention. Call your ex-wife. I want her to hear the *condition* you're in."

Norman finished his drink then was rolling a spliff, licked the rim of the paper, fired it up, drew deep, coughed, said, "No shit, but that's great fucking shit." And then he looked right at Perry, though his eyes were unfocused.

Perry pushed, "Make the call to your ex-wife."

The bedroom door opened and a young Hispanic man, looking all of maybe sixteen, dressed in a small fluffy towel round his middle, sauntered into the room, put one hand in Norman's receding hair, lisped, "I'm Pedro, the pool person." He then took the spliff out of Norman's hand, took a long pull, coughed, muttered, "Oh, this sucks." Made the accompanying sound.

Norman shrugged, said, "Tell you, cleaning those water filters is a pain in the butt."

"Jesus." Perry sighed. No use. This fool was gone.

Outside, it was dark, just the lights from Norman's beach house vanishing into the bluffs. Perry took a deep breath, then another. He needed something to clear his head after that. He got on his cell, made the call he'd wanted Loki to make, to Julia Drusilla, said he had to see her but it would be late. She told him to come, that she never slept so it didn't matter. Then he called the East Hampton PD, tried again to reach Gawain. Impossible. Some local incident, a 7-Eleven stick-up gone bad. But Gawain had left him a message, which the deputy read: "Officer Gawain says to tell you that nothing incriminating has turned up in the prelims, the car is clean. No blood. No nothing. Appears to be simply abandoned."

"Anything else?" Perry asked.

"Nope. That's it. You have something you want me to report back?"

Yeah, thought Perry. *Tell him I'm sick to death of the Hamptons.* But he said, "No."

12

LISA UNGER

Perry could not get Norman Loki out of his head. He puzzled over the guy's insane behavior during the whole ride back to Manhattan. The guy was stoned and drunk beyond reason. His daughter was missing. He'd been living a lie, hiding his sexual orientation. Who knew about his homosexuality? Did Angel? Did Julia? Was the guy medicating his personal misery, or was he simply out of his mind? He could not shake the questions, even as he parked, then made his way to his client's apartment for some answers.

Perry checked his watch. It was almost ten thirty. He'd made good time, but all that driving had him feeling like an old man—back aching, legs stiff. He could still feel that Hamptons chill that had settled somewhere deep inside him. Not that it was any warmer in Manhattan, but the frigid city air was less damp, less invasive somehow. It hurt in a whole different way.

He pulled Nicky's scarf tighter and dug his hands into his pockets, bracing himself against the painful cold that chewed at his face and snaked down his collar. Just one more block; he was counting the seconds until he felt the warmth of the lobby. He tried to keep his mind on the errand at hand.

Angel's car turning up—it may or may not mean anything. On

the other hand, the finding of an abandoned vehicle in a missing-persons case was never a good thing. He could have, maybe should have, given Julia Drusilla the news over the phone. But he wanted to see her reaction—watch her face, her hands. People said so much without ever saying a word.

And then, yes, the rush of warmth as he brushed past the doorman who was opening the door.

What was it about the rich? thought Perry as he stepped from the chill concrete night into the overwarm, marble opulence of Julia Drusilla's Park Avenue apartment building. There was a scent and a texture to wealth, an unmistakable aura. It colored the walls, brought out the pink veins in the marble floor. Was it the same calla lily arrangement, which sat high and proud on the round lobby table, or a new one? It was taller than his daughter and probably cost more than Perry made in a week. His mother always used to say, *Money will buy what money will buy.* And that never made any sense to him then. But lately, he got it. Some people were just barely making it, while others were drifting on a cushion of money high above the rest. And you knew 'em when you saw 'em. They spent money on flowers, while you clipped coupons and bought the day-old bread.

There was a woman wrapped in a black shearling coat in the lobby. Her golden hair flowed long and shimmering; her jeans tried hard to look tattered. She had a black standard poodle on a long leather leash, and she and the dog shared a kind of lean, aloof look. They were waiting for something, something important. The woman stared at her smartphone, tapping with a single, perfectly square pink fingernail. *Tap, tap, tap.*

"May I help you, sir?" The voice bounced off the walls and the hard floor. The young woman didn't even look up.

Had the doorman leaned on the word *sir* with just a touch of irony? Perry didn't like to think so. But the guy had the same look as the poodle, owned by wealth. Pampered, in a sense, manicured by association, well kept. Perry strode over to the desk and locked the other man in his hardest, nowhere-to-hide cop stare, and was gratified to see the other man squirm. A poodle, while smart enough, was no match for a pit bull. And there was much less blood shed if everyone knew this going in.

The woman and her dog left in a cloud of Chanel No. 5—which Perry recognized because it was the scent Noreen used to wear. Even though he could ill-afford it, he always made sure Santa left a bottle of the cheaper eau de toilette in her Christmas stocking, and she made sure to use it only sparingly. And that's how normal people afforded little luxuries. Thinking of it, how he'd never been able to give her what she wanted, not really, made something inside him go hollow and angry. After so many years, one would think he could move on. But that was the thing about a pit bull; when he sunk his teeth in, you might have to break his jaw before he could let go.

Suddenly, he felt self-conscious about the fray on the collar of his trench, his old dress shoes, the jagged conditions of his cuticles. But he wouldn't show it. No, never. A real man didn't feel bad about his appearance.

"She's something," Perry said. He'd watched the doorman's dark brown eyes drift after the young woman and her poodle. "Man. For real."

The young Latino gave Perry a polite half smile. "May I *help* you?" he said again.

"I saw her checking you out," said Perry. "You didn't notice?"

The doorman issued a little snort, but Perry saw the color come up in his cheeks. "Not likely."

"I don't know," said Perry. He let the sentence trail, singsong and light. It was the same doorman from his first visit, though the guy didn't seem to recognize or remember him. Perry noticed he had manicured nails, not polished but shaped and buffed. His skin was so dewy and fresh that he might have just come from a facial.

"Anyway," Perry went on. "I'm here for Mrs. Drusilla. She in? Name's Christo. I've been here before."

The doorman looked him over again, then picked up the phone and dialed.

"*Detective* Perry Christo." He saw the kid's eyes brighten a bit. Everyone thought he was living in a *Law & Order* episode when you said you were a detective. It was definitely a pop-culture advantage. People just loved to talk—about themselves, about everybody else.

"There's a Detective Christo here for you, Mrs. Drusilla." A pause followed by an obedient nod. "Of course."

Of course. It was in the lilt of his words that Perry picked up on something he'd missed. The doorman probably hadn't been checking out the girl. He might have been admiring her shoes or her hair—but not her ass.

"You may go up, sir," he said. "Twenty-fourth floor. That's the penthouse. Penthouse A."

"Thanks," said Perry. "I know." He started to move toward the elevator.

"Be careful," said the doorman. He lowered his voice to a sly whisper. "She *bites*. But maybe you know that, too."

Oh, an invitation to dish. *Sometimes,* Perry thought, *you just get lucky.*

"Is that so?" He moved back slowly. Somewhere outside a siren wailed.

"Um-*hmm*," the doorman said. Perry leaned in close. He knew that he might not have polish—he needed a shave, could stand to pull a brush through his hair—but Perry knew what he had, and he wasn't shy about using it.

"She been in tonight?" he asked.

"Oh, she's been in all right," the doorman said. The tag on his uniform read LUCAS. He tapped on it. "You can call me Luke."

"So, she's been in all night, Luke?"

Luke raised his eyebrows and nodded slowly. Perry saw that there was something dark to him, dark appetites, dark sense of humor, something moving beneath the smooth, practiced surface. Perry suddenly liked him better.

"Alone?"

The doorman made a show of organizing his desk—pen in its little mesh cup, papers in a tidy pile. He lifted a logbook and opened it.

"You must see it all here, huh?" asked Perry. "The rich are different, right?"

"Oh, no," Luke said. "They're not different at all. They're as dirty and mean as any thug in the projects. They're just prettier."

There were about three different notes of bitterness in the young man's tone, and Perry planned to play them all if he had to.

"So who was here tonight?" he asked.

He saw a battle play out on the guy's face between what he wanted to say and what he knew he should say. Finally, as though remembering what had gotten him talking in the first place, he leaned in closer to Perry.

Perry could smell the other man's cologne. To be honest, their proximity made him a little uncomfortable. But he stayed where he was.

"There was a man earlier," he said. Luke leaned back, brought a hand to his throat, and rubbed. It was a self-protective gesture; something about the encounter had left Luke feeling threatened. "I've never seen him before. Cute. In a vapid, shallow sort of way."

Perry looked down at the leather logbook in Luke's hand. "Is his name in here?"

Luke shook his head. "He didn't give his name," he said. "He wouldn't."

"And you didn't insist?"

Luke gave him a tired look. "Doormen don't insist, Detective. We do as we're told."

"But Mrs. Drusilla probably wouldn't want you talking about her visitor, right?"

Luke shrugged and put his hand to his throat again.

Something about Mrs. Drusilla made Luke nervous. Perry couldn't say that he blamed the kid; she was about as warm and cuddly as a python.

"Good night, Detective," said Luke.

Perry slid a card over the marble countertop. "Anything interesting, give me a call."

Luke pocketed the card, but he didn't say anything else, just cast his eyes down to those manicured nails. Perry had been dismissed. By the doorman. At least he knew where he stood on the totem pole.

The elevator carried the scent of the calla lily arrangement up to the penthouse. The elevator chimed at each passing floor: eleven, twelve, thirteen . . . Perry thought that there weren't any thirteenth floors in New York City, something about bad luck for the building. The people in this building might have thought they were above all of that. And maybe they were. Maybe rich people didn't have any bad luck that they couldn't buy their way out of.

At the end of the long, carpeted hall, the door to Penthouse A stood ajar. Perry pushed on the gold knob and took in the place for the second time, the towering ceilings, the panoramic view of Manhattan, the black marble floors, the low, white leather couches—it was his ex-wife's dream apartment. If she died and could create her own little piece of heaven, this would be it. *You shouldn't have married a cop,* he'd teased, *with dreams like that. You're setting yourself up for disappointment.*

Now *you tell me,* she'd joked. Or had she been joking?

Maybe it was him, but the place seemed colder as he moved from the foyer into the main room. And it wasn't just the fact that his client kept the air-conditioning going in the dead of winter. There was no place soft or cozy to sit, nothing out of place. It would be hard to be a kid in a place like this. Every spill a disaster. Every trip or fall into some hard edge. He found himself wondering what it was like to be Angel. She hadn't grown up with her mother, not after the divorce. Of course the beach home in Montauk was no less opulent. And clearly, Daddy Dearest was a lunatic in his own right. Maybe Angel never had a soft place to land.

He heard his own daughter's voice. *You're hardly ever here, Daddy. Sometimes I don't even know who you are.* The sting of those words had never faded, mainly because they were all too true, even if he knew she loved him.

"Detective."

Julia Drusilla didn't walk; she glided. It was as if there wasn't enough weight to her so that she actually had to touch the earth. She had that delicate, brittle look. He'd taken a minute to surf the Internet on his phone, found pictures of her as a younger woman, at this gala or that one, on the social scene from the time she was a girl; and of course, she'd always possessed that patrician thinness that was inherited and not simply "achieved." But age and illness had robbed her of any of the lushness youth had once bestowed. Once again, Perry took in her collarbone, which seemed to strain against her skin, and the knobs on her wrists that were as round and hard as marbles.

"What news?" She looked at him eagerly, wringing her bejeweled hands. She drifted over to the window, her dove-gray silk robe trailing behind her like a cloud.

He had waited this long to tell her in person in order to judge her reaction, so he wasn't going to soften his delivery. "We've found Angel's car. But no Angel. You told me not to lie. This isn't good news."

She bowed her head into her hands and released a strangled

sound. He almost moved to comfort her. But she had too many hard edges. He found himself remembering what Luke had said. *She bites.*

"Mrs. Drusilla," he said carefully, "I think it's time to call in the cops. This is a real missing-persons case, and now we have evidence of foul play."

She looked up at him. Though her face was a mask of sadness and fear, he couldn't help noticing that her eyes were dry.

"No," she said vehemently. "No."

"Mrs. Drusilla—" he began. But she raised her hand.

"I'm begging you," she said. She moved over toward him, took his hand in hers. "No police."

"The police have resources that will be helpful in finding Angel," he said. "It's the right thing to do."

"It will be a media circus," she said. Here she issued a little cough and seemed to swoon. He led her by one spindly elbow to a low couch, where she sank, leaning back. But was it an act? He wasn't sure. The white silk pajamas beneath her robe—it all seemed to coordinate perfectly with the room around her. The ivory walls, the plush slate-colored area rug, the glossy gray and white tables. Above the fireplace, that gigantic Jackson Pollock painting dominated—a rage of black and white and gray splatters, with some angry slashes of red.

The coughing started lightly and seemed to pick up pitch and intensity. She pointed off behind the fireplace, and he assumed she was indicating where he could find water. He found his way to the granite and stainless steel kitchen, which was enormous and so spotlessly clean that it looked never to have been used to prepare food. He rummaged through the cabinets for a glass, ran some water from the faucet, then rushed back.

She took some tentative sips, and Perry looked on helplessly. He felt guilty now for doubting her. Finally, the hacking subsided. Then she found her voice again.

"I'm dying, Detective. You know that."

"I'm sorry."

She took a shuddering breath. "Spare me your pity," she said. He thought he detected a flash of nastiness, but it passed quickly. When she spoke again, her voice was soft and pleading. "I need you to find Angel before I die. I want her to know what belongs to her. But more than that, I want her to know that even though I wasn't the mother I should have been, I loved her. I need her to know that."

It was a variation on the same speech she'd given before.

He wanted to say something to convince her that the police could help her better than he could, but she went on.

"I can't afford red tape, bureaucratic delays, institutionalized incompetence. I don't have that kind of time. I need you to find her, Perry."

Her face was slack, and she stared out through the glass doors that led to the wide terrace spanning the length of the apartment. Outside millions of lights glittered like jewels on a blanket of velvet.

Every light is a life, a story, his wife used to say. *The Manhattan skyline is a little bit of everything isn't it? Life, death, joy, misery, love, hate, murder, rescue— it's all playing out right there*

"Do you know what it is to fail your child?" She asked the question as if she already knew the answer. Maybe one failure could recognize another. It was a mark they wore, visible only to other bad parents.

He didn't answer her. He didn't sense that she was interested in whatever tale he had to tell.

"I need to make this one wrong right before I die." She was staring at him, searching his face, and he felt a creeping discomfort. She wanted something from him that he wasn't sure he could give. But he *wanted* to give it to her. He *needed* to find Angel, to be the one to bring her home to her mother. He wanted that for a million reasons, none of them pure or right or having anything to do with Angel.

"What will it take?" She reached for him again, got his hand in her cold, hard grip. "There's nothing that's wrong in your life that I can't fix, provided it can be fixed with money."

What would money solve in his life? He'd already lost everything: his job, his wife, his only child. Sure, he lived in a tiny apartment. But even if he lived in a palace, he'd live there alone, without the only people who meant anything to him. He couldn't buy his way out of failure like Mrs. Drusilla seemed to think she could. The rich *were* different.

"I don't want your money," he said.

"Then what?" she said. She looked flustered, confused, but suddenly rejuvenated. She had the creamy skin of a much younger woman, a pretty blush to her cheeks. And her eyes glittered. Right now he wouldn't have known she was ill if she hadn't told him so. Even in her terrible thinness, there was something intense and vital about her. "What do you want?"

He wanted not to be the man he was, a disgraced cop, an ex-husband, a part-time father. Maybe finding Angel wouldn't change all of that. But maybe it was a start. His dad used to say, *Every morning, you gotta face the guy in the mirror. Make sure you like him.* He couldn't remember the last time he truly liked himself. What did that even feel like?

He pulled his hand from hers and walked over to the fireplace, his eyes scanning the room. Nothing had changed. There was not a photograph or a personal item in sight, not a book, an open magazine. Everything in here was for show, even the lovely, wasted woman on the couch.

"Your ex-husband—"

"Yes," she said flatly, as if the conversation about Loki already bored her.

"I just saw him, and he was—"

"Drunk?"

"More than drunk. He was completely out of control, belligerent, barely making sense, and—"

"Were you expecting me to be surprised? When Norman drinks, he becomes a totally different person. I told you that. Alcohol is poison to him. It's one of the reasons we—" She sighed. "You have to excuse him, Detective. If he was drunk, I'm certain he had no idea what he was doing or saying. He is upset by Angel's disappearance: that's why he's drinking. It's no excuse, but . . ."

"And do you know that your ex-husband is . . ." Perry stopped. Did it really matter?

"That he's gay?" She offered a mirthless smile. "Of course. Norman and I led quite separate lives."

"And Angel?"

"I have no idea what Angel knows or doesn't know about her father."

Once again Perry found himself wondering what it was like to be Angel with these two people as parents.

"Where would Angel go?" he asked, half thinking aloud. "If she was afraid, in trouble, if she just needed a break, where was her haven?"

Julia shook her head, then sank it again into her hand. "I have no idea. Isn't that awful? A mother who knows nothing about her daughter."

She released that strangled sobbing sound. But when she looked up at him, her eyes were still dry as dust.

"A childhood friend, a boyfriend, a godparent?" he asked. He found himself watching her, for what he didn't know. "Anyplace she felt safe, not judged."

"I hardly speak to my daughter," said Julia. "She judges me, thinks everything is my fault. That's the way it is with young people—everything's black and white, no shades of gray."

He found himself agreeing, a way to keep her talking. "They're so sure of themselves, aren't they?" he asked. "So harsh in their judgments."

"Age brings wisdom, at least," said Julia. "At least we're smart enough to know that we don't know anything—especially about each other."

"You had a visitor tonight," he said. Just thought he'd toss it out there, see what kind of a reaction he'd get.

She was too cool to startle, but he saw a micro-expression dance across her face. Anger, fear—he couldn't tell. It wasn't pretty, but it was gone as quickly as it had come.

"My massage therapist," she said. She looked away from him, started twisting a ring on her hand. The chunky emerald was as big as a Volkswagen. "He works wonders. I'm carrying so much tension. I'm sure you can imagine."

She coughed a bit, reached for her water, took a long sip.

Is she using the illness as a prop? he wondered. "He's been here before?"

"Many times," she said. Again a little flash of something across her face. "But never so late. It was an emergency; I'm in so much pain."

A massage emergency—that was a new one. He thought about pressing her. Wouldn't the doorman have known her masseur? But she'd covered that by saying he'd never come so late. Still, why would the masseur refuse to give his name? Something off about that, but her fragility kept him from pushing her too hard. After all, she'd hired him to find Angel. If she was having a handsome young man up to meet whatever emergency needs she had, what business was it of his?

"So you'll keep working?" she asked. "No police?"

It wasn't right. It was a matter for the cops. But he found himself nodding, reaching out a comforting hand, which she took and squeezed.

You never could resist a damsel in distress, his wife used to tease.

But it was more than that, wasn't it? He wanted to be the one to find Angel. It was his case. He'd started it, and he wanted to finish it. And there was a tangle of other feelings knotting up in his gut, too, many, too complicated, too messy to contemplate.

Outside, he pulled his too-thin coat tight around him and wound Nicky's scarf even tighter. The cold air snaked up his cuffs and down his collar, chilling him to the core. Fatigue, which he'd been holding at bay with caffeine and junk food, was now a weight on his back, pulling down his shoulders, making every step feel as if he was slogging through mud. Trekking down the street, he pulled out his phone and dialed his daughter's cell. He didn't want to talk to his ex-wife, endure her snipes, all delivered in the happy lilt of her voice. She *was* happy—rich new boyfriend (whom Perry's daughter *just loved* by the way), living in the boyfriend's nice big apartment in Brooklyn Heights, working in a preschool (she'd always wanted more kids; now she had 'em). He wanted to be happy for her. But he wasn't, because he was a prick—as she was fond of reminding him.

"Hey, Dad," Nicky answered. "Where are you?"

"Heading home," he said. "Sorry to call so late. What are you doing?"

"Ugh," she said, "calculus." He heard the television going in the background, some sitcom with laugh tracks. It sounded tinny and strange on the line, almost mocking.

"With the television on?"

"Its helps me concentrate," she said. "A little noise helps you focus, you know. It's proven."

The kid was a brainiac, a 4.0 average, star of her track team, frighteningly gorgeous—as pretty as her mom and then some. Every time he saw her, he just wanted to wrap her up in blankets and hide her away somewhere. Did they still send girls to the nunnery? Was that an option?

"You sound tired," she said.

Kid, you have no idea. I'm tired to the bone. I could sleep for a thousand years. "No," he said, forcing himself to sound bright. "I'm good. I'm great."

"Are we getting together tomorrow?"

Shit. Was that tomorrow?

"I've got a case," he said. The words stuck in his mouth, tasted bitter, like a piece of gum he'd chewed way too long.

"No problem," she said, light, resigned, as if she was used to being disappointed by him. She expected very little. *Do you know what it is to fail your child?* Julia had asked him. Of course he knew. Of course, he did. He hadn't abandoned her, no. He wasn't a deadbeat. He'd always paid his alimony and child support on time. He was saving for her education. He'd never missed a birthday. But he'd failed her in a million little ways. It added up. She'd learned she couldn't count on him, and now she didn't. Not at all.

"You didn't let me finish," he said. "I just need to do it a little earlier."

"It's okay."

"No, really. Tomorrow is Saturday, so how about brunch? I have an eight o'clock appointment and—"

"Oh my God. Not at eight."

"No. After. It will be closer to nine thirty or ten. You can handle that, right?"

They chatted a while longer about how her best friend was going out with a jerk, how Mom and Cornelius wanted to take her to the Bahamas for spring break, how calculus was so hard—who ever needed calculus in the real world, anyway? And then they hung up. And even though the talk had been good, that hollow place he'd felt open in the lobby of Julia's building grew wider and wider until he thought he might disappear in there, never to be heard from again.

Finally at home, he tossed and turned before falling into an uneasy sleep. He dreamed that he stood on the balcony of Julia's apartment, looking down those long twenty-four floors to the river of traffic below.

"We all go there sooner or later, Detective," Julia said.

She was beside him, her gnarled hand on his shoulder. When he turned to look at her, the silk pajamas were gone, replaced with a black cloak and hood. In her hand, she held a sickle. She pulled back her hood to reveal the gray, twisted face of an old crone.

He backed away from her, a scream of horror caught in his throat. In the enormous living room was Angel's car, dark and abandoned. He looked inside and saw only empty leather seats and a Gucci bag opened on the floor.

He heard a strange knocking and realized quickly that it was coming from the trunk. But he didn't have the key. The knocking grew ever more panicked and insistent, and his fear ratcheted to a crescendo. He started banging on the trunk.

"Angel," he yelled. *"I'm coming, baby."*

But then Angel was standing there, golden and willowy, smiling. She issued a little chuckle, as if the whole thing was terribly funny. He reached for her, but she shimmered like a mirage.

"Don't worry," she said.

She clicked the small black remote in her hand, and the trunk opened with a *pop*. He raced to it, and inside he found his own daughter curled tight into a fetal position. She was purple pale and so, so still. He called her name over and over and took her into his arms, rocking her the way he'd done when she was a child.

"I'm sorry," he said. "I'm so sorry." But they both knew it was far too late.

Perry continue to rock her, but then she was gone and everything was black and it was raining hard and he was trying to get across the street, to get somewhere, anywhere.

13

S. J. ROZAN

In the morning Perry was still trying to shake off the dream.

Half an hour later he circled to the sidewalk, down the four flights of creaking, slanted stairs. He'd showered, he'd dressed, but his caffeine was still to come. Last week, his Mr. Coffee had busted spectacularly, frying the ancient fuse, plunging half the tiny apartment into darkness. He'd fixed the fuse, but before he'd gotten around to a new machine, he'd realized he'd rather drink his coffee at the counter at the diner than at his cheerless kitchen table—though the diner's coffee always tasted burned. He turned up his collar against the dispirited drizzle and walked the half block to the diner. He didn't take his customary counter stool today, though. He ordered his coffee to go. It was some kind of commentary on his life, one he was careful not to shine too bright a light on, that even sipping burned take-out coffee from a cardboard cup on the street on a gray and spitting morning like this was preferable to starting the day at home.

Home? He lived in that shabby fifth-floor walk-up, had for years now, but home?

Get out and move, that's what it was all about.

Well, not quite all. Sometimes it was about sitting still, but that

was only with Nicky. As it would be later today, when they en-
sconced themselves at that overpriced café in Brooklyn Heights that
she liked so much and she told him, between bites of burger and
spoonfuls of hot fudge sundae, what her past couple of weeks had
been like.

He couldn't wait.

Meanwhile, though, he had work.

That's what it was: it was work. Angel's face—a face he'd never
seen except in a photo—drifted into his mind and lodged there. He
told himself, as he walked, slurping coffee, skirting puddles, that this
was normal; this was the way he always worked. He told himself that
it had been this way even in his cop days, that he'd fixate on a suspect,
on a victim, who'd haunt him and who he'd find he couldn't shake.
He crumpled his coffee cup and tossed it into a trash can on top of
other sodden garbage.

He didn't believe a word he was saying.

He threaded his way along the sidewalk, occasionally passing one
of his well-heeled neighbors, more often a member of the army that
served them: nannies, maids, dog walkers, delivery guys. The well-
heeled neighbors took cabs on days like this.

Turning right at the corner of Sixty-seventh and Lex, Perry pulled
up his collar again and tied Nicky's scarf around his neck, took a
breath, and trotted up the sidewalk. He was early for his eight a.m.
appointment, but he knew Henry would be early, too—not waiting for Perry, just getting a start on his work. Slick with February
rain, the 19th Precinct again loomed before him. He stopped, not
quite ready to go in, and surveyed the majestic old building for the
umpteenth time—a delaying tactic, his looking at the decorative
brickwork, elaborate cornice, old-fashioned wood windows. At
least, majestic and old was what it looked like. Behind the landmark

facade, which had been supported like a stage set during the building's reconstruction which he'd lived through—the 19th was totally
new: concrete, vinyl, fluorescent lights. Perry wondered if there was
such a thing as a reverse metaphor, because the NYPD itself worked
the other way. Every few years, new policies and new procedures
made it look like the department was starting fresh. Inside, not a
damn thing ever changed.

Enough delays.

The sergeant at the desk was too young to be from Perry's day.
Perry braced himself anyway, but the sergeant didn't react when
Perry stated his name and his business, just handed him a card.

"You'll need this. Watson left it for you."

"Right," said Perry.

The sergeant nodded to the stairs, and said, "Squad room, second
floor." Perry knew that—both that the detectives occupied the second
floor, and that Henry would be up there, waiting for him. He took
another breath—he'd learned that in a yoga class Nicky had dragged
him to: to breathe deeply whenever his heart started pounding—and
headed up. The concrete stairs in the concrete block staircase hadn't actually gotten steeper or longer over the past five years, he was sure of it.

It only seemed that way.

He swiped the card to get onto the second floor then pushed his
way though the heavy steel door into the squad room. Three of the
guys sitting around inside were nodding acquaintances of Perry's,
though he couldn't have dredged up their names. Not that any of
them nodded. They just followed him with their eyes as he crossed
the room to Henry's desk. Perry wished he remembered who at least
one of them was, then he could give him a hearty, "Hi, Joe!" and
watch him crap his pants. Just the idea that people might know you
knew Perry Christo was enough to give a cop nightmares.

Unless the cop was Henry Watson. "Hey, Perry," Henry grunted, tipping his chair forward and standing, sticking out his hand.

As they shook, Perry felt eyes slip from him as the other detectives scuttled back to their work. Except for Mr. Donald Duck tie, who walked in and gave Perry a sneer then sagged behind his desk and started typing. Perry returned the sneer.

"Damn," Henry said. He looked Perry up and down and scowled. If Henry hadn't been born scowling, then he'd been the only kid in history whose features actually did freeze when his mother warned him not to make that face. "You look like crap, buddy. You get any sleep since I saw you?"

"Not much. Been driving back and forth to the Hamptons. Exhausting."

Watson nodded and looked down.

"Shit, and you're still wearing the old dress uniform shoes. What the hell did you do to them?"

Perry shrugged. "Been wearing them around. And it's been raining, you notice? But why the hell not? Don't have much other use for them."

Henry gave him a laser look, then dropped himself into his desk chair. It groaned under the load.

"How many of those things do you go through in the average year?" Perry asked, sitting opposite.

"Ignore it, it's just looking for attention. So, really, how're you doing?"

"I'm vertical. You manage to get me anything?"

Another brief stare from Henry; then he grunted and opened a file folder. Perry had asked the favor only yesterday, but the folder was already creased, bore two coffee rings, and was smudged from the only writing instrument Henry ever used: a blunt pencil.

"I got your girl," Henry answered. Perry's heart leaped ridiculously, but before he could say anything, Henry went on, "At least, I got her Visa card. She bought an LIRR ticket into Penn Station and paid for a taxi in la-di-da East Hampton to get to the train."

"Or someone did."

"Yeah, okay, someone did."

"When?"

"Yesterday."

Perry considered. "Could be good. What about the phone? I know you don't have a warrant, so whatever you were—"

"Who the hell needs a warrant?"

Perry blinked. "For the phone?"

"You PIs, whaddaya know? I guess it's because you just break the law all the time. It's a cell phone." To Perry's blank look, he said, "Things've changed since your day, buddy."

"No shit."

"Mostly for the worse, but sometimes for the better. They clarified all kinds of crap about cell phones. I need a warrant to listen in on a conversation, but not to dump the phone. Or, assuming it has a GPS, to find it."

"I know all that, but—"

"Like I said: I got your girl. Or"—forestalling Perry's question—"besides her Visa card, I also got her phone. Last phone call she made was to Brooklyn."

"Or someone made."

"Yeah, someone made. You okay?"

Perry nodded. He couldn't explain, to Henry or to himself, the chill that had just passed through him. Maybe it was the words *last phone call*. Just because Perry had traced a call to Angel's phone, it didn't mean Angel had made it.

It didn't mean Angel was alive. Nothing they had found so far could be said to mean Angel was alive.

Perry shook his head, shook off the chill. "Who's the call to?" he asked.

"One Athena Williams."

"Who is she?"

"Some damn model citizen with no record. Law on that hasn't changed. I can't dig any deeper into her without—guess what?—a warrant. Jesus, Perry, don't look so depressed. Good old Henry's got your back. I got two more things for you."

"Well . . . ? Or do I have to wait until after the commercial?"

"One: this Athena Williams lives at 354 Washington Avenue, in Brooklyn. For that I didn't need a warrant, just a phone book."

"How do you know you have the right one?"

"For Christ's sake, how many Athena Williamses do you think there are? In Brooklyn? And."

"And?"

"Your girl's phone is there. You're welcome."

On the way to his car Perry debated calling Angel's parents to find out who Athena Williams might be. One of them might know, and it was always better to go into any situation with more information rather than less. He thought of Angel's mother, who'd hired him to find her daughter; or her father, from whose home Angel had run away. He could ask either. Or both.

But Perry didn't call because he didn't trust them. Either of them. Why? Plenty of reasons. But more important, before his troubles he'd been a cop, and a good one. Gut instinct, he'd found, was always based on something: something indefinable, something too buried or too tiny or too new to bring into the rational mind and look at. But that you couldn't explain it didn't make it wrong. In a situation like this he had no problem doing what his instincts told him, and looking at it later.

• • •

Traffic moved well along the FDR but bogged down on the Brooklyn Bridge. There were days when Perry wouldn't have minded that—he felt on top of the world here, Manhattan spread beneath him on one side, Brooklyn on the other, the East River forever dividing and connecting the two—but today the clouds hung low and the rain still spat, and Angel might be ahead of him, right down there on Washington Avenue. He fought an urge to lean uselessly on the horn.

He inched along through the low gray clouds until he finally made it to the Brooklyn side. He had checked the address on his iPhone and it was in Fort Greene, right near the Pratt Institute. He'd just swooped down the endless bridge approach when the black Toyota he thought he'd glimpsed in his rearview mirror—and knew for sure he'd glimpsed a couple of days ago—appeared again, two cars behind him.

No question now: this was a tail. Again. He spun a fast left then a right then another left. No one with two brain cells to rub together would bumble around like that to actually get anywhere, but as Perry turned onto DeKalb Avenue the car was still behind him.

Damn.

The light was changing as Perry slammed on his brakes, jumped out, and charged back toward the black Toyota. Other cars honked, irate people cursed, and the car responded by cutting into the oncoming lane and peeling out before Perry could get to it, or even get a look at the driver. Or the plate. The Toyota raced past him, narrowly missing getting creamed by a milk truck.

Damn.

Perry stood in the rain, staring, then gave the honking, irritated drivers around him an irritated wave and got back into his car. His cell phone buzzed. He pulled around and stopped on Clinton. A text—Henry? With something new? He pulled it out.

dad—what time do u think u'll b here? n.

Nicky. Oh, God, Nicky!

Perry checked his watch. Almost ten. If he headed over right now and traffic was with him, he could still get to the café before she did.

He typed, *Baby, I'm soooo sorry—I'm in Brooklyn on a case, so not far away. Should be done in an hour. Rain check (haha) until a little later? Lunch? And ice cream? I love you—Dad.* He had to retype some words more than once, his thumbs were so clumsy. He hated texting. *Then why didn't you call her,* he asked himself. Instead of answering, he started his car and made his way toward Fort Greene.

Fuck! Fuck! Fuck!

Your hands are shaking on the steering wheel while you sit on the goddamn Brooklyn side street trying to catch your breath, the vision of the PI charging out of his car coming toward you like some goddamn madman replaying in your head, along with the sound of cars hitting brakes and blasting horns, and for a minute how you thought it was over, all your hard work over, all your hopes and dreams over. Fuck.

But no way you could let that happen, so you just pressed the gas pedal against the floor without thinking, without looking, praying the whole time, praying to God as you turned the car into the oncoming traffic, gritting your teeth as that goddamn milk truck came at you, hearing the crash in your mind and bracing for the impact, eyes half closed when the truck swerved at the last second, just clipping your back fender, but you held on, kept the car steady as it bumped back over the divider and you cut across two lanes of traffic, more horns like wild geese quacking, and you just kept going, driving without thinking, speeding, turning down one street then another, around corners and now, finally, finally, you sit and wait for your pulse to slow and your breathing to return to normal, the panic you felt only minutes ago replaced by rage that fuels you as you start the car again and pick up the trail, backtracking through the Brooklyn streets, thinking you cannot lose him, will not lose him, because everything depends upon it and you know you're close—you can feel it in your flesh and bones.

So you drive up and down the streets searching, your heart in your throat and burning hatred in your soul, and together they keep you going until you see it, that junk heap of a car with the license plate you have memorized, making its way down the Brooklyn street, and you thank God because He is obviously on your side.

This time you keep enough distance because you can't risk his spotting you again, because you think this might be it, exactly what you have been waiting for, and you steel yourself because if you are right, if this is the moment, you must be ready to act, must be ready to kill.

14

DANA STABENOW

Traffic had eased, and no one felt the need to curse at Perry or flip him off as he drove. Still, he had the same itch between his shoulders since losing the tail, one eye on the rearview mirror as he made his way into Fort Greene.

Washington Avenue was a wide street of mostly five- and six-story brownstones and a few big old houses with front yards featuring black metal fences and garden gnomes wading hip deep through the swiftly melting remains of last week's snowfall. The address Henry had given him, 354, was one of the old houses, the door painted bright red with a fanlight and brass fittings and a coachman's lights placed precisely at each corner. He knocked with the feeling that there were eyes on him from behind every lace curtain on the street.

The woman who answered the door was dressed in designer jeans and a boat-necked, three-quarter-sleeve sweater in a crimson that nearly matched the door. She had skin the color of eggplant, teeth like JFK, and hair like Michelle Obama's. The only things sixtyish about her were her eyes, guarded and suspicious, carrying a memory that had neither forgotten nor forgiven the fire hoses and the attack dogs.

She had herself planted in the doorway like a glacial erratic, and short of dynamite he didn't see any way outside of honesty to move her from it. "I'm as white as you can get without bleach and I'm on your doorstep uninvited," he said. "I figure, one more strike, I'm outta here, probably on the toe of your boot. How could you turn down that opportunity?"

There was an infinitesimal relaxation in the muscles around her eyes. She didn't ask him in, but at least she hadn't slammed the door in his face, and he took that for assent. "My name is Perry Christo, and I'm a private detective. You Athena Williams?"

"Her mama send you?"

There wasn't any point in acting surprised and even less in denial. "Yes, Mrs. Drusilla says her daughter has been missing for more than two weeks. She's concerned—"

He stopped abruptly when Athena Williams's expression shifted beneath the black, polished skin. There was no bullshitting this woman. "Her daughter stands to inherit a lot of money, but only if she shows up to sign for it, and time is running out."

Athena Williams's eyes narrowed. "How much does Ms. Julia get?" The "Ms." was heavily accented, and not out of respect.

"I'm not at liberty to say."

Athena Williams snorted. "And I'm not saying anything at all."

"But you worked for them?"

"I was Angel's nanny, if that's what you're asking."

"Have you seen Ms. Loki recently?" he said.

"No," she said.

He didn't believe her, but then she wasn't trying to convince him all that hard. "Ms. Williams—"

"Mr. Christo," she said, "I haven't seen Angel, and I wouldn't tell you if I had. Now, is there anything else? My mama raised me not to slam doors in people's faces, but I'm always willing to make at least one exception to every rule."

"You sound like you graduated from Bryn Mawr," he said unwisely.

"Black folks ain't supposed to talk English right?" she asked.

He sighed. "Ma'am," he said, "all I'm trying to do is find Angelina Loki."

"And if she doesn't want to be found?"

He looked at her for a moment. "Yesterday, the East Hampton police found Angelina Loki's car abandoned on a deserted road." He paused. She didn't twitch so much as an eyebrow. "The only good news—if you can call it good news—is that she wasn't in it."

"Plenty of public transportation," she said.

"I didn't know anyone from the Hamptons ever had to learn how to walk," he said.

She almost smiled.

He waited.

After a long moment, she stepped back, holding the door wide. "Come in, then, if you won't go away when you're told to."

The living room was comfortably furnished with a dark blue overstuffed couch and matching chairs. There was a thirty-two-inch flat-screen television mounted on one wall, and the area rug had not been bought at Home Depot. Nannying must pay better than he'd thought.

She went so far as to bring him coffee on a tray with cream and sugar. It was a hell of a lot better than the industrial-strength cleaner Henry Watson had served up that morning, and he drank gratefully and felt the better for it.

He set his cup down and looked across at her. She sat with a straight back, her knees and ankles together and her hands loosely clasped in her lap, but she looked a lot more approachable than she had seemed at the door. "Why are you looking for Angel, Mr. Christo?" she asked.

Her voice was a little louder than it had been on the doorstep. He wondered if someone else was in the house, also waiting to hear his answer. Who it was could determine his answer, which might or might not be a long way from the truth.

There was a collection of photos on the wall, all children, all white. Three of them were snapshots with Athena Williams, swinging, building a sand castle, riding a merry-go-round. The fourth was an eleven-by-fourteen studio portrait in what looked like a solid gold frame. Even at, what, thirteen—fourteen at most—Angelina Loki's sheer physical presence made itself felt. She stood barefoot on a wooden parquet floor, looking directly into the camera, unsmiling. A mass of tousled hair the color of a Saint-Gauden's double eagle, wide blue eyes, a full ripe mouth, skin like cream velvet.

Most people would have stopped at the personification of rich white privilege, but if you looked a little longer, the photographer had caught an air of vulnerability about the eyes, a hint of desperately held control in the line of the mouth, a chin more defiant than determined. Perry looked a little longer, and then he looked at Athena Williams, saw her narrowed eyes, and sat back in his chair. It was a very comfortable chair. "The easy answer is, because I'm paid to," he said.

She waited, her eyes steady on his face.

He shook his head. "Look, Ms. Williams, it doesn't take a genius to see that she's in trouble. Her mother says she only wants to be reunited with her estranged daughter, whom she hasn't seen in a year. Her father, with whom she has been living, hasn't seen her for two weeks and doesn't appear to be too concerned about it. Her best friend says she hasn't seen her and told me to check with Ms. Loki's boyfriend. The boyfriend says he hasn't seen her in a week and to check with a new boyfriend, and either he isn't the jealous type or he never gave a shit in the first place."

He took another appreciative sip of his coffee. "The new boy-friend comes with so much baggage they wouldn't let him on a seven forty-seven, even if he was flying up front. As in he's married with three children and more than the swing vote on the local town council. And he won't admit to having seen her in the last two weeks."

He felt his voice beginning to rise and cut himself off, taking another deliberate pull at his coffee. "All I know is she's missing," he said, "and nobody I talk to knows or will say where she is."

"You're that concerned over a girl you haven't even met?" There might have been pity in her voice, although it might equally have been contempt, or maybe it was a combination of the two.

"You knew she wasn't in her car," he said. "You didn't even blink when I told you the cops found it. So where is she, Ms. Williams?"

Her face closed up again. No sale. The silence stretched out between them.

"She's just a kid," he said.

"She's not just a kid," Athena Williams said. "She's never been just a kid. But she's smart—smartest child I ever took care of—because she had to be."

She looked annoyed, more with herself than with him, probably for volunteering information.

"Seems like somebody ought to be looking out for her," he said mildly, "and nobody is." He thought of Nicky, and again he felt the oppressive guilt of the absentee father press down on his shoulders. But his ex, Noreen, wasn't Julia Drusilla, thank God, and he wasn't Norman Loki.

"I looked after her," Athena Williams said.

The words wrenched themselves out slowly, one phrase at a time. "I looked after her as best I could. As best as they would let me."

He kept his own voice low and without expression. "How did you come to be Angelina Loki's nanny?"

"A woman with my education, did you mean?" But she closed her eyes on a sigh, and for a moment only looked her age, and tired. Her eyes opened again, and the moment was gone. "I got my degree from Brown University. And then my mother got sick." Her smile was twisted. "It turns out that a professional nanny, especially one with a master's degree, earns a lot more than a high school history teacher. Angel was my fourth job."

"How long were you with her family?"

"From the week Angel was born," she said, "until her graduation from high school."

"So you spent time with her after the divorce?"

"Yes. Mama died when Angel was eight, and I could have quit, but by then . . ." She shrugged.

He looked around the well-appointed room. "You're retired now?"

She followed his train of thought with no difficulty. "I have feathered my own nest nicely, haven't I?"

He thought of his employer, the thin, bitter matron in her big, sterile penthouse on Park Avenue. "I have no doubt you earned every penny twice over, Ms. Williams."

She almost looked over her shoulder and stopped herself, but not before he noticed. "Only the best butter, Mr. Christo."

Again, he wondered who else was in the house. "I'm not asking you to betray any confidences, Ms. Williams," he said, raising his voice a little. "When I find Ms. Loki, if she doesn't want me to, I won't tell anyone I have."

"I thought that was what you were paid to do."

He smiled. "I didn't say I was any good at it."

She did smile this time, reluctantly.

"At this point, I'd be happy to know she was all right. And if I can help her, I will."

He pulled out his wallet and extracted a card. "You can call or text me twenty-four/seven at that number, or e-mail me at that address."

She took the card gingerly, as if merely by holding it between finger and thumb meant that an agreement of some kind existed between the two of them, and she was far from willing to accept anything of the kind. "I haven't seen her," she said, and this time even she could hear the lack of conviction in her words.

"When you do," he said.

He stood on the doorstep and took a deep breath. The air pollution in Brooklyn wasn't as bad as it was in Manhattan, and you could still smell the ghosts of the roses of summers past. He looked down the street both ways, and saw the curtain at the first-floor window across from 354 fall hastily back in place.

That could account for the feeling that he was being watched. It would not account for the tail he'd shaken that morning, or the uncomfortable feeling that he hadn't so much shaken the tail as the tail had done a better job of following him the second time.

He checked his watch, not quite ten thirty, as he came down the steps and turned left to head for his car.

"Mr. Christo! Mr. Christo, please wait!"

He turned and saw the girl from the photograph standing on Athena Williams's front step.

His first feeling was relief that the first time he saw her in person she wasn't looking up at him from a body bag.

His second was the sudden realization that whoever was following him could have followed him right to Angelina Loki's hiding place.

15

VAL McDERMID

The photographs had been no preparation for the reality. The full impact of Angel's beauty was available only in the flesh. Perry was so occupied with scanning his personal database for comparisons he lost all sense of urgency and just stared.

It soon came to him. The impossibly young Lauren Bacall of *To Have and Have Not,* but without the carefully constructed coiffure. Angel's toffee-blond hair had a tousled, bedhead look that the prudish Hollywood studios could never have tolerated. But the feline eyes, the full-lipped mouth with the tilt of a smile even in this moment of distress—all of it a dead ringer for Bacall at her most vulnerable.

She'd stopped short a couple of feet from him after shouting, "Wait," in a frantic voice just the right side of a scream. She drew her breath in sharply, emphasizing the full breasts beneath her skimpy black T-shirt. She had a coat on, but she'd only draped it over her shoulders. She folded her arms across her midriff, but not so fast that Perry didn't notice the tremble in her long fingers. She tucked her chin down and gave him the up-slanted look that Bacall had made her own.

"Angel?" Perry knew it, but he couldn't quite believe it. There had been something dramatic, almost film noir, about the places this commission had taken him so far. He usually dismissed high-flown romantic ideas like that as idle fantasies designed to make him feel better about the routine repetitiveness of the job. But being confronted with a woman who could have stepped out of the pages of Dashiell Hammett was deeply unsettling.

And it was Hammett that came to mind, not Chandler. This girl— no, make that this woman—was bristling with raw sexuality. Her photograph had attracted him; her physical presence mesmerized him.

"Who are you?" she demanded. "Who are you *really*?"

"Like I told Athena, my name is Perry Christo. I'm a private eye. Your mother hired me to find you." He didn't have to work at injecting his voice with warmth.

She shuddered, and it wasn't just from the cold, her arms folding even more tightly round her slim body. "Are you the one? Is that what this has all been about? My goddamn mother finding me?"

He couldn't make sense of what she was saying. Was he so dazed by her beauty? "I don't know what you mean. Am I the one? What one?"

She unfolded her arms and ran a hand through her hair. Even in the gray light of an overcast day, it shimmered bright gold against the dull green of the garden's evergreen foliage. "The one who's been stalking me," she said impatiently.

"Stalking you? Someone's been stalking you?"

She gave him the haughty stare that youth reserves for the dim adult world. "But I don't suppose you'd call it that, Mr. PI." Her top lip curled in a sneer.

"I've not been stalking you, tailing you, following you, or anything that might come under that heading." He took a step backward and spread his arms out in a placatory gesture. "Swear to God. I've been trying to *find* you, sure. But today's the first time I've clapped eyes on you, Angel."

Angel frowned, her cat's eyes narrowing, her expression considering. "I don't know . . . You *look* like you're telling the truth. But somebody's been stalking me."

"Is that why you took off from Montauk?"

She drew back, her arms clamping against her midriff again, jittery as a stand-up comic waiting to go onstage. "How did you know that if you're not the one?"

"I told you. I've been looking for you. All I had to go on was what your mother knew. She sent me to your father's house, but all he could tell me was that you'd taken off. He pointed me toward your buddy, Lilith. And that's how I found out about you and Randy going on the run." Perry shook his head, desperate to impress her with his truth. Usually, he didn't give a damn what the targets of his investigations thought of him. But Angel was different. He wanted her to think well of him, and that made him uncomfortable.

Angel sneered again. "'I thought he'd, like, protect me?" Her voice rose at the end of her sentences. It was her generation's habit to make the most commonplace statement sound like a question. *Her generation,* Perry reminded himself. *She's hardly more than a child, and you're a man heading straight down the slope toward middle age. Get ahold of yourself.*

"And he didn't?"

Angel looked sideways. "I got scared. I was sure someone was on my tail, but Randy, all he cared about was . . . Well, you know. He just blew me off, told me I was paranoid. I figured if he wouldn't take me seriously, I was better on my own."

Perry remembered his own uneasy sense of being followed—and it was more than paranoia, he was sure about that. Still, it was easy to succumb to paranoia when you were out on the edge. He knew that from living with his eyes on the rearview mirror. It saddened him that this beautiful young woman was already prey to such fears.

Quickly, he scanned the street. Seeing nothing suspicious, he focused on Angel again. It wasn't exactly a hardship. Perry chastised himself for the thought and forced his mind back to the job in hand. "So you took off again?"

She nodded. "I figured I'd be safe with Athena. The one person in my life who never betrayed me." She sighed and gave him a half smile. "And then you showed up." For a moment, she brightened. "You think maybe the person who was stalking me was another PI my mother hired?"

Perry shrugged. He didn't think Julia Drusilla was a belt-and-suspenders kind of client. "It's possible," he hedged, trying to keep the doubt out of his face and his voice. "She's certainly keen to find you."

Angel unfolded her arms and put her fists on her hips. It was an attempt at taking control of the conversation. *Attempt* being the operative word. Whatever subterfuges she'd learned over the years, hiding her feelings hadn't been among them. He could read her body language as easily as the morning headlines. He could see anxiety in the tightness of her stance and the rigidity of her features. "Did she tell you why?"

Perry smiled, trying to reassure her. "There are some papers you need to sign so you can both claim an inheritance. It's money your grandfather left in trust for you. You can't access the money until you're twenty-one, but you both have to sign the papers."

"Did she tell you how *much* money?" Angel's chin came up. Perry thought she was trying for assurance, but she just came off like a defiant little girl.

"Let's just say she made it clear that the stakes were high. For both of you."

Angel shook her head in disgust. "I'll say they're high. High enough for her to want me dead so she can get her claws on all of it."

It was a melodramatic moment. Perry had long years of

experience watching families tear themselves apart, and it wasn't the first time he'd heard an accusation like this against a parent. But no matter how often a child spat out such words, it still cut him like a blade. All those broken relationships started in the same place—the innocent eyes of a newborn gazing into the face of someone who owed them a duty of love and care. And they'd all taken a journey down a twisted highway littered with shattered dreams and broken hearts to a place from which there was no retreat. If Angel truly believed this about her mother, there was no way Perry's mission was going to have a happy ending.

Just as well, he thought, *happy endings are for Pixar.*

"You don't really believe that," he said.

Angel snorted. "All she cares about is *money*. She tried to stop me from finding out about the inheritance. She hid the papers and letters, anything about them. I only found them by accident when I was . . ." Her voice trailed off as she tried to figure out a way to make herself the good guy. Inspiration lit her face. "When I was looking for my birth certificate so I could apply for a passport."

The lie didn't come anywhere near fooling him. *But why lie?* "That doesn't mean she wants you dead," Perry said firmly.

"You don't understand." She cast a quick, nervous glance around her and put a hand on his arm. "Look, let's go someplace we can talk properly about this. I'm cold."

Perry moved away from her touch. "We could go inside to Athena's."

Angel shook her head. "I don't want to burden her with this. She doesn't deserve to have this shit in her head."

He wanted to suggest his car. Sitting side by side, so close he could smell her, an intimacy impossible to ignore. "There's a coffee shop on the corner," he said, his voice gruff.

"Okay," she said. They set off down the street. Perry kept a couple of feet between them, fearing and distrusting the attraction he felt.

He eyed the cars parked on the other side of the street, checking that they were empty.

But it wasn't the parked cars that were the problem. As they reached the end of the street, Perry picked up the high note of an accelerating engine behind them. He swiveled in time to see a black sedan racing up the street toward them. Dimly, he heard Angel scream as the car mounted the sidewalk in a screech of rubber. The rest was a blur of movement and color.

Afterward, Perry reconstructed what had happened. He'd known exactly where Angel was, and he'd jumped straight backward, knocking her off her feet and over the low iron railings of the last house on Washington and St. James. Then he'd thrown himself sideways to land painfully on his hip beside her. He'd struggled to his feet, but the car had already been lost in traffic. Worst of all, none of the nearby pedestrians seemed inclined to break step in their busy day to offer support or witness. Nobody even started yelling about the damage they'd done to the shrubs. So much for a friendly neighborhood.

Angel scrambled to her feet and threw her arms around Perry. "Now do you believe me? Now do you get it? She's trying to kill me. She wants me dead so she can steal all the money." She was quivering in his arms like a frightened animal. Which, he supposed, was exactly what she was. And she certainly provoked all his animal instincts.

Gently, Perry tried to pry her free. But she wasn't ready to let go. "You have to help me," she pleaded. "You're the only one who's taken care of me. If I'd been with Randy, I'd be dead right now. Please, Perry, I need you." She planted a kiss on his cheek, her smooth skin soft against his weathered cheek.

Perry caught himself feeling he could be a hero. He would be the one she could depend on, the one she trusted, the one she wanted to wake up with. Then his better self kicked in, and he reminded himself he was a sorry sack of a middle-aged man seduced by the needs of a beautiful—and terrified—young woman. The oldest story in the book. He should know better than that. Hell, he was better than that.

He unpeeled her arms from his body and stepped back over the railings onto the street. A line of wrought-iron spikes was just what he needed between them. "I believe you, that somebody is trying to kill you. But I don't think it's your mother. Whoever was behind the wheel of that car had to be waiting for an opportunity. He or she knew just where you were. If your mother knew that, she wouldn't have needed to hire me."

Angel pushed her tousled hair away from her face and climbed over the railings. "Maybe she bugged you. Maybe she's got a trace on you. Like in that movie."

Perry had no idea which movie she meant, but he didn't care enough to ask. "We need to go to the police."

She shook her head. "No way. As soon as that happens, I'm public property again. I'm going back to Athena. I'm safe there. She won't turn me in. And she'll protect me till you find out who's behind this." She angrily tapped his chest hard with her index finger. "And I guarantee you it will be my evil, fucking mother. And then we'll go to the police." Then she smiled, that slow, feline Bacall smile. "You and me. Together."

Angel's shift from fury to seduction was as smooth as a jaguar, and possibly quite as lethal. She ran the tip of her tongue over her upper lip and smiled again.

This time, it didn't work. Because this time, Perry's brain was working harder than his hormones. He knew who was to blame for what had nearly happened. He didn't believe Angel's crazy notion that he'd been bugged. But he knew he'd been followed. He should have figured out what was going on, who was on his tail, before he led them straight to Angel. Instead, he'd been so puffed up with his own ability to track a fugitive that he hadn't covered his back the way he should have. And a young woman had almost died as a result.

"You have to promise me you'll stay out of sight at Athena's. No rushing down the path to chase the next guy who shows up looking for you." He took her elbow and marched back down the street to Athena's place.

"I promise," Angel said breathily. "Whatever you say, Perry. You saved my life. I'm going to do whatever you tell me from now on." She paused on the path leading to the front door, stood on tiptoes, and planted a kiss on his surprised mouth. Then she was gone, the door closing behind her with a sharp click.

Perry drew in a shuddering breath. He felt as if he'd had more than one narrow escape. But he wasn't so shaken up that he'd forgotten how the world worked. Somebody knew about Angel's safe house. And Angel herself wasn't to be trusted to take good care. Maybe Angel wasn't to be trusted at all. Still, he needed backup. He pulled out his phone and called Henry.

"How's it going, Perry? You find your gal?" Henry sounded clipped, the background noise suggesting a busy squad room.

"I did, thanks. Trouble is, I'm not the only one. Somebody just tried to pull a hit and run on us, Henry."

Henry gave a low whistle. "Time you brought her in, Perry. You need to make this official."

Perry sighed. "I wish. But she's running scared. She thinks coming to you guys will leave her in the wind. I'm working on it. But I could use a pair of eyes on the girl till she's ready to come into the fold." What he couldn't admit to Henry was his niggling doubt about trusting Angel. Something she'd said, or something she'd done had set his mind jangling.

Henry sucked air through his teeth. "You don't make life easy for any of us, do you?"

"I try."

"Tell you what. I know the captain at the local precinct out there.

I'll have him put a uniform on the block. That should be enough to scare off anybody with the wrong idea about your gal."

Henry's words drove some of the tension from Perry's body. He leaned his head back and let out a long, slow breath. He noticed a tiny patch of blue at the heart of the thick gray cloud cover. Maybe he was finally starting to see daylight on this case. Maybe it was time to find out whether he was a player or just being played. It was time to find out just what Julia Drusilla was up to.

Whatever it took.

Maybe confronting Angel's mother would take his mind off Angel's kiss. Impatient, Perry scrubbed his hand across his lips, as if that could wipe away the impact of her mouth on his. He wished he could have believed in its sweetness.

That damn private eye.

Eyes in back of his head.

Too late now to go turn around and try to run them both down again.

You've got to think. Got to make a decision.

And you do. You will take care of the PI first because he knows about you now, and he's going to be looking for you, trying to stop you, and you can't have that. You have to get rid of him—doesn't fucking matter if he sees you because it's going to be the last goddamn thing he ever sees.

So you wait a little longer then follow him, knowing exactly where the girl is, and once you have taken care of him, once he's dead, you'll come back and take care of her, too.

16

Perry looked over his shoulder for one fleeting glance. Timmy Knox, the cop he had left guarding the house, was a nice young guy, but fresh out of the police academy. He had the build of a young Arnold Schwarzenegger and looked as though he could tackle a gorilla. *That would make him a great bodyguard,* Perry thought, but he wasn't convinced Timmy was what his mother used to call "a deep thinker." In fact, if Timmy had been standing there when the car had come lunging at Angel, Perry would have bet that instead of pushing Angel aside, Timmy would have tried to take down the license number of the car.

But at least he made a solid-looking obstacle to anyone who just might be trying to get into the nanny's house.

He called Julia Drusilla and got her voice mail. He left a message saying that he had news for her and that he'd come by soon, though he was glad she was out. It gave him some time to see Nicky.

Perry heard a faint rattle in the engine as he drove into Brooklyn Heights. *I just had a complete overhaul two weeks ago,* he thought. *I just hope the mechanic did it before he started celebrating the Giants winning streak. I should have asked him that,* he thought.

Because he was late, there was naturally a fender bender about three cars ahead of him. With a heartfelt groan he realized that two lanes would be out of service, but then reminded himself that at least he would get around them pretty fast. *Pity the poor jokers who are going to start piling up behind me,* he told himself.

Getting back to the nanny. She seemed like a nice lady, but he wouldn't have wanted to have been the one to take care of Angel for so many years. No wonder the poor soul looked so exhausted. *What was it,* Perry thought again, *that had made me doubt Angel?* Was it just the way she toggled so easily from fear to anger to seduction? His gut told him it was more than that. But what man could think straight around a girl like that?

Perry was trying to avoid looking at the clock on the dashboard, but he couldn't help stealing a glance at it. Oh God. He was getting even later for his lunch with Nicky. He had called to say he'd been delayed. Then he'd called to say he was still delayed. Should he call again? No, Nicky would wait for him. *Maybe if I tell her about Angel, she'll understand,* he thought. *I mean, she wasn't that interested in my last case, when I traced a phony moving van to a secondhand furniture shop, but Angel is different.* He even had a picture of her with him. Nicky liked to read *People* magazine, and Angel looked like a movie star.

Large drops of rain were beginning to fall. Automatically, he switched on the wipers then listened to the usual screeching as they fought their way back and forth across the windshield. *The mechanic supposedly changed them,* he thought. *Even Cyclops could see they were listed on the bill he gave me.*

He inched the car up to and around the spot where the accident had occurred. The drivers were standing around and starting to shove each other. Perry's instinct as a former member of New York's finest was urging him to stop before there was real trouble, but then he heard the unmistakable sound of a police car speeding toward the scene.

They're all yours, pal, he thought as, finally in the clear, he put his foot on the accelerator. His thoughts immediately switched back to Angel. She should be safe enough with that block-of-granite cop outside the door. As long as she didn't go out. That possibility left Perry light-headed. She had promised that she would stay with Nanny dearest, but how many times had Angel changed location in the roughly fifty-two hours he'd been on the case?

Should he call her cell phone and warn her again? No, if she was out, she'd probably lie to him. You didn't have to be a detective to know that Angel was not a truth-teller. What had the nanny said about her? *She's never been just a kid. But she's smart—smartest child I ever took care of—because she had to be.*

Yeah, Angel was smart all right, and cunning, he could see that.

His shoulders slumping, Perry went back to worrying about how upset Nicky would be when he got there. They'd now changed their date from morning to afternoon and from meeting at the coffee shop to meeting her at home. And how upset would her mother be? Noreen was a stickler for promptness. Hadn't one of the problems in their marriage been that the meals she'd prepared had gotten cold while he was chasing some thief who had robbed an old lady at gunpoint? Well, that hadn't been the only problem . . .

Maybe that's a bit of an exaggeration, Perry conceded. *She probably got upset that I had a few beers with the guys when we went off duty after tackling some guy.*

Fifteen minutes later he was looking for a parking spot on the street where Nicky lived with Noreen and her new boyfriend. *This is a nice area,* he thought. *In summer when the trees are out, it's really pretty. And the building has an elevator. Sure wish mine did. Those five flights of stairs are a killer.*

He found a parking spot, a very small one. *Back in my squad days the guys used to say that I could park an elephant in a teacup,* he remembered with a sigh. He tried to find something to feel cheerful about but could only come up with the fact that it had stopped raining.

He got out of the car, locked it, and walked down the block to Noreen's building. As he got close to it, he looked up and could see Nicky watching for him from the window. He waved, but she didn't wave back. Harry, the superintendent, greeted him with the same cliché, "How you doing, Mr. Christo? Been solving any crimes lately?"

"Yeah. I just found the Maltese Falcon. It's in the trunk of my car." Perry forced a smile. He was tired of trying to figure out a comeback that Harry would get. Bracing himself for the recriminations he knew would be coming his way, he headed for the elevator and pushed the button. Thankfully, the elevator was already there. *At least twenty seconds saved,* he thought.

When he got to the sixth floor, Nicky was already in the hall waiting for him. "Daddy, you're always late," she said accusingly as she threw herself at him.

Perry wrapped his arms around her and felt the familiar rush of love that engulfed him when he held his daughter. *God, she's gotten even taller in just a couple of weeks,* he thought. *She's going to be sixteen. I've missed so much of her life.* "Oh, baby, you don't know how glad I am to see you," he said. He tilted up her face. "I didn't think it was possible, but you're even prettier than last time."

"You said that last time."

"And the time before that because it's true."

She's the image of Noreen, he thought, not for the first time. *But with a sense of humor, thank God.* His arm wrapped around her and they walked down the hallway to the apartment. The door was ajar, and as they crossed the foyer he could see that Cornelius Barker, Noreen's boyfriend, was stretched out in the reclining chair with his feet on the hassock. Perry knew that was his way of showing that he was the man of the house.

"Hi, Corny," Perry said with mock cheer. "Been setting the world on fire lately?"

"Daddy!" Nicky said reproachfully, even as he knew she was trying not to laugh.

"Well, *you* certainly haven't been since we laid eyes on each other." The crisp voice came from Noreen as she emerged from the kitchen. "And his name is Cornelius, or Neil, if that's too long a word for you."

Noreen's auburn hair was twisted in a bun. Her superb figure was enhanced by a clingy white top and flowing black pants. Her slender high-arched feet were in shoes that consisted of a few scraps of velvet and silver heels.

Noreen was always around when he came to pick up Nicky. And even though she always needled him about something, she always made it her business to look terrific. And she always made it a point to play chef for Corny Barker, so the aroma of something good in the oven was drifting through the apartment.

Perry always felt that, on some unconscious level, Noreen was showing him what he was missing. A nicely decorated comfortable apartment, a good meal, and *her*. *All of which is true*, he thought. Not that he hadn't met some interesting ladies along the way, including one who loved to golf almost as much as he did. Noreen thought that chasing a ball through the grass was, as she put it, "a trivial way to spend the day."

The trouble with the golfer was that she was a nonstop talker, even when he was about to swing a club. She hadn't lasted long with him.

Now Nicky was giving him the look that said, *Please, Daddy, don't get into an argument with Mom.*

"Hello, Noreen," he said. "May I say you look lovely? And I think I can detect the delectable scent of a pot roast simmering in the Crock-Pot. Am I right?"

"You know perfectly well that's a roast chicken," Noreen snapped. "Unless you've taken leave of all of your senses, which of course is possible. And it really is terrible that you kept Nicky waiting so long, and you do it every time. Every single time."

"Not every single time, and I never do it deliberately. I'm sure when I tell her about the case I'm on, she'll more than understand." Perry resisted his desire to kick the hassock out from under Cornelius's feet. "Nicky, why don't you grab your coat so that Mommy and Cornelius can dive into that chicken together?"

"Wear your heavy jacket, Nicky, the one with the hood," Noreen ordered. "I'm sure your father doesn't have an umbrella in the car, and it may start raining again."

"Detectives don't carry umbrellas. They carry guns," Perry protested, heatedly forgetting for the moment that he wasn't an NYPD detective anymore. Before Noreen could come back with a zinger that, thanks to his getting into trouble he'd been thrown off the force, he added firmly, "or they should."

Before she could reply, Cornelius lowered his feet from the hassock and heaved his body from the chair. "I may have been a top-drawer tennis player, but it's left its mark on the bod," he groaned.

Cornelius never missed making that speech whenever he got up. Perry wondered if he even said it when he slid off a barstool. The guy had made the quarter finals at Forest Hills twenty-five years ago, lost all his games, and then dropped like a stone from competition. Now he sold tennis clothes and equipment for a manufacturer and occasionally was invited to comment on a minor league tennis match.

"Noreeny," Cornelius said in an intimate tone that made Perry want to belt him, "we planned a big lunch for an hour ago. I'm worried that the chicken that your detective ex thought was a pot roast will get tired of waiting for us." He smiled the too-white smile that lit up his salon-tanned face and brushed back his fading blond hair.

Noreen turned from Perry to him. "Oh, sweetie, I'm sorry. Sit down at the table. I'll bring the salads out." She turned back to Nicky. "Warm jacket," she said firmly. "And don't be late. You didn't finish your calculus homework, and you have a test on Monday."

"Mom, please."

The ringing of Nicky's cell phone interrupted another round of acrimonious dialogue. She answered it and clasped her hand to her forehead. "Oh my God. I totally forgot. She did text me, but she's always texting about something. You'd think this show was going on Broadway. Is she mad? Tell her I'll be right there."

Nicky snapped the cell phone closed. "I have a rehearsal for the play. Oh my God, how did I forget it?" She grabbed Perry's arm, raced into the foyer, and reached into the clothes closet with her other hand. "Dad, can you drop me off at school then bring in a pizza to the auditorium? We can eat lunch together there. I don't come in until the third act, but the director insists we be there for the whole rehearsal. She said otherwise we don't absorb the uncertainty and sadness of the human condition."

Perry barely had time to yell, "Bye, Noreeny, bye, Cor-*nel*-ius," before he was out the door. Before it closed he had the intense satisfaction of inhaling the distinct odor of something burning coming from the kitchen.

He and Nicky raced to the car. "Oh, Dad, I'm so sorry," Nicky gasped. "The director moved the rehearsal time. I totally forgot because I was looking forward so much to seeing you. But of course you were late, so it's not like it's my fault that we don't have much time. It's yours."

"Your mother could not have put it better," Perry sighed as he unlocked the door for Nicky and jumped into the driver's seat. "What's the play?" he asked as he pulled out of the spot with the same Houdini-like dexterity with which he had gotten into it.

"It's *Our Town*. Last year we did *Little Shop of Horrors,* remember? I really liked that one. This one makes me cry. I mean, Emily dies; little Wally dies because he has a burst appendix. A neighbor who wants to go to Paris only gets to Gettysburg every other year. George throws himself on Emily's grave. Too much."

"It's considered a classic, honey. I think you'll appreciate it more when you're in college."

"But I like being in it. I play 'first dead woman.' I don't have a big line, but I like being onstage."

Perry remembered that he had played the male lead in *Our Town* when he was a sophomore in high school. *Gigi Jones played Emily,* he thought. *She was one hot cookie.*

"My line is, 'She lived on the same road we lived on, mmm-hmm.'" Nicky shrugged and switched subjects. "I think Mom is getting sick of the tennis champion, Daddy."

"It's a miracle she didn't get a blinding headache the first time she was introduced to him," Perry said, then was annoyed at the secret thrill of satisfaction at hearing his daughter's words.

"It's like I've been thinking it through. I think you and Mom still love each other, but you don't like each other very much. Billy and I have discussed it a lot, and we're synched on it."

It was raining again. Reluctantly, Perry turned on the windshield wipers. Raising his voice over the screeching sound they emitted, he asked, "Who's Billy?"

"He's my boyfriend. He's the guy who plays the milkman in the show. You'll meet him later. His mother and father are getting a divorce, but they can't afford two apartments so his father sleeps in Billy's room with him. There are twin beds. His father snores, so Billy is totally going nuts."

They were pulling up to the school. "The auditorium door will be open, so drop me over there. Maybe you'd better get two pizzas.

Some of the other kids might want a slice. And bring some Cokes. Okay?"

Nicky did not wait for an answer as she hopped out of the car. Nor did she pull the hood of her jacket to cover her head as she made the dash to the door through the now-teeming rain.

Before he started the car again, Perry called Angel, and her cell phone immediately switched to "Leave a message."

"Angel," he said, "I want you to call me back right away. And be sure to stay inside with . . . Athena." It had taken him a moment to recall the nanny's name.

Twenty minutes later he was back at the school, the pizzas and soda balanced in his arms. His visit with Nicky consisted of everyone not onstage coming over to share the pizza. By luck, he managed to get one slice. The director ordered perfect silence in the auditorium during the rehearsal, so his time with Nicky consisted of watching the rehearsal as it dragged on interminably.

It did give him time to worry about Angel. If she was right and someone was trying to kill her, who could it be? Her mother? But her mother was his client. Was he turning into an enabler by tracking down Angel and then reporting where she was to her mother? At least he hadn't done that so far. But should he do it?

Finally, Nicky was onstage. The director had them do the final scene at least twenty times. "You're not sad. You're not glad. You're matter-of-fact that Emily is dead, too," she bellowed.

At last the rehearsal was over. "How was I, Dad?" Nicky breathed.

"You were good," he said. The idea of acting brought Angel to mind. Had she been acting, too? Something in his gut kept saying yes.

"You had what the director was looking for." Perry searched his head for the right words, which he actually meant. "You had that thoughtful remembrance tone in your voice, which is what the part calls for," he tried.

Nicky's sunny smile was sufficient reward for knowing that, at least for once, he had supplied the on-target response he'd been praying for. As the rest of the cast grabbed their outer garments, Nicky turned and pulled over a baby-faced guy with a head of curly hair and a timid smile. "Dad, this is Billy. He was helping backstage. That's why you haven't met him yet."

"Hello, Billy."

"Hello, sir."

My God, the kid has manners, Perry marveled then warned himself not to prejudge. It got him thinking about Angel again. How had he judged her? He still wasn't sure. But something about her act didn't sit right. Even so, he was supposed to be protecting her.

"Billy, sorry this is a rush. Hope to see you another time. But Nicky has homework to do, and her mother wants her home."

"Dad," Nicky whined. "It's a Saturday."

"Tell that to your mom," Perry said, and repeated his apology to Billy.

"That's okay, sir. I just want you to know that when your daughter is with me you have nothing to worry about, like, I mean, I'm not like a lot of guys."

"Oh, Billy, shut up," Nicky said, her face turning into a full-fledged blush.

Methinks he doth protest too much . . . maybe, Perry thought, but he did seem like a nice guy, and if there's one thing he was sure of, Noreen kept a close watch on Nicky. "Come on, Nick," he urged. "Nice to see you, Billy."

"On the short drive home, Nicky was unusually silent then burst out, "That was a totally stupid thing for Billy to say. It's not like . . . I mean . . . ever . . . I haven't . . ."

The ring of truth. Thank God for the ring of truth. "I believe you, baby, and keep it that way. Let's change subjects. I'm minding this"— he searched for an adjective—"ditsy twenty-year-old who claims her mother wants to kill her."

Instantly distracted, Nicky laughed. "Does she know Mom? Maybe there's a club they both belong to." Then as they turned onto the block heading to the apartment, a car went around them. "Dad, see that car?" Nicky asked, "the one that looks as though it got rear-ended? It was behind you when you parked. I saw it drive by when I was looking for you from the window."

Perry felt the hairs on the back of his neck begin to bristle. "Are you sure it's the same one?"

"Oh, I mean, I *think* it is. How many cars look as if they're banged in the same spot?"

Like father, like daughter, he said to himself.

"Who knows? There was a fender bender when I was on my way over. Can you believe it? There's a spot in front of the building. But pull your hood on anyhow. Let's make it look good for Mom."

He stopped the car, and Nicky leaned over to kiss him. "I love you, Daddy. Try to be on time next time."

"I'm going to the door with you."

"That's silly."

"No, it isn't."

Harry the doorman was opening the door for Nicky. "Good night, Sherlock Holmes," he said to Perry.

"I'm taking her up to the apartment," Perry said. "I'll just be a minute. Keep your eye open for flying objects."

This time they waited for the elevator to descend from the twelfth floor. "Daddy, you're worried because I told you about that car," Nicky said.

"Nicky, I'm on a funny kind of case. If you see it again in this neighborhood or around the school, you've got to promise you'll tell the nearest adult that I'm worried about it and then call me. And if possible get a license number but don't get close to it. This isn't fooling around. Okay?"

The elevator came, and they got into it. "If anyone is tailing your car, they're after you, not me, Dad. You be careful. Promise."

"Promise."

They got off the elevator and Perry waited as Nicky unlocked the door. "I won't make any final farewells inside. Let Mom and Corny split the wishbone in peace." He hugged her. "Talk to you tomorrow, Nick. Who loves you?"

"You do. And I love you."

Perry checked his phone. There were no messages. Time to see Julia.

He went back downstairs, through the lobby, and out to his car. He had left it running and the windshield wipers were screeching. Forestalling any comment from Harry, who was holding open the door for an elderly couple, he jumped into the car and drove away. The rain was pouring down, and try as he might he had no way of knowing if he was being followed as he approached the Brooklyn Bridge.

And then he saw it, a dark car inching up on him, then trying to pass, way too close for comfort. He sped up. The black car did, too. He weaved in and out of the traffic, and the black car followed. No doubt it was a tail. Then as he was halfway across the bridge the car sideswiped him. The sound of scraping metal was loud in Perry's ears, and his Datsun skidded on the wet road.

Clutching the wheel, he tried to keep his car from flipping over. It lifted into the air, teetering for a breathtaking moment before slamming down on the road instead of going directly into the railing.

Even with the hopeless flapping of the windshield wipers, Perry could see that the car that had sideswiped him had a battered trunk. Jamming his foot on the accelerator, he pursued his aggressor, darting in and out of traffic to the tune of frantic honking and slamming brakes, until he was over the bridge and in the maze of city traffic, where he lost his would-be assailant.

Damn—Damn—Damn—

You punch your fist against the steering wheel as you try to navigate the traffic of the Manhattan streets. You try to breathe normally, your mind spinning.

So you didn't stop him, didn't send his piece of shit car over the side of the bridge.

So what?

Forget him.

A car horn beeps and you jump. You check the rearview mirror for the tenth time. But it's not him, you've lost him. You're okay. Better than okay.

You drive through the streets, your blood pumping, your head throbbing. It's time. You've got to do it already—what you planned to do from the beginning, why you followed the PI in the first place.

You've got to take care of it. Now. You can't wait anymore.

Do it.

You repeat the words, your hand tapping the steering wheel: Do it. Do it. Do it. Do it. Do it. Do it. Do it. Do it. Do it. Do it. Do it.

17

C. J. BOX

ire and ice, Perry thought as he gritted his teeth and gripped the wheel so tightly his knuckles were white as he cut off FDR Drive at Seventy-first Street and headed toward East Seventy-fifth and Park Avenue. His nerves were jangling from the close call on the bridge, and despite the cold February day, he felt pinpricks of sweat on his scalp and beneath his collar. His heart was still racing.

He powered the driver's-side window down as he drove and welcomed the sharp-toothed bite of the icy air. Suddenly there was the boiling sound-track cacophony of New York—horns blaring, steam rolling out from sidewalk grates, snippets of conversation from bundled-up shoppers and pedestrians. Messengers on bikes weaved through stop-and-start traffic, and sidewalk vendors called to potential customers in balloons of vapor. The rain had eased, but the late afternoon sky was gray and mottled and close, as if someone had placed a lid over the city to prevent anyone from getting out.

Not the worst idea, Perry thought. Clamp that lid on tight and turn the heat up on Julia Drusilla. Make her uncomfortable, make her start to sweat the way he was. Make her tell him what was *really* going on, and why she *really* wanted her daughter found.

When she spilled, he thought, *he could eventually find the assholes who kept trying to run him off the road. And when he found them . . .*

But what about Angel? She seemed to know all about her inheritance. So why did she run? And what was it she'd said—something to do with her mother or . . . Perry tried running their conversation in his mind but kept losing the thread. The scenario he thought was clear to him—the framework of the case itself—seemed to be coming apart at the seams, and he was suddenly doing a clown act, juggling the pieces in the air, trying to reassemble them before they crashed down around him and took him down, too.

Perry had driven in New York traffic long enough that he could sense it bottling up ahead of him long before the jam-up was actually visible. It didn't improve his mood. He'd nearly been killed again, and he was in a hurry.

Traffic didn't flow in the city. It moved spasmodically; sprinting to the next stop, fidgeting, looking for an opening to squeeze through. So much of every day was simply spent trying to get from Point A to Point B. It was maddening.

He swung into the far left lane to pass the taxi that was slowing down ahead of him, and he accidentally cut off a bike messenger whistling through an open chute. The messenger swerved, wildly cursed at him, and thumped the top of the car with the heel of his hand before squirting away between two cars ahead.

Perry entertained a thought he'd had often where he threw his driver's-side door open just as a bike messenger tried to sizzle past him. Someday, he vowed, he'd do it. That would show them.

Julia Drusilla's building was still four blocks away when he saw the lights ahead. Red and white flashes from the light bars atop RMPs strobed the sides of the buildings and bounced off windows. Something near Julia's building had attracted an army of cops.

"Where were you back there on the bridge when I needed you?" Perry asked aloud.

Traffic was crawling but not *good* crawling, like it was poised to break loose. It was crawling to a stop.

Perry cranked on the wheel, fitted the nose of his car between two yellow taxis with inches to spare on each side, and bolted down a shadowed side street. Screw the traffic.

It was a narrow street lined with parked cars, and he felt blessed when a four-door turned out onto the pavement, leaving a space. Perry didn't look around or hesitate; he took the space before anyone else could take it. He'd park and walk the rest of the way—it would be quicker.

As he swung out of his car he saw the signs posted on the poles lining the street: NO UNAUTHORIZED PARKING. RESIDENTIAL PERMITS ONLY.

He shrugged.

"Hey," a thin and pinched woman called to him from where she was walking her tiny dog on the sidewalk, "you can't park here."

Perry reached into his breast pocket and pulled out his PI certification and flashed it so quickly she'd have no chance to note his name.

"I just did," he said, and left her with her dog and her thoughts.

On the street in front of Julia's building was a blue wall of uniformed cops standing shoulder to shoulder to prevent foot or vehicle traffic. Inside the cordon was a fire truck, a paramedic van, and several crazily parked police cruisers, lights flashing.

A growing knot of people stood and gawked, trying to see over or through the uniforms. They were tightly packed, and Perry had to shoulder his way through.

A Rastafarian with a sheep-size coil of dreadlocks was talking to a fat man in an overcoat holding two overfull bags of groceries. The fat man was complaining that the cops wouldn't let him through to get to his building.

"They won't even tell me when I can get through," the fat man said, his voice rising. "It's an outrage. I'm *outraged*."

"There was a jumper, man," the Rasta said in a rhythmic baritone cadence. "A jumper."

"What?" the fat man asked, surprised. "Somebody jumped from my building?"

"Yeah, man."

"Who was it?"

"Don't know," the Rasta said with a chuckle. "I don't know any of these rich white folks around here."

"Was it a man or a woman? My God—I might know them."

"Don't know, man. I didn't see it happen but I *heard* it. Yeah, I heard it."

Perry paused, interested.

"What, did you hear a scream or something?"

"No scream, man. I heard it hit the ground. It was horrible, man. You know what it sounded like?"

"No," the fat man said cautiously.

"Like, you know what it sounds like when you buy a bag of ice at the store? But the ice is all stuck together so you can't use it right away? So you drop the bag of ice on the sidewalk to break it apart? You know that sound it makes when it hits, man?"

"Yes."

"That's what it sounded like. Like a bag of ice being dropped onto concrete. That smashing sound, you know, man?"

"Ugh."

"No shit, man. I won't forget that sound for a while."

Perry winced, and pushed through. A uniformed cop with a wide Slavic face and little pig eyes reached out and grabbed his shoulder.

"Where do you think you're going?"

"To that building. I've got a client who lives there."

"Can't you see me?" the cop asked. "Am I invisible to you?"

Perry fished his PI credentials out and handed them over. "I've got to see my client."

The pig-eyed cop took it and read it.

"I'm a private investigator, and I've got business inside that building. I've got a right to get through. I'd suggest you call somebody if you don't believe me."

The cop smirked and handed it back. "It don't mean nothing to me."

Perry held his tongue. One of the few cops in the NYPD who had not heard of him. Any other time he'd be thankful. The cop watched him and grinned. There were cops like this on every force—men who wore the badge solely for the pleasure of asserting power. Perry used to work with a few of them. He'd long before had his fill of the type.

"You know what you can do for me now, mister?" the cop said.

"And what would that be?"

"You can stand back and let me do my job, or I'll cuff you and take you back to my shop."

Perry didn't budge. The cop's eyes narrowed, as if he were girding himself for a fight and really looked forward to it.

At that moment, Perry saw Henry Watson inside the cordon talking to a pair of paramedics.

"Henry!"

Watson heard his name and looked up. The cop glanced over his shoulder, then back at Perry. He seemed disappointed.

Watson held up a finger to the paramedics for them to wait and walked toward Perry. His face was clouded, and he looked preoccupied.

The cop said, "If you think that's going to get you in . . ."

Watson said, "Perry, get in here. I need you to see something."

The cop grudgingly stepped aside. As Perry passed him, he said, "I won't forget this."

But a knot formed in Perry's gut. What did Watson want him to see?

You look like crap," Watson said as he led Perry through the uniforms and vehicles toward the building.

"Thank you, I try," Perry said.

"It's only gonna get worse."

"Oh, good." Then: "There was talk back there about a jumper."

Watson nodded his head.

"Was it a resident of the building?"

"Oh, yes. Which is why I'm glad you showed up. This way we don't have to go out and find you."

Perry glanced up at the building and his eyes climbed the floors, the rows of windows. They came to a rest at the open glass doors on the twenty-fourth floor's terrace. It seemed like a half a mile up there, but he could still see the doors were open and pushed out to welcome the cold February day.

"Oh, no," Perry said. "I think that's the penthouse apartment of—"

"Julia Drusilla," Watson said, finishing Perry's thought. Watson asked a paramedic to step aside, and when the man did Perry could see the body.

She was facedown on the pavement, arms and legs splayed out at broken angles, the fan of her hair resting on her shoulders, one shoe on and one shoe off. A single rivulet of black blood snaked out from beneath her and serpentined across the pavement square until it pooled in the gutter around a comma of ice.

"Jesus," Perry whispered. He felt as if he'd been punched in the gut. There was no mistaking her. Even in death she had a bad attitude.

Perry felt other detectives move in on him, from behind and on his sides. Watson just stood there, trying to read something from Perry's face that would give him some kind of insight.

"You were working for her," Watson said. "So you know more about her than we do right now. Like maybe why she decided to jump out of her window."

Perry shook his head. He couldn't believe it. Julia Drusilla was too damn mean and had way too much money coming to kill herself.

Watson said, "We're going to leave here and go get a nice warm room at the station. And Perry, you're going to tell me everything you know about Julia Drusilla."

Perry assented with a stunned grunt.

As Watson led Perry toward a waiting cruiser, the pig-eyed cop looked over his shoulder and said, "Say good-bye to your meal ticket, Christo."

18

MAX ALLAN COLLINS

The desk sergeant barely looked up as Watson swiped his badge to the second floor, Perry right beside him.

As they moved through, Watson's latest partner—a smirky kid named Fleming, maybe working his first dead body—joined them as they wound their way back to one of the interview rooms.

Fleming was in his late twenties, fair-haired and fresh-faced. He looked a lot like a junior-league Watson in his slightly better suit, a gray pinstripe; the older detective's was navy blue and, as usual, as rumpled as an unmade bed. Perry hadn't met Fleming the other day, and he didn't think he was going to like him.

Watson and the kid cop dropped into chairs on one side of the table and Watson waved Perry to a chair opposite, then reached forward and hit Record on the small digital recorder that was the table's tiny metallic centerpiece.

Still standing, arms spread with his palms up, Perry asked, "An interview room? Recording me? Henry, am I a suspect?"

Patting the air between them, Watson said, "No, no, but she was your client, after all. Just have a seat."

Reluctantly, Perry did so, as Watson told the recorder the date and time, adding the name of the interviewee, of course.

Perry said, "Yes, she was my client."

"Why did she hire you?"

"You know why."

"This is for the record." Watson nodded at the recorder and gave Perry the edge of a smile.

Perry saw nothing to gain by dodging the question. Julia was dead, and there wasn't a damn thing to be done about it. "She hired me to find her estranged daughter."

"The daughter have a name?"

"Angelina Loki."

"Spell that please."

Perry did.

"And it was *her* cell phone you had me run down?"

"You already know that."

"It's for the record. I'm sorry, but I have to do my job here—you know that."

Perry knew the pressure would be on Watson, that Julia Drusilla's body was his jurisdiction, suicide or not. He nodded.

"Verbal response, please."

"Yes. Her cell phone."

"Did you find her?"

"I found her."

"So, then . . . I assume your client was pleased?"

Shrugging, Perry said, "I never had the chance to tell her. When I got to the apartment, she was . . . you know."

"Splattered?" Fleming said.

Watson shot the kid a look, but Perry didn't react. He wouldn't give the smart-ass kid the satisfaction. And if Watson had set up the ancient good-cop/bad-cop wheeze, he wouldn't dignify that with a reaction, either. Was his old friend trying to put some distance between them? Was that what this was about?

Watson asked, "So . . . Julia Drusilla never knew you found her daughter?"

"That's right. She didn't." Would it have made any difference if he'd reached her as soon as he'd found Angel? Perry wasn't so sure. At the time he'd been happy for the delay. Now he was sorry.

"What was the story?"

Perry settled in. "Julia Drusilla told me she was dying and wanted to straighten things out with her estranged daughter."

"Angelina."

"Angel. Ms. Drusilla wanted me to track her down."

"You had the cell number and came to me?"

Perry supposed a cop, even his friend, going on the record, had to ask questions he already knew the answer to, but that didn't make it any less irritating.

Watson sighed. "Look, I know we've been through it, but I need to file a report."

"On me?"

Watson's jaw twitched. "On Drusilla. But you came to me, remember, got me involved. So now I've got to include that in that report."

So that was part of it: his good pal wanted to make sure he looked clean and pure, none of the old Christo stain on him. The two men stared at each other a moment.

"First," Perry said, "I went out to Long Island and met Norman Loki, Julia's ex. When that marriage went bust, Angel moved to Long Island with her father."

"Uh-huh," Watson said, nodding.

"Then I met an artist, Lilith Bates—Angel's best friend. She gave me the name of the motel where Angel and her boyfriend Randy had taken off to, and were supposedly shacked up in."

Fleming was frowning. "They weren't *at* the motel?"

"No. But I spoke to the boyfriend, Randy Hyde, and he'd been there, with her. And I spoke to the motel manager, too . . . but no Angel. Not anymore."

Perry left out that he thought Randy—or that crooked politician Angel was playing with—might have been driving the car that tried to run him off the damn Brooklyn Bridge. That wasn't part of the story—that was personal, and he'd keep it to himself.

"Then?" Watson asked.

"Then I had you run the cell number. I'm sure you remember." He tried to keep the edge out of his voice but failed.

"Yeah." Watson nodded. "I remember."

"And?" Fleming asked.

"And that sent me to Brooklyn to see Athena Williams."

"Who's she?" Fleming asked.

"Angel's nanny. She might be the only real friend that girl has in the whole world. That's where I found my client's daughter."

"But you never got a chance to tell Ms. Drusilla?" Fleming asked.

Perry just shook his head.

"Verbally, please."

"No, I never got that chance. I *already* said that."

Watson finally asked the question the PI had been waiting for this whole time. "Why was Julia *really* looking for her daughter? If she wanted to 'straighten things out,' she'd had years to do it. Why now, all of a sudden?"

"Why now? She was dying, and there was the matter of an inheritance."

"Details, please."

Perry shrugged. "Angel would be eligible for that in a few days. When she turns twenty-one."

"Her mom's estate," Fleming said, not a question.

"Which was quite sizable," Perry said, nodding. "Mommy got a bundle when her own parents died."

"When was that?" Fleming asked.

But it was Watson who answered: "Julia's old man died in a crash. Him and his wife, both."

"Car accident?" the young detective asked.

"Yeah. He was a big shot, filthy rich, plus he had tons of life insurance coverage on the whole family. Then, wham—his car runs into an eighteen-wheeler. Fell asleep driving, maybe. Anyway, he and his wife die, and presto, Julia's got herself quite the little nest egg."

That was a nasty way to put it, but Perry skipped a comment and finally asked a question of his own. "Any chance that it *wasn't* an accident?"

"State boys handled it. They didn't come up with anything indicating foul play that I know of." Watson glanced at Fleming, as if he needed to explain. "I came across it when I was looking into this business for Christo. It's all a matter of public record." He tugged at his collar then looked at Perry. "Last time I told you about this, you didn't have much to say. You have any new thoughts in light of what's happened?"

Given what had happened to him on this case, Perry wasn't sure he believed in accidents anymore. Her parents had died "accidentally," and now Julia had slipped off her balcony or jumped.

And even if he did still believe in accidents, Perry sure as hell didn't believe in coincidences. He wanted to know what was really going on, but that was hard to do when you were the one under the microscope.

"Anyway," Perry said, trying hard to keep it matter-of-fact, "while Julia would get half the money, supposedly the other half was due Angel on her twenty-first birthday. Assuming the papers were signed in time."

"Why look for the daughter?" Fleming asked, frowning. He'd gotten interested enough to stop playing smart-ass. "If she didn't sign the papers, wouldn't Julia, her mom, have kept it all?"

"Maybe Julia was less . . . pragmatic than you, Detective."

"Especially if she was dying," Watson put in. "She wanted to find the daughter, repair whatever it was that got broken between them, then make sure her daughter was set for life."

"That's what I don't get," Perry admitted. "If all that's true, then why the hell did Julia jump *before* she knew whether or not I'd found her daughter?"

Watson seemed about to reply when a burly detective stuck his head into the room. "Henry, someone here to see you."

"Busy," Watson said, waving off the detective.

The big cop raised an eyebrow. "It's Angelina Loki," he said.

The three seated men traded looks.

Watson said, "Send her in."

They all rose as the burly detective stepped aside and two women entered the interview room. The blond and beautiful Angel Loki appeared tiny next to Athena Williams, the African American woman who ushered her in, a firm arm wrapped around her charge.

As Perry made the introductions, the burly detective brought in another chair, placed it next to the one Perry had used, then exited and shut the door.

Her hair tied back in a conservative ponytail, a single strand of pearls riding her black silk blouse, Angel already seemed to be dressed in mourning clothes. The tissue clutched in one hand, occasionally dabbing at her eyes, confirmed that.

The nanny had changed, too: a dark dress instead of the designer jeans she'd been wearing when Perry last saw her. She carried a purse so big and heavy that Perry half expected her to pull out a small lawyer, should one be needed.

Stepping forward, Watson said, "We're terribly sorry for your loss, Ms. Loki."

"Thank you." Her voice sounded like it was coming from far away.

The detective waved them to the two chairs, while he and Fleming took the other two, leaving Perry to lean against a wall.

Sitting, Angel said, "So, then . . . it's true? My mother is . . . she's dead?"

"Unfortunately, yes," Watson said. "We were searching for you to inform you—how did you hear?"

Angel turned to her nanny as if unable to respond.

"One of those twenty-four-hour news channels," Athena said. "It's on the TV already. They were just guessing, of course . . . but Angel, she knew it was her mama right away."

Perry ran a hand over his face. Damn twenty-four-hour news cycle meant the vultures were pouncing faster than ever; speculation had long since replaced reporting. They didn't give a good goddamn about the families. But then, how would Angel know it was her mother if the news hadn't actually said so?

"What made you think, *know* it was your mother, Angel?" Perry asked.

"Well, they—" Angel stammered. "They gave the address, so I just thought—"

The nanny stepped in. "That's a rude question at a time like this, Mr. Christo."

"What happened to my mother?" Angel asked, now choking back sobs.

"I thought you saw it on the news," Perry said.

"I did but—"

Perry studied her, the tilt of her head, the tissue to her eyes. He watched Watson grow uncomfortable, and even the smart-ass

Fleming was doing his level best to disappear into his chair. Angel had that effect on men.

Finally, the older detective said, "We're still gathering evidence, and waiting for the coroner's report. But it would appear your mother took her own life."

Angel's eyes widened, but still there were no real tears that Perry could see. "How?"

"I'm sorry. Indications are that she jumped from her balcony."

While one arm remained around Angel's shoulders, Athena's free hand shot to her mouth, clutching at herself.

Looking toward the PI, Angel said through splayed fingers, "Mr. Christo must have told you that my mother was terminally ill. She probably didn't want to . . . to go through the pain of a long, slow death." Bitterness now edged the sorrowful little voice. "She hated pain . . . probably even more than she hated being married to my father."

Perry thought that the illness might explain a leap to her death—despite the horror of the fall, the pain from a drop at that height would be over in an instant. Not that he was convinced. But why now the remark about her father and mother's marriage? And why the look of shock if she had watched the news report and already knew it was her mother who had jumped? He was about to ask when Watson cut in.

"I know this is difficult, Ms. Loki, but there are some questions I need to ask you."

"Now?"

"I'm sorry, yes. Suicides fall under the broader umbrella of homicide, and the more quickly the facts can be gathered in any homicide, the more likely we can ascertain what actually happened."

She processed that momentarily, then nodded.

"I need to know where were you today?"

Angel's eyes widened again. "What . . . am I a *suspect*? I thought you said this was a suicide."

Watson shook his head, though there was no enthusiasm in it. "At this stage, it's a suspicious death. Procedure requires asking all family members and close friends this kind of question." He gestured to the little recorder. "And I should note that our conversation is on the record."

Angel drew in breath loudly, but her "All right" was barely audible.

Watson repeated his question.

Wiping away a stray tear, eyes moving with thought, she said, "I was . . . I was napping in Athena's back room."

The nanny nodded her corroboration.

"All day?"

Angel said, "After speaking to Mr. Christo, well . . . that was so emotional. I'm sure you understand, Detective. Hearing that my mother wanted to make amends, and realizing all that money was coming, it was very . . . I just needed . . . to rest for a while."

"All right," Watson said, with a couple of barely perceptible nods. "Since you brought it up, was your meeting with Mr. Christo the first time you'd heard about the inheritance from your grandfather?"

"No. My father told me."

Not exactly the way she'd explained it to me, thought Perry. He replayed the conversation they'd had in Brooklyn, how Angel had appeared to know all about it when she'd asked . . .

Did she tell you how much money?

Let's just say she made it clear that the stakes were high. For both of you.

I'll say they're high. High enough for her to want me dead so she can get her claws on all of it.

"You and your mother didn't get along," Fleming said, not a question.

"That's true," Angel said without hesitation. "I blamed her for breaking up her marriage to my father. That's why I chose to live with him on Long Island, rather than with her."

After Norman Loki's recent drunken performance, Perry found it tough to buy that Angel would have chosen the guy; but maybe he was the lesser of two evils.

Watson now: "When was the last time you saw your mother?"

"Almost a year ago. Mother made this big production out of us burying the hatchet, but we argued so much that . . . we almost ended up burying it in each other." Her laugh was small yet large with bitterness. "It was a disaster."

"So, then . . . the two of you were still feuding?" Watson asked.

"At that time," Angel said, tissue dabbing at her eyes again. "But . . ."

"You didn't contact her?"

"I thought she was still angry. It wasn't until Mr. Christo here came around, and said my mother wanted to make peace, and told me about the money. Truly, I believed with all my heart that she still . . . still *hated* me." She looked at Perry. "I know it sounds terrible to say, but all she ever seemed to care about was her stuff—her jewelry, her homes, and her great big Jackson Pollock painting."

Then, the tears came, and the nanny was patting Angel's shoulder as if tending to a grieving child. And wasn't she? Or was it a performance? Perry wasn't sure, but it didn't add up. Angel had just said her father told her about the money. What else had he told her? And when?

Before they could continue, the burly detective stuck his head in again.

"What now?" Watson boomed.

"Now *Norman* Loki is here."

Hands spread, palms to the sky, Watson threw a look to Perry. "Apparently, Mayor Bloomberg couldn't tear himself away today."

The burly cop didn't react to the sarcasm.

Watson sighed and said, "Show him in, show him in—might as well have the whole family in here."

What's left of it, Perry thought.

Within seconds, the big detective was leading Norman Loki in. Father immediately went to daughter, and the two hugged, though there was something tentative about it on Angel's side, Perry thought.

The nanny immediately took a step back, as if she didn't want to be anywhere near Norman Loki.

Still holding his daughter, Loki said, "I drove in from Long Island, soon as I heard."

Perry almost asked why before remembering this wasn't his interview, at least not his side of it. Better to keep his mouth shut.

Loki wore a sport jacket, a Hawaiian shirt with parrots on it, lightweight slacks, and loafers with no socks. Somewhere along the way, he had confused Fire Island in the summer with Long Island in the dead of winter.

Watson told Fleming to take Angel and her nanny to the break room and get them some coffee while he spoke to Mr. Loki.

The younger detective did as he was told, and Perry continued leaning against the wall, staying mum.

When the room was cleared, Watson sat down opposite the dead woman's ex-husband, Perry positioned in the background between them, like an umpire presiding over a tennis match.

"We're sorry for your loss," Watson said, an opening lob.

"Thank you," Loki said.

Watson informed the man that their interview was being recorded. Then they volleyed over how Loki had heard about his wife's death, why he thought she might have jumped, and so on until Watson finally started in with questions geared toward winning points.

"Mr. Loki, did you stand to inherit your wife's estate?"

He shook his head. "No, Angel will inherit almost all of Julia's estate. I'm the executor, so I receive a nominal fee, of course, and our divorce provided me with a small . . . stipend . . . but otherwise, I will get nothing."

Point Loki.

Except that Perry wasn't buying it. He cleared his throat. "First time I saw you, you denied any knowledge of the inheritance papers."

Watson gave him a look but didn't say anything.

"Frankly, I didn't think it was any of your concern. And I didn't see how it would help find my daughter."

Clearly, he'd had time to firm up his story.

Watson asked, "Do you think Angel may have hated her mother enough to kill her?"

"Hell, no!" Loki said, and if that was supposed to be outrage, it came out undecided, at least to Perry's ears. "There was no gain in it for her. She was going to get half the estate—more money than she could ever need, and on her twenty-first birthday, just around the corner. No, no, that makes no sense."

Perry wondered if Loki was trying to convince them or himself. And what was it Angel had just said that was gnawing at him?

Before they could go any further, the burly detective popped in again, and Watson snapped, "What the hell is it now?"

"The ME just sent up the preliminary tox screen," the big cop said. "I'm not tryin' to set a record for interrupting an interview . . . just figured you'd wanna see this, toot sweet." He handed Watson a file folder.

"Yeah, thanks," Watson said, with a faint tone of apology, to the detective's exiting backside.

Watson scanned quickly, gave Perry an unreadable glance, then turned his attention back to Loki.

"Did your ex-wife take drugs?" Watson asked.

Loki shrugged. "I wasn't in charge of her even when we *were* married. But as far as I know . . . when we were married, anyway? No. Never did know her to take drugs. Well . . . almost never."

"You're going to clarify that, right?"

The husband sighed. "I know I shouldn't say this, but lately . . . during all this unpleasantness with Angel's disappearance . . . I gave Julia a bunch of my sleeping pills. She asked, and I gave. I'm sure she could have gotten them from her doctor, but I had them, so I didn't see anything wrong with it . . . Why, is there a problem?"

Watson was shaking his head, and Christo felt as if he already knew what was coming; but he still felt a little sick when Watson said, "Your ex-wife had tranquilizers in her system when she died."

A hand that went to Loki's mouth, but he stayed quiet.

"We'll have to wait for the full autopsy," Watson said, "but it does make it look like Julia may have taken her own life . . . Again, I'm sorry for your loss. I need to speak to Mr. Christo a moment alone. If you could just wait in the hall, briefly . . . ?"

Loki nodded, sighed, took a long time getting to his feet but no time at all leaving the room.

Then Perry sat down across from Watson again, though the former leveled the first question to the latter.

"Come on, Henry. You know something doesn't feel right about this one."

The detective shrugged, his expression both weary and frustrated. "What? The woman was terminally ill, distraught. She took some pills and threw herself off the balcony. What's not to feel right?"

Perry shook his head. "I told her I was close to finding Angel. If you hire a PI to find your estranged daughter, and you know he's getting close, is that the time you pick to kill yourself?"

"You and I both know suicides always leave a lot of questions be-hind," Watson said. "If she was in pain, hell . . . maybe it just got to be too much for her."

"Maybe," Perry said with no conviction.

Watson let out his biggest sigh yet, and that was saying something. He clicked off the little digital recorder. "That's it. For now."

As Perry rose and walked out of the interview room, he couldn't help but feel that he was missing something important. And so was Watson.

Suicides were unpredictable, all right. But mothers, where the welfare of their children were concerned, were among the most pre-dictable creatures on the planet. And he could not see Julia slipping over that ledge when possible reconciliation with her daughter was so nearly at hand.

19

MARK BILLINGHAM

Coffee and doughnuts . . .

Police stations smelled of coffee and doughnuts, that's the way Perry *remembered* it anyway . . . whenever he found himself sitting up late with a drink in his hand and thinking about these big, ugly buildings he'd once spent so long in. The dingy corners and the crowded hallways and the squad rooms that had made his blood pump just a little bit faster as he walked into them every day, until six years ago when everything . . . changed.

That's the way he dreamed it.

Rose-tinted spectacles. Didn't sound right when you were talking about the way a place smelled, but it was the best he could come up with sitting there now and breathing it in.

"Somebody taking care of you, buddy?" A young cop—one whom Perry didn't know, and who didn't know him. He was glad.

"I'm good, thanks."

Piss and puke was more like it, and something else that was hard to put into words but that all cops recognized the moment they caught a whiff of it.

Police stations smelled of fear.

Perry sat on the edge of a scarred, wooden bench on the second floor of the 19th Precinct Station House. Twenty feet to his left was the small, brown door to an interview room, which he had glanced at every twenty seconds or so since he had been asked to leave and the Lokis had been ushered back into for a second round of questioning.

"You sure?"

Perry looked up again at the uniformed cop standing over him. The man had a shaved head and a face like a forgotten potato in the bottom of the refrigerator. "Yeah, like I said." He sniffed and leaned back. "Just waiting on somebody."

The cop sucked his teeth and straightened his belt, and as soon as he had turned away, Perry stole another glance at the door to his left. He rolled his head around on his neck. He let out a long, slow breath and dropped his gaze to the patch of scuffed gray marble beneath his feet.

"Yeah, well, that's bullshit!"

"Try telling someone who cares."

"I know my rights."

"Good for you . . ."

He might have been wrong about the smell of the place, but it was every bit as noisy as he remembered. While the argument echoed up from the floor below, a radio was playing somewhere and raucous laughter drifted toward him from a room at the other end of the hallway. There were high ceilings in here. There was plenty of air. Sound carried in a place like this, and you could hear a whispered plea or a muttered curse from fifty yards away.

He remembered a cop saying once, "Don't even *think* out loud in here."

Once or twice in the last few minutes he had thought he'd heard voices coming from the interview room. Not raised voices, just the gentle to and fro of a conversation, but even so he had struggled to resist marching across and pressing an ear to that small, brown door. Struggled, until he'd drawn the attention of the potato-faced sergeant and thought better of it. He looked up now, and the cop was still watching him, making a bad job of pretending he wasn't and looking away just a second too late. For a moment or two, Perry wondered if the cop *did* know who he was.

He looked at the door again.

Cigarettes, too, back in the day. A station was always thick with the fug and stink of cigarettes, and, even though it seemed like a lifetime ago, he suddenly found himself wanting one.

No, not suddenly.

Ever since he'd stood looking down at Julia Drusilla, at what was left of her.

It was guilt as much as disgust, he knew that. After all, it didn't seem like five minutes since he had been thinking that the woman might have been trying to kill her own daughter, to kill *him,* and now they were hosing her off the sidewalk. Scraping bits into a bag. How could he have gotten it so wrong? When it came to trusting people, he had always been slow off the mark and with damn good reason, but up until now he'd always been able to trust himself at least, to have faith in his own judgment. Whatever else happened, he'd always been able to count on that.

He put a hand on his knee and pressed, tried to stop the tremor in his leg.

Now, Perry wasn't so sure.

A door opened a little way down the hall, and Perry looked up to see Athena Williams stepping out of what he guessed to be the ladies' restroom. He watched the nanny straighten her skirt and softly dab a hand against her hair before moving toward the stairs.

Perry stood up and hurried to catch up with her.

"May I speak to you, Ms. Williams?"

The woman glanced at him, kept on walking. "You were rude to Angel back there, Mr. Christo. I have nothing to say to you."

"I just want the truth," Perry said. "Isn't that what we all want?"

"Some things are better off left alone, Mr. Christo."

"What kinds of things?"

"You don't know this family."

"Oh, I think I'm starting to . . ."

The nanny began walking a little faster suddenly. Perry kept pace with her and dropped a hand onto her shoulder. She stopped and looked at him, waited for him to remove his hand. "I love Angel," she said. "Do you understand?"

"That's very touching."

"I've got nothing else to say."

"Do you love her enough to lie for her?"

"Good-bye, Mr. Christo . . ."

Perry could do nothing but watch her leave, before he turned and walked back the way he'd come. The nanny's face right before she'd marched away certainly suggested that he'd touched a nerve.

He was good at that, but it didn't seem to be getting him anywhere.

He was a few feet away from the door to the interview room when it opened and Angel and Norman Loki stepped out into the hall. They waited for a few seconds, their heads bowed, until Detective Henry Watson followed them, closing the door behind him.

The argument downstairs had petered out, and it was quiet suddenly.

Perry was pleased that his old friend had called them back for a second round. There were certainly a few questions—*more* than a few—that needed answering, and Watson rarely gave anyone an easy ride, least of all when there was a body involved.

Watson cleared his throat and reached out to shake hands with Norman Loki. He said, "Once again, I'm sorry for your loss. And for having to put you through this."

"Thank you," Loki said.

"We won't need to bother you again."

"It's really no trouble."

"You need a ride anywhere?"

Angel laid a hand on Watson's arm, the fingernails bloodred. "That's sweet of you," she said. "But we'll be fine."

"You're *kidding* me, right?"

They all turned to look at Perry, who was shaking his head in disbelief. He had been talking to himself as much as anything, but his words had carried, and he was fine with that.

After returning Perry's stare for a second or two longer than anyone else would find comfortable, Angel turned back to Henry Watson. "Well, then . . ."

Loki nodded. "Thanks again for being so thorough."

Perry had to fight the laugh that rose up, foul-tasting, in his throat.

Angel linked arms with her father, and the two of them turned away from Henry Watson. They paused for a few moments, each taking a deep breath. Then, at a pace that was nicely pitched between funereal and unseemly, and taking care to keep their eyes on the floor directly ahead of them, they began walking down the hall toward Perry.

With her hair tied back and now with an oversize pair of very dark sunglasses, she looks every inch the grieving daughter, Perry thought, watching her. Or an actress playing the role of grieving daughter. She leaned against her father, who looked equally stricken, and, as they walked, Norman Loki appeared to be getting as much support from his daughter as she was from him.

It was all very convincing. But the two of them were playing at . . . something.

What was it Angel had said before that had flipped a switch in the back of Perry's brain, that had convinced him she was lying?

When they were only a few feet from him, Angel's heels *click-clack*ing against the marble floor, he watched her raise a hand and delicately push fingers behind the lenses of her dark glasses. It was a simple enough gesture, an obvious one. It was the way somebody would oh-so-subtly wipe away tears, but short of dashing across and snatching those expensive sunglasses from her face, there was no way to be sure there were actually tears there to begin with.

Perry would not have been surprised to find that she could manufacture them at will.

It was clear that neither Angel nor her father had any intention of acknowledging Perry's presence. With Norman Loki it made sense, but why the sudden change in Angel? Clearly, she had not liked his questions, but he wasn't going to stop till he had all the answers.

They began to walk just a little faster and looked the other way, returning the uniformed sergeant's respectful nod with thin and grateful smiles. Perry waited a few seconds, then stepped casually forward. He fell into step and walked alongside them.

"It's funny," he said. "Julia told me she was going to die the first time I met her, but I really don't think she thought it would be quite so soon."

There was no visible reaction from Angel or her father.

"I mean, even if she *was* dying, and you know I'm really not convinced that's true . . . she didn't strike me as the type to kill herself." Perry shrugged, pretended to think about it. "Maybe it was an accident." He looked sideways at Angel and her father, who were now moving a little quicker than before. *"Maybe . . ."*

Now, Norman Loki stopped and snapped his head around to look at him. "What's the matter, Christo? You worried that now your client's dead, you aren't going to get your fee? I'm sure I don't need to tell you that your services are no longer required. We'll send a check to you next week—you needn't worry."

Perry saw a smile flicker briefly at the corners of Angel's mouth.

"Why should I be worried?" Perry said. "I know there's still plenty of money around. I mean, Angel stands to inherit a bundle." He looked at Angel, then turned back to Loki. "And as you're the executor, I'm sure there'll be a few dollars coming your way, too. Maybe a lot more."

"You know nothing about it," Loki said.

"You said earlier that you wrote the terms of this weird inheritance. And we both know that everything hinges on Angel's twenty-first birthday, which is just a couple of days away now." He widened his eyes, as if he had only just been struck by something that he'd actually been thinking ever since Julia Drusilla's so-called suicide. "Whatever the hell happened to Julia, the timing's awfully convenient, don't you think?"

"Are you making some kind of accusation?"

"Just talking things through."

"Good," Loki said, looking around. "Just keep talking nice and loud, okay, because when I sue your ass for slander, I want there to be plenty of witnesses."

"Shame there were no witnesses around when your ex-wife took that dive from the twenty-fourth floor," Perry said. "Maybe if there had been, you two wouldn't be walking out of here."

"How dare you!" Loki took a step toward him. Angel made a show of trying to hold her father back. "Where d'you get off saying things like that? Julia has just *died,* for Christ's sake."

Perry raised his hands and nodded, mock-impressed. "It's nice to see that you're so upset. I'm a little surprised, though, tell you the truth. It's not like you and Julia had a . . . conventional relationship, is it?"

"What's that supposed to mean?"

"Come on, Loki. You forget telling me all about it when you were drunk—you really want to get into that here and now? We can talk about your pool boy and bathhouses and underground nightclubs if that's what you want, but in front of your daughter? I mean, isn't she upset enough already?"

Loki glared, and Angel tugged at her father's arm. "Let's go, Daddy."

Loki was breathing heavily, and the bones in his jaw pulsed against the skin as he clenched his teeth. He managed the thinnest of smiles then turned and began to lead Angel away toward the stairs. Was he running the show now? Had he been all along?

Perry followed, a step or two behind. "I mean, you *are* upset, aren't you, Angel?" She kept walking, but he could see the tension in her shoulders. "You certainly *look* upset, but it's so hard to tell with you. I mean, I *thought* you were upset when you told me about why you ran away, when you told me how scared you were. But you also told me that you knew about your inheritance, that the stakes were high, remember? You know, I'm thinking that maybe you're pretty damn good at getting people to think all sorts of things. The boyfriends who all think they're special. That politician who seems to think you're worth cheating on his wife for." Perry's voice was raised now, and people in the corridor were staring as the three of them marched toward the top of the stairs. "All of them happy to believe whatever the hell you want them to believe . . ." Perry needed to get a rise out of her. He wanted her to prove to him she was innocent. He *needed* her to, and yet . . .

A few steps farther on, Angel stopped suddenly. Loki kept walking, then stopped to wait for her when he reached the stairs.

"Me, too," Perry said. "That's the stupid thing." He walked slowly toward her. "You had me believing . . . all sorts of things." Damn it, what was it she'd said that he was trying to remember? "For a while, anyway."

Angel moved toward him until they were only inches apart. She removed her sunglasses, and he could see that her eyes were wet. Then that smile flickered again, just for a second, before she raised her arm and slapped him hard across the face.

Perry closed his eyes for a few seconds against the pain, and when he opened them again, he could see the potato-faced sergeant bearing down on him, shouting.

"Everything okay, here?"

"Everything's fine," Angel said, her face set hard, the sunglasses already back in place.

As the sergeant took a firm hold of Perry's arm, he could only watch as Norman and Angel Loki turned and walked casually away down the stairs without looking back. He tried to yank his arm from the cop's grip, and just as the struggle threatened to become something Perry might easily have been arrested for, a familiar figure appeared at the sergeant's shoulder.

"I got this, Jimmy," Watson said.

Spud-Face nodded and reluctantly let go of Perry's arm. He walked away, seemingly frustrated at not being given an excuse to throw a punch. Perry watched him go, equally disappointed.

"In there." Watson hissed in his ear, and pointed back along the corridor toward the interview room with the brown door. "Now!"

"What the hell do you think you're playing at?"

Perry dropped into a chair and undid a button on his shirt. Cold as it was outside, the interview room was hot and stuffy. There were no windows. "What am *I* playing at?"

Watson folded his arms, eyes narrowed. "Okay then, let's hear it. It's not like you can make yourself any *less* popular."

"Why did you let them go?"

"No reason to keep them."

"Come on, Henry, you really think Julia Drusilla killed herself?"

"For Christ's sake, Perry, we already went through this. The woman was sick."

"You got any proof of that? A doctor's letter? Hospital records?"

"You got any proof of *anything*? You got *any* reason at all to be harassing these people. They make a complaint, I'm not going to think twice about busting you."

"Sounds like they did quite a job on you," Perry said. "Father and daughter. Angel sitting where I am now, drying her big doll's eyes and wrapping you round her little finger. Jesus . . ."

"You need to drop this," Watson said. Steel inside the whisper.

"I can't."

"That wasn't advice, Perry."

Perry blinked. "You ask them where they were when she died?"

"You think I'm a moron? You heard her, she was with her nanny—and the nanny confirmed it."

"And Loki?"

"He was on Long Island, remember?"

"Who says? His pool boy? Come on, Henry . . ."

"He's vouching for her, and she's vouching for him."

"That's convenient."

"Doesn't mean it isn't the truth."

"*None* of these people are telling the truth—you need to know that." Perry leaned across the small table. "I have a feeling Julia was lying about being sick, her old man's lying about who he likes sleeping with, and you can tell Angel's lying because she's breathing. I swear to you, Henry, it's like that entire family has DNA that's ninety percent bullshit."

"And you know this because—"

"Because . . ." Because of the way both Angel and her father kept changing their stories: she didn't know about her inheritance, then she did; Loki didn't write the trust papers, then he did. The way Angel shifted so easily between wrath and seduction. The way Loki shifted between drunken fool and savvy lawyer. They were up to something. Maybe together. Maybe each of them alone. Perry couldn't say. He just knew it, felt it in his gut.

"I can't arrest people for lying," Watson said.

"You don't seem that keen to arrest anyone for murder, either."

"Don't push it—"

"It's about the money—"

"What's that thing they tell us about at the police academy? It's on the tip of my tongue . . . oh yeah, *evidence*."

"So . . . find some."

"Find some, that what you're saying? Or *invent* some? You're really the last person who should be talking to cops about cutting corners, all things considered."

Perry pushed his chair back hard. "You got something to say, Henry?"

"Just that you don't have too many people on your side anymore." Henry stabbed a finger against his own chest. "Maybe just *this* idiot. So if you want to lose the only friend you've got around here, go right ahead and continue doing what you're doing. But don't say I didn't warn you."

Neither of them spoke for a long few seconds, and the only sound in the room was the gentle shushing of hot water in the radiator pipes.

Perry stood up and walked to the door. "Your client dies, and you've got an obligation," he said. "That's how it works. I need to know how Julia Drusilla died and who was responsible. I care about that, okay? Even if you don't."

"Get out, Perry . . ." Watson let out a long sigh, the breath rattling in his chest. He lowered his head and began scratching at the edge of the table.

Perry did as he was told.

The city lights turned the night sky slate gray above, the sullen gray smear of the river away to his right, and the dirty gray trunk of the Buick that stayed just a few feet ahead as Perry crawled slowly through the traffic on the FDR.

His frustration quickly blossomed into anger. He muttered curses then shouted them. He slammed his palms against the wheel and leaned on his horn, but it did nothing to speed his progress and only tightened the knot of guilt and confusion in his gut.

There was only one way to unravel it. One place to go, if he ever got there.

He leaned on his horn one more time, for the hell of it.

It was like he'd told Watson; they were all lying, but somebody was telling lies a damn sight less white than the rest of them. It was time to find out who that was. And to find out how Julia Drusilla had died and why.

Was Norman Loki hiding more than just his sex life?

Was Angel really capable of setting up her own mother's murder?

Were they in it together? Was this whole thing a ruse?

He'd been a cop and a PI long enough to know when the pieces didn't fit, and these didn't even come close.

As the gray Buick accelerated away from him and the traffic began to move a little faster, he thought, too, about his argument with Henry Watson. His friend had been angry, obviously. Perry had pushed all his buttons and had known damn well he was pushing them.

It was more than anger, though, or impatience.

Maybe just this idiot . . .

Sitting there in that sad and stuffy interview room, shoulders slumped on the other side of the table, Henry had looked . . . disappointed. Convinced that Perry was out of line. That he was being stubborn only because the case had got away from him, that he had everything the wrong way up.

Perry put his foot down.

He decided that he would prove Henry Watson wrong. That he would prove them all wrong. He had to.

He was still in the outside lane when saw the sign for the Queens–Midtown Tunnel. He sped forward, only inches from the car ahead then swerved hard and fast across two lanes. An old man at the wheel of a Subaru sounded his horn.

Perry gave him the finger as he hit the off-ramp.

20

Angel and her father had close to an hour's lead, but it didn't matter. Perry knew where they were going. He just had to get there before they had time to bury any evidence. Before they had time to plan. Before they had time to disappear.

But they wouldn't disappear. Not yet. Not until Angel's birthday, which was still a few days away. No one runs away *before* she inherits a fortune.

Traffic had ended, night had descended, and the LIE was moving. Perry's foot was heavy on the gas pedal, and he was weaving in and out of traffic. He checked the rearview mirror. No tail this time, at least none he was aware of.

But why stop tailing him now?

Because whoever had followed him was after Angel and she had been found. But was she still in danger? Or was she the biggest danger of all?

He pictured the black car racing down Washington Avenue directly at Angel. Then he pictured Angel in a car, sitting beside her father.

Her father. If there was anyone Perry did not trust, it was Norman Loki.

Loki, the one who had written the terms of the inheritance and had lied about it.

He checked his mirrors again. Still no tail he could see. But maybe he'd been wrong, maybe the tail was just a diversion, and Julia Drusilla had been the target all along. But Julia's whereabouts were no secret, never had been.

And leaping to her death?

Not a chance. Not the steely woman who told him she never went out on her terrace.

I'm not a fan of heights.

People with a fear of water did not drown themselves. People with a fear of heights did not jump from penthouse terraces.

Then someone had pushed her. But who?

They were all in his mind now, everyone he'd met in connection to Angel.

Lilith Bates, who had lied about knowing Randy Hyde then followed him to make sure her dirty little secret stayed buried. But was it more than that? Could she possibly have been in cahoots with the mechanic to get rid of Angel? But what would she get out of Angel's demise? Randy. Maybe. But did she really want him that bad, a sex machine who she was ashamed to be seen with?

And what about Randy? With sex and money to offer, Angel could probably get that oversexed grease monkey to do anything, even kill her mother for her. But the guy didn't seem smart enough to pull it off, to sneak in and out of Julia's penthouse unseen. Though Angel was smart enough to do anything. What had her nanny said about her?

She's never been just a kid. But she's smart—smartest child I ever took care of—because she had to be.

Yeah, Angel was smart all right. But even the smart ones messed up; Perry knew that. And there it was again, lurking at the fringe of his subconscious, something Angel had said, something simple and innocuous, which had made him know she was a liar. *But what was it?*

Perry rolled down his window for a blast of cold air, something to clear his head.

And what about that shady politician, Tweed? Now there was a man with plenty to lose. Had Angel been pressuring him to leave his wife? Or was he worried she'd expose their affair and he wanted her out of the picture? *He could have been the one to send a killer after Angel,* thought Perry. But why would he send someone to kill her mother? Nothing to be gained in that.

And it was about gain, wasn't it?

Didn't it always come down to that, to money?

And Angel had the most to gain. And maybe her father.

The two of them conspiring to get the money. All of the money. It was the only thing that made sense.

Unless Perry was wrong. Unless his instinct had failed him.

The lights of Forest Hills high-rise apartments slid by like a million tiny comets. Then the Unisphere, that odd 1960s remnant of the World's Fair. It looked to him like a prop from some low budget sci-fi movie. He drove past Kissena Boulevard and Utopia Parkway until Queens was an afterthought and he was driving through Nassau County, where the lights grew dimmer and traffic thinned.

Perry pictured Angel the last time he'd seen her, hair pulled back, pearls around her neck, already looking like the wealthy matron she was about to become. He saw the dark glasses and then the tears in her eyes, and he wanted to believe her but he didn't.

He stared through the windshield, the voice of his old friend in his head: *So if you want to lose the only friend you've got around here, go right ahead and continue doing what you're doing. But don't say I didn't warn you.*

He thought: *I have to prove to Henry Watson that I'm still a good detective.*

Then he thought: *This isn't about proving anything to Henry. It's about proving it to myself.*

No way he could fuck up again. No way he would be the fool, the dupe, the guy who walked away with his tail between his legs.

Window up, down, cold air, then heat, he couldn't get it right. Couldn't get any of it right, all the conflicting thoughts of this case buzzing in his brain.

Did Angel need more than a couple of hundred million on top of whatever money she was already getting?

Did Norman Loki?

Julia had said her ex-husband was well taken care of, and it looked it. But who knew what sort of debt the man might have. He was a liar and a chameleon, a weed-smoking, aging hippie one minute, a vicious drunk the next.

Perry tried to picture him pushing his ex-wife off the terrace, but the man didn't seem brave enough.

And what about Angel? Would her nanny really lie for her?

Perry could see Athena Williams defending her charge to the death, but covering up a murder? Not that.

So what was he missing?

Window down again, another blast of night air needed to jog his addled sleep-deprived mind.

He drove through Hauppauge, Patchogue, Nesconset—towns with Native American names that hadn't seen an Indian for hundreds of years.

He pictured the gold-framed photograph at the nanny's home—the teenage girl with feet planted firmly on the floor, her cool blue eyes and defiant chin. A tough little girl. Not the trembling siren he'd held in his arms, the gorgeous creature who made it impossible for him, for any man, to think straight.

Perry stared into the dark road ahead. What was it she'd said that had lodged in his brain, something that had caught in the lower register of his psyche, something that had made him think she was lying? *Know* she was lying. What the hell was it?

He tried to get at it, but all he could see was Julia Drusilla splayed on the sidewalk like a broken marionette and his last friend in the police department accusing him of reckless behavior.

But it was there somewhere, a word or two buzzing in the back of his brain like a gnat.

Perry turned off at the Manorville exit that would lead to the smaller roads connecting to the Hamptons. The moon was out, almost full, its silvery light illuminating the edges of the huge *Stargazer* sculpture on the deserted field by the side of the road. He knew it was supposed to be an abstract deer, but tonight it looked like something ferocious.

It brought him back to another night in the Hamptons, a night with no moon, no stars. Just a madman he had tracked and almost killed. A madman who had almost killed him. Another missing-persons case, another young woman. One he had not been able to save.

Like a phantom limb his side began to throb where the bullet had gone through flesh and muscle and the face of Derace McDonald was in his mind, a specter that never truly left him.

He saw other faces, too—the girl's parents, who had hired him to find their child when the police and FBI had failed. McDonald was locked away now, a mad lab rat for psychiatrists to study. But the girl Perry had been hired to find was dead. And despite the fact that the cards had been stacked against him, that the police and the FBI had not found the girl, it didn't matter because she had died. In the end, he had failed and had almost died himself.

The reason, Perry knew, that he had taken this case: to get it right this time. To save a girl. To save Angel. And he'd found her and she wasn't dead. But still, his client had died, even though there was no madman like Derace McDonald coming after his client or after him.

Or was there?

Perry thumped his palm against the steering wheel, his adrenaline pumping, nerve ends tingling.

Was it possible her father had set it all up, that right now he was arranging for Angel's death so that he would inherit all of the money? No one had asked where the money went if both Angel and Julia were dead, and Norman Loki was the logical benefactor.

Perry put more weight on the gas pedal, broke the speed limit on the quiet two-lane road through Water Mill, then Bridgehampton, then East Hampton.

He pictured Norman at the station house, a protective arm around his daughter; then he pictured him so drunk he'd barely made sense. He saw Angel, too, tears in her eyes asking how her mother had died but not acting shocked when she'd gotten the answer.

He drove through Amagansett, trying to remember the exact words that had made him doubt her, and for a split second he could hear her voice and what she said before it disappeared into a tangle of ganglia.

Had he imagined it?

Maybe he was wrong about Angel. Maybe she was a victim—or about to be.

The road to Montauk was dark, just a few lights flickering in houses on the dunes but almost no cars. Perry gripped the steering wheel. Another mile flew by, then another, until he saw it: the turnoff to Norman Loki's house.

Perry switched off his headlights and headed slowly down the private lane. He cut the engine halfway to the house and took the rest on foot.

An icy chill blew across the dunes and bluff, and he shivered as he walked, head down, collar up, not sure what he was going to do when he got there.

And that's when it came to him: what Angel had said.

Up ahead he could see the house, the cars; he could just make out Norman Loki's Jeep and Mercedes in the moonlight.

The downstairs windows were lit up and smoke billowed from the chimney. *It looks like it's out of a storybook,* he thought, *cozy and tranquil.* But he knew better.

Nicky's striped scarf whipped around his face as he got closer, then he spotted the car on the side of the road under a thicket of gingko trees, a black Toyota, moonlight playing off the dented back fender.

The car.

His stalker.

Here.

Perry laid a hand on the hood. Still warm.

He got out his cell and made a call. "Get here soon as you can— and keep the phone on." He gave the address then pressed the Mute button.

Dirt and pebbles crunched under his shoes; ocean waves broke in the distance and the wind howled.

Crouching now, light from the large bay window falling across him as he moved to the side and caught a glimpse of them, Angel and Norman, being ushered to the sofa by the dark silhouette of a man.

Perry leaned closer, could hear muffled voices though not what was being said. A few steps along the side of the house, past another window, and this time he saw him: a man with dark hair, holding a gun. And he recognized him.

Perry moved faster now, making his way around the house until he found the back door, closed but unlocked. He tried to picture the interior as he turned the doorknob and then he was in, spinning through the door into a small mudroom off the kitchen. He could hear voices as he slowly made his way across the room and into a dark hallway that separated the kitchen and living room, the cell phone still in his hand, the whole time holding his breath.

Halfway down the hall he stopped. He heard them before he saw them.

"You're crazy!" Angel's voice rang out, a mix of arrogance and fear.

"You dare call *me* crazy!" It was the dark-haired man. "You, of all people. You have no idea, no *fucking* idea what I've been through!"

Perry dared a few steps closer. Back flattened against the wall, he could see them.

Angel and Norman were side by side on the couch. The man faced them, his back to Perry.

"Just take it easy," Norman said.

Perry let out the breath he'd been holding, unsure of his next move. No quick moves, no leaps into the room until he was absolutely certain.

"Let's talk it over," Norman said. "I'm sure—"

"Sure of what?" There was a high-pitched edge of hysteria in the man's voice.

"I'm sure we can work this out," said Norman. "Whatever it is."

"Oh, so you don't know me?"

"Should I?"

"Why would you recognize something thrown away, cast off, a piece of your wife's garbage."

Angel turned to her father. "Daddy, do you have any idea who this—"

"If it's money you want," said Norman, "I can—"

"Oh, it's money all right. Why she sent me. To collect what's right-fully mine."

"Who?" Angel look back and forth between her father and the dark-haired man.

"Tell her," the man said. "You know, don't you?"

Norman Loki shook his head, but even from a distance Perry could see he was lying.

"We made a deal. Me and Julia. I'd take care of Angel; then we'd split the money fifty-fifty."

"Take *care* of me?" Angel was up now, arms at her sides, hands in fists. "What the hell are you talking about?"

"Sit down. Or I'll shoot you." The man aimed his gun at Angel.

Perry stiffened, tried to gauge an attack. He could lunge, but what if he miscalculated, was a second too late, and the man fired his gun?

"Angel—" Norman reached out a hand to his daughter. "Please. Sit down."

"Explain it to her," the man said.

Angel sat, and Perry watched the scene like a play. He could see the man in profile, the tightness of his jaw, hand gripping the gun. Flames danced in the fireplace, casting eerie shadows around the room.

"He's Julia's son," Norman said to Angel, almost in a whisper.

"See?" the man said. "It didn't take you long to figure that out."

Perry was putting the pieces together: The late-night visitor to Julia's apartment, the masseur. And the man sitting beside him at the bar of the Memory Motel. *My mother says I'm too dramatic.*

"What?" Angel's voice, strident.

The man took a step closer to Angel, and Perry got ready, every muscle in his body poised for attack.

"You didn't know you had a big brother, did you? I'm your

mother's secret, her bastard, the baby she gave away when she was fifteen, the orphan passed from one foster home to another, while you,
her dear little *angel,* got everything."

"Oh, please." Angel folded her arms across her chest, her face a
mask of incredulity and disdain.

The man waved the gun at Norman. "*Tell her.* She needs to know
the truth before she dies."

"There's n-no reason to hurt anyone," said Norman. "Please."

"No? She got everything—private school, tennis lessons, clothes—
while I got a pittance, an anonymous allowance, just enough to keep
me off the street, paid off in dribs and drabs. But that's how I—"

"If you only knew," said Angel, voice dripping with irony, "what
my life has been like."

"*You?* You had a home—*two* homes! You know what it's like to
have nothing? No family, no one who cares about you." His voice was
quavering. "That lousy allowance was all I had. Julia tried to make
it anonymous, but—" He turned to Norman. "You arranged that
pathetic stream of guilt money. That's how I found it, by tracing it to
your defunct law practice. It took a long time, but I finally figured it
out. At first Julia wanted nothing to do with me, but then she admitted it—because then, *she* wanted something from *me.*"

"This is absurd," said Angel. "Tell him, Daddy."

Perry saw the look of horror and dread bouncing around Norman Loki's face. "I . . . she . . . we . . . didn't want you to know, Angel.
There was no reason—"

"But it's true!" the man shouted. "You don't want to know it, but
it's the truth! You hear what your father is saying, Angel? Now listen." He took a step forward, and Perry readied himself again. But
the man was still talking, wanting to, needing to.

"Your mother had me follow the detective, told me it was the
perfect opportunity, that you were already missing, so when I found

you and killed you, no one would be surprised. You see, she hired the detective as a guide for *me,* and to make it look like she cared about *you.*"

Perry flinched at the thought of being used.

"Julia did her homework. She chose him, see? Because he was kicked off the force, she figured that no one would believe him when it was all over."

Perry flinched again, then took a deep breath, tried to calculate out how he could tackle the guy before he fired a shot.

"Your mother—*our* mother—said to make it look like an accident, like you were drunk or taking drugs. She said no one would be surprised—that you're a tramp, that they'd blame one of your boyfriends or think you OD'd or—"

Angel shouted, "Shut up!"

"She said once you were dead, she'd get all the money and split it with me. But now, I'll get it all."

"You're insane," Angel said. "My mother—I'm not surprised by anything she'd do—but she would never have given you anything, not a dime."

"It doesn't matter now. After you and your father are dead, I'll inherit it all. You see, I'll be the only heir." He aimed his gun.

Perry got ready to pounce, but Norman Loki put up his hands.

"Wait. Listen. Angel is right. Julia used you. She lied. She always lied. You have no idea what she was like. She orchestrated her own parents' deaths. Had them run off the road. You can't imagine how furious she was to discover that her father had locked away the bulk of his estate for his grandchild until her twenty-first birthday and that *she* couldn't get at it." Norman shook his head. "As if she didn't have enough."

"Nothing was ever enough for her," said Angel. "You think I had it good with a mother like that! A monster without a heart?" She barked a laugh. "You were the lucky one! Getting away from her. From all of this."

"So that's why you killed her?" the man asked. "Because you hated her? Or was it just for the money?"

"Wh-what are you talking about?"

Perry could see Angel shifting her weight from foot to foot.

"You know exactly what I'm talking about, dear sister," the man said.

"You're crazy."

"Am I? After you two are dead—a family feud the way I see it, your father shot you then himself, or maybe the other way around. It doesn't really matter. Either way, the two of you will be dead and then, a few weeks from now I'll announce my existence and I'll get all the—"

"Um, no." Norman cut in. "No."

"No, what?"

"Angel's right. You will not get any money, not a cent."

"Of course I will! I'm Julia's flesh and blood. Her heir. The only one. Everything will come to me."

"I'm . . . I'm afraid not. You see, I wrote the trust papers, and they do not allow for any half siblings. Other than Angel, no one can get his or her hands on that money."

"You're lying!" The man took a step toward Norman. "And now you're a dead man."

Perry slipped his cell phone into the pocket of his trench coat. Then he charged.

So did Angel. Lunging at her half brother, the two of them struggling over the gun as Perry sprinted and the gun went off and then Norman Loki was on the floor, blood leaking from his head. Perry knocked the man to the floor, and the gun flew from his hand.

"Oh my God—my God—Daddy, no!" Angel was shrieking, but she had gotten the gun and was aiming it at her half brother.

"It's okay," Perry said to Angel. "Take it easy."

The man was struggling, but Perry had him in a headlock, under control when Angel fired the gun and he sagged in Perry's arms, a hole in his shirt, a red stain spreading.

Angel dropped the gun, and Perry kicked it away.

"Why?" Perry asked. "I had him. You saw that."

"He killed my father, and he was going to kill me." Angel stared at Perry. Her face looked like stone. "I had no choice. Anyone could see that," she said, her voice calm.

A hand gripped Perry's arm, the man coughing up blood, fighting to speak. "It was . . . her. After I left you on the bridge I—I turned around because it, it was my chance . . . she was alone and you didn't matter anymore. But when I got there she was creeping out from the back of that house on Washington Avenue, and I, I followed her . . . from Brooklyn to Park Avenue . . . waited across the street to, to see what she was up to and—"

"Shut up!" Angel screamed. "You're crazy!"

She went for the gun again, but Perry got it first.

"Go on," he said, and pressed a hand into the man's wound to staunch the bleeding.

"I, I was outside when . . . when Julia came flying off the terrace. Five minutes later I saw her, Angel, slip out of the building and . . . and lose herself in the crowd."

"Liar!" Angel screamed. "You crazy, fucking liar!"

"It was"—his breathing was labored, blood bubbling at his lips— "her." Then his eyelids fluttered, his grip loosened on Perry's arm, and he slid to the floor.

"Hang on, damn it, hang on!" Perry glared at Angel.

"You don't believe him, do you?" Angel's blue eyes were wide, filled with her unique brand of manufactured innocence. "He's insane. God knows if *anything* he's told us about his life is true. I think he made it all up. This pathetic story about being Julia's son and, and—" She sniffed, holding back sudden tears. "Oh, it's all so, so awful. My father, my mother— That crazy murderer, that liar!"

Perry stood up, took a few steps toward her, spoke softly but firmly. "I think it's you who is lying, Angel."

"How dare you? After all I've—"

"After all you've done to make sure you get all the money? That's what this was all about, wasn't it, Angel? Money."

She swiped her tears away, and Perry saw the tough little girl in the nanny's photo, jaw set, the look of determination in her eyes.

"You'll never prove that."

"No?" Perry had them now, the words she'd uttered, what he had been trying to recall. "The Pollock," he said.

"The . . . what?"

"The Jackson Pollock painting in your mother's apartment."

"What about it?"

All she cares about is stuff—her jewelry, her houses, her great big Jackson Pollock painting.

"You mentioned it, just before, at the precinct."

"So?"

"It's new. Your mother just bought it."

"So what?"

"So it means you were in your mother's apartment. Recently. Very recently."

"No." Angel shook her head, ran a hand through her blond hair. "I haven't been there but, but . . . My mother told me about it."

"But you said you hadn't spoken to your mother for a year, and she said the same thing."

"Then I, I must have read about her buying it. That's it."

"Where?"

"The *Times*, I think. I can't remember." Angel waved a hand. "What does it matter?"

"The buyer's name was withheld, Angel."

"So?" Her face softened, and she took a step closer to him, her voice that seductive purr Perry remembered when he'd held her trembling body against his in front of her nanny's home. "It's just a painting, Perry. Not important. What's important is us."

"*Us?*" Perry looked into those wide blue eyes, no tears now, just a deep void.

"You and me," said Angel. "Why not? There's plenty of money— or there will be. You don't want to scratch out a pathetic living as a private eye for the rest of your life, do you, Perry?" She eased the back of her hand across his cheek, fingernails flicking against his skin, and he felt a chill. "We can go anywhere. We can—"

Perry grabbed her hand. "*We* are not going anywhere, Angel. And neither are you. I think the police will be interested to know that you were in your mother's apartment."

Angel tugged her hand away, her face going hard. "Try to prove it," she said, her purr now a rasp. "Oh, I can just see it. A disgraced cop trying to hang a murder on the casual mention of a painting." She laughed. "That's rich."

Perry knew she was right. It wasn't enough.

Angel's lips curled into a smile. "And gee, all the witnesses are dead, aren't they?" She looked down at her half brother and her father and shrugged. "You know, Perry, I don't think you're going to say anything."

There were sirens in the distance.

Perry returned her cold stare. "You made a mistake, Angel, and my guess, you've made others. I'm going to start by having your mother's building canvassed, every apartment, every doorman, every maid, and every maintenance man. *Someone* will have seen you come in or out or passed you in the stairwell. We'll get you, Angel."

"The cops will never do that, Perry. They won't listen to you. Why should they?"

"Who said anything about the cops? I'll do the canvass myself."

"And I'll be long gone."

The sirens were louder now, just outside.

Angel mussed her hair and rubbed at her eyes, looked at Perry briefly, then dropped to her knees beside her father, turned on the tears, and cried, "Daddy, Daddy," as the front door opened and East Hampton's Sergeant Gawain burst in, two deputies beside him, a half-dozen uniforms and a couple of medics just behind.

"Jesus Christ," said Gawain, taking in the scene.

"Yeah," said Perry.

"You okay?" Gawain asked.

Perry nodded.

Gawain looked at Angel, cradling her father's head and rocking slightly. "She okay?"

"Angel? Oh, she's just fine."

Angel looked up, her eyes locked on Perry's, a smile behind the tears just for him.

"This the half brother?" Gawain asked.

"He's not my brother," Angel said. "He made it all up. He's just some lunatic."

"She shot him," Perry said.

"I had to! He shot my father and probably killed my mother!"

A medic tore open the man's shirt, stethoscope to his chest. "There's a pulse, weak, but it's there." He nodded to the EMTs who strapped an oxygen mask over the guy's face and got him onto a gurney.

Angel watched, that secret smile of hers gone.

"I hope he makes it," said Gawain.

"It's a shoulder wound, mostly blood loss," said Perry. "I think he'll be talking."

The medic was leaning over Norman Loki now. "He's gone," he said.

Perry took the cell phone from his pocket and handed it to Gawain. "You heard most of what went down here, didn't you?"

"Enough," said Gawain. "But a lot was garbled."

"I'll help you ungarble it," Perry said. "And there are computer programs that will help, too." He looked at Angel kneeling beside the medics who were strapping her father's body onto a stretcher. She was crying, her hands fluttering around her beautiful face, but her brows were knit as she strained to hear what Perry was saying.

"I'd better cuff her before she runs away again," said Gawain.

"You do that," said Perry.

It was cold out on the dunes, but after Gawain had handcuffed Angel and the police and EMTs had all driven away, Perry lingered a while, looking up at the stars and moon. He thought about Derace McDonald and the girl he had found but could not save, and he thought about Angel, the girl he'd found who didn't need saving.

The police sirens had long faded, replaced by the sound of the ocean and the howl of the wind, and Perry wondered who was going to inherit all that money. Then he decided he didn't care.

He wound Nicky's scarf around his neck and turned away from the ocean, thinking about his daughter and how he would call her in the morning.

Acknowledgments

Organizing twenty writers can be a difficult task, but this one was made easy. First, because David Falk entrusted me with the assignment; second, because of Michelle Howry's astute editing; third, because Stacy Creamer stood back and let me do my thing with her blessing; and fourth, because I was following in the footsteps of Andrew and Lamia Gulli, who edited the last serial novel and got the ball rolling.

Of course the real thanks must go to the writers. I don't think there is a more supportive or generous group of writers around, all of whom understood that we were playing with three or four noir classics at once, who followed the plan and yet made each chapter their own. They were indeed a dream team.

—JONATHAN SANTLOFER

ABOUT THE AUTHORS

MARK BILLINGHAM is one of the UK's most acclaimed and popular crime writers. His series of novels featuring D.I. Tom Thorne has twice won him the Crime Novel of the Year Award and been nominated for seven CWA Daggers. Each of his novels has been a *Sunday Times* Top Ten bestseller. A television series based on the Thorne novels starred David Morrissey as Tom Thorne. Mark Billingham's latest novel is *The Dying Hours*.

LAWRENCE BLOCK has been writing for so long he's accumulated several life achievement awards—his colleagues' gentle way of telling him his future lies largely in the past. One can but hope he'll get the message. Meanwhile his latest book is *Hit Me,* the author's fifth novel about that wistful urban lonely guy, Keller, philatelist and hit man.

C. J. BOX is the *New York Times* bestselling author of fifteen novels including the award-winning Joe Pickett series. Box has won the Edgar Award for Best Novel as well as the Anthony, Macavity, Barry, and Calibre .38 awards. His novels have been translated into twenty-five languages. Box lives outside Cheyenne, Wyoming. His most recent novels are *Breaking Point* and *The Highway*.

KEN BRUEN is the author of over twenty novels, and has a doctorate in metaphysics.

ALAFAIR BURKE is the bestselling author of nine novels, including *If You Were Here, Long Gone,* and the Ellie Hatcher series. A former prosecutor and graduate of Stanford Law School, she now teaches criminal law and lives in Manhattan.

STEPHEN L. CARTER is the bestselling author of five novels and eight non-fiction books. He is the William Nelson Cromwell Professor of Law at Yale, where he has taught for more than thirty years. He is a graduate of Stanford University and Yale Law School and lives near New Haven, Connecticut, with his wife, Enola Aird.

LEE CHILD has been a television director, union organizer, theater technician, and law student. He is the author of the Jack Reacher novels. He was born in England but now lives in New York City and leaves the island of Manhattan only when required to by forces beyond his control. Visit www.leechild.com for more information on his books, short stories, and *Jack Reacher,* the movie starring Tom Cruise.

MARCIA CLARK, former O. J. Simpson prosecutor, has published three novels that feature Los Angeles special trials prosecutor Rachel Knight: *Guilt by Association, Guilt by Degrees, Killer Ambition,* which is due out in June 2013. Marcia is a frequent legal commentator on television and radio, and her books have been optioned by TNT for a one-hour drama series, currently in development. Marcia is attached as an executive producer. She's currently at work on her fourth novel.

MARY HIGGINS CLARK's books are worldwide bestsellers. In the United States alone, her books have sold more than one hundred million copies. Her latest suspense novel, *Daddy's Gone A Hunting,* was published by Simon & Schuster in April 2013. She is an active member of Literacy Volunteers. She is the author of more than thirty suspense novels, three collections of short stories, an historical novel, a memoir, and two children's books. She is coauthor with her daughter, Carol Higgins Clark, of five suspense novels. Two of her novels were made into feature films and many of her other works into television films. Mary Higgins Clark is married to John Conheeney and they live in Saddle River, New Jersey.

MAX ALLAN COLLINS is the author of the *New York Times* bestselling graphic novel *Road to Perdition,* made into the Academy Award–winning film. His other credits include such comics as *Batman, Dick Tracy,* and his own *Ms. Tree;* film scripts for HBO and Lifetime TV; and the Shamus Award–winning Nathan Heller detective novels. His tie-in novels include the bestsellers *Saving Private Ryan, Air Force One,* and *American Gangster,* and he is working with the Mickey Spillane estate to finish a number of works by Mike Hammer's creator. He lives in Muscatine, Iowa, with his wife, Barb, with whom he writes the popular "Trash 'n' Treasures" mystery series (*Antiques Roadkill*).

JOHN CONNOLLY was born in Dublin, Ireland, and is the writer of the Charlie Parker series of mystery novels, the latest of which is *The Wrath of Angels;* the stand-alone novel *The Book of Lost Things;* and the Samuel Johnson stories for younger readers. He is also the host of the 2XM radio show *ABC to XTC,* which allows him to indulge his love of the music of 1977 to 1989.

JAMES GRADY's first novel became the Robert Redford movie *Three Days of the Condor*. Grady has received Italy's Raymond Chandler Medal, France's *Grand Prix du Roman Noir* and Japan's *Baka-Misu* literature award. In 2008, London's *Daily Telegraph* named Grady as one of "50 crime writers to read before you die."

HEATHER GRAHAM is the *New York Times* and *USA Today* bestselling author of more than a hundred novels, including suspense, paranormal, historical, and mainstream Christmas fare. She lives in Miami, Florida, an easy shot down to the Keys, where she can indulge in her passion for diving. Travel, research, and ballroom dancing also help keep her sane; she is the mother of five, and also resides with two dogs and two cats. She is CEO of Slush Pile Productions, a recording company and production house for various charity events.

BRYAN GRULEY's Starvation Lake series has been nominated for an Edgar and won the Anthony and Barry awards. Gruley also is a Pulitzer Prize–winning journalist for Bloomberg News in Chicago, where he lives with his wife, Pam. He's working on his fourth novel.

CHARLAINE HARRIS, author of more than thirty novels, is best known for her novels about telepathic barmaid Sookie Stackhouse. A daughter of the South, she now lives in Texas.

VAL McDERMID escaped from a mining community in Scotland to Oxford University. She abandoned an award-winning career in journalism for fiction and has published twenty-six crime novels. Her bestselling books are translated into more than forty languages and she has won many awards including the Gold Dagger, the Los Angeles Times Book Prize, the Lambda Pioneer Award, and the Diamond Dagger for lifetime achievement. She lives in the north of England with her American wife, her son, and their dog.

S. J. ROZAN, the Edgar-winning author of fourteen novels and dozens of short stories, was born in the Bronx and lives in Manhattan. Her latest novel, as half of the writing team of Sam Cabot, is *Blood of the Lamb*.

JONATHAN SANTLOFER is the author of five novels, including *The Death Art-ist,* which has been translated into eighteen languages and the Nero Award–winning *Anatomy of Fear.* He is the coeditor, contributor, and illustrator of *The Dark End of the Street;* editor and contributor of *L.A. Noire: The Collected Stories;* and editor, contributor, and illustrator of Akashic Books' *The Marijuana Chronicles.* Also an artist, Santlofer has been the recipient of two National Endowment for Arts grants and sits on the board of Yaddo, the oldest arts organization in the United States. He lives in New York where he is at work on a new novel.

DANA STABENOW has written twenty-nine novels, many short stories, has edited anthologies and wrote the "Alaska Traveler" column for five years for *Alaska* magazine. She lives in Alaska.

LISA UNGER is a *New York Times, USA Today,* and internationally best-selling author whose novels have sold more than one and a half million copies in the United States and have been translated into twenty-six languages. Her novels have been hailed as "masterful" (*St. Petersburg Times*), "sensational" (*Publishers Weekly*), with "grip-ping narrative and evocative, muscular prose" (Associated Press). Her next novel, *In the Blood,* will be released by Touchstone in January 2014. She lives in Florida with her husband and daughter.

SARAH WEINMAN is news editor for *Publishers Marketplace* and the editor of *Troubled Daughters, Twisted Wives: Stories From the Trailblazers of Domestic Suspense* (Penguin). She writes the "Crimewave" column for the *National Post* and contributes to the *Wall Street Journal,* the *New York Observer, Slate,* and other publications. Her fiction has appeared in *Ellery Queen Mystery Magazine, Alfred Hitchcock Mystery Magazine,* and several anthologies. Weinman lives in Brooklyn.

2 Lafayette Street, 3rd Floor NY NY 10007
T 212.577.7700 F 212.385.0311 www.safehorizon.org

safehorizon
moving victims of violence from crisis to confidence.

About Safe Horizon

Crime writers, much like the perps who populate their pages, couldn't succeed at their work without victims. A murder mystery will offer up at least one corpse; and when a serial killer is on the loose, the body count grows even higher. Some bad guys choose their victims with great care; others catch toddlers or little old ladies in random cross fire.

I was a prosecutor in New York for thirty years, during which time I started my own career as a crime novelist. When I began the job in 1972, there were no victim advocates anywhere in America. Prosecutors represent the state or federal government; and as much as they may empathize with someone who has been assaulted or robbed or burglarized, they are not lawyers for the victim.

When Safe Horizon was founded in New York in 1978, it filled an enormous void, stepping up to provide support and promote justice for victims of crime and abuse, their families, and their communities. Its twenty-four-hour toll-free hotlines are gateways to assistance for so many of the 250,000 crime victims whose lives we touch each year. We are the largest provider of domestic violence services in America, offering innovative programs to support women—in collaboration with the criminal justice system—as they navigate the complexities of leaving abusive relationships and building safe futures. We have state-of-the-art child advocacy centers that aid more than four thousand sexually and physically abused children and their families every year, pioneering the model of fully co-locating police, prosecutors, doctors, social workers, and mental health professionals in one facility so that the child victim is not exposed to repeated interviews in hostile environments.

Safe Horizon has more than fifty-seven programs in courthouses, schools, precincts, and in our own havens and shelters. Our counseling center helps clients regain a sense of control over their lives, a sense often lost after a violent and traumatic event. Since 1979, we have worked with family members who survive homicide victims—their spouses, siblings, parents, and children. We also advocate nationally for policies on behalf of those affected by violence and abuse.

How especially fitting, then, that this brilliant cast of contributors—some of the finest writers in the genre—have pooled their considerable talent to support Safe Horizon, the largest and best victims' services agency in the United States. While the writers hold us spellbound with their storytelling, our friends at Safe Horizon will continue to do their work on the side of the angels, using this support to help move victims from crisis to confidence.

LINDA FAIRSTEIN
crime novelist and board member of Safe Horizon